THE STREET ARAB

The Story of a British Home Child

SANDRA JOYCE

WELLDONE PUBLISHING,
2011•TORONTO, CANADA

Library and Archives Canada Cataloguing in Publication

Joyce, Sandra
      The street Arab : the story of a British
home child / Sandra Joyce.

ISBN 978-0-9877640-0-3

      I. Title.

PS8619.O966S77 2011   C813'.6   C2011-905993-2

Cover design and Images: Leigh Voigt
Printed and bound in Canada at Gauvin Press

This is a work of fiction, and the characters in it are solely the creation of the author. Any resemblance to actual persons - with exception to historical figures - is entirely coincidental. When historical figures consort with fictional characters, the results are, necessarily, fiction. Similarly, some events have been created to serve fictional purposes.

Welldone Publishing
105 Burgess Avenue
Toronto, Ontario
M4E 1X2

www.sandrajoyce.com

THE STREET ARAB

The Story of a British Home Child

FOREWORD

Sandra Joyce witnessed the second Reading Debate of my British Home Child Day Act on February 10th, 2010, at the Ontario Legislature in Queen's Park, Toronto. The act was to declare September 28th of each year as British Home Child Day in Ontario, recognizing them for their tremendous contributions made to the social, cultural, and economic fibre of Canada and the province of Ontario. The year, 2010 had already been declared The Year of the British Home Child by the Federal Government.

That day, I introduced Sandra to my colleagues and to those watching on the Parliamentary Channel on television. "Sandra Joyce is with us, too, and I welcome her to this Chamber. Her dad, Robert Joyce, came over to Canada from Quarrier's Home in 1925. He was fifteen years of age and his brother twelve. Robert worked on farms in the Brockville and Smith's Falls area, but at the age of twenty years he made his way to Toronto where he enlisted in the Canadian Army and was stationed in both Northern Africa and Italy in World War II."

Sandra was there for her dad and the many other descendants of Home Children, remembering the more than 100,000 children sent from Great Britain, to work as farm labourers and domestics in homes in Ontario and across Canada. These were boys and girls, anywhere from six months to eighteen years of age, sent out from the British Isles as part of the child emigration movement, from the late 1860's to the late 1930's.

The story of the British Home Children is one about courage, strength and perseverance, a subject that has been largely untold. It was rarely talked about by the British Home Children themselves to their descendants. Although my Private Members' Bill passed, it died on the Order Papers, when the Legislature prorogued.

With the same determination as the British Home Children, and as a descendant of one, I brought forward the same act, twice in 2011, and on May 19, 2011, when Bill 156 was debated in Second Reading, it finally received unanimous Second and Third Reading votes in the Legislature, with the support of my colleagues and co-sponsors of the bill, MPP Steve Clark (Leeds-Grenville) and MPP Cheri DiNovo (Parkdale-High Park).

The British Home Child Day Act finally received Royal Assent on June 1, 2011, when Chief Justice Warren K. Winkler signed the bill into law, in the Lieutenant-Governor's suite at Queen's Park.

Sandra Joyce's book, "The Street Arab", is her story to the world that her dad, Robert Joyce, despite many challenges along life's journey, did endure, and that his story is an important part of Ontario's culture and heritage. Bill 158, the British Home Child Day Act, is now Ontario's reminder to the world that we should pause for a moment, each September 28th, to remember the spirit of determination and perseverance of our province's British Home Children. It is my hope that "The Street Arab" will help all of us to better understand the life and times of one young 'Home Boy'.

As the MPP for the Riding of Stormont-Dundas-South Glengarry, I congratulate Sandra Joyce on taking the time to put thoughts into print. Thank you, Sandra, for sharing this with us, and for unlocking one of the many stories that would never have been told, if not for a loving descendant.

"The Street Arab" is a wonderful legacy to one of Scotland's and Quarrier's finest boys. God bless Robert Joyce.

Jim Brownell, MPP
Stormont-Dundas-South Glengarry

This novel is for Robert Joyce, the Home Boy, on whom it is based and his descendants: Lynda, Sandra, Leigh, Claire, Cynthia and Penelope.

Dad, if I had only known, before you 'went up north', what I now know.

Love you and miss you.

Lest we forget.

"At first Matthew suggested getting a "Home" boy. But I said "no" flat to that. "They may be all right - I'm not saying they're not - but no London street Arabs for me," I said, "Give me a native born at least. There'll be a risk, no matter who we get. But I'll feel easier in my mind and sleep sounder at nights if we get a born Canadian."

Anne of Green Gables, L.M. Montgomery

THE STREET ARAB

The Story of a British Home Child

PART ONE

Lochoal, Scotland, April 1915

CHAPTER ONE

The mining village's unimaginative name was a combination of its two most important features: loch, a tiny water hole, so inconsequential that no one cared to find out its original name; and coal, black gold – Scotland's most important resource.

The squat houses of which Lochoal was built, hewn quickly from local stone a few years prior, had been plunked down back to back, in drab, straight rows with no regard for community or weather. Behind the rows, there was a barren area, the width of two houses, for the communal privies, washhouses and clothes drying areas.

To the women's despair, the wind often whipped dark, grey dust through that space to soil their freshly washed laundry where it hung drying. And depending on the wind's direction and strength, they had to close their windows, even in the heat of the summer, against the stench of the privies. The greenery covering the ground was sparse.

In the washhouse, Mary shielded her eyes from the early morning sun, soapsuds running down her forearm, as she looked at the women walking towards her. Realizing that the North Sea wind was fiercer today than usual, they had wrapped their shawls tightly around themselves. Spring was late.

When her neighbours reached the washhouse, they grew silent, afraid of breaking the trance they thought she was in. They passed around lit cigarettes, while Mary, reddish brown wisps of hair escaping from her scarf, swirled the frothy water; eyes squinting in the steam.

They were hoping that Mary would 'see' their men.

The Great War had deepened. And for this generation of women, a life without men was settling in after the proclamation of war last summer. Lord Kitchener's cunning recruiting strategy that let pals who had joined together, stay together, had been an overwhelming success. During the first month of the war, in what the *Daily Mail* called "August Madness", enlisting offices were in cheery, riotous chaos. That month, thirty thousand men between the ages of eighteen and thirty-five enlisted every day.

As the men stood in queues under posters of 'Kitch' pointing accusingly at them, the words, "Duty, King and Country" rang out. Later on, in the pubs, without his stern countenance overseeing them, one could hear: "We'll show those bastards." And then, after a few pints: "To French women!"

Many, like Mary's husband, Duncan, and William, Helen James' husband, had left Lochoal together to travel to their hometowns to enlist. Employers proudly supported the recruits by promising to hold their jobs open for them until they returned. Everyone agreed the war would be over in just a few months. With God on their side, they would surely show those German bastards "right quick".

With the men gone, many of women had to fill in at the mines and factories, but Mary, covering as best she could for Dr. Lister, who had also enlisted, survived on what she received for her healing and midwifery. Her best friend, Helen, was given an allowance to support her two children. The two women managed to make ends meet.

***

Mary's first visions had started four years ago while doing her laundry. She noticed something strange was happening to the water, cloudy with dirt and soap. An image was developing. She put her hand out to touch the surface, fingertips causing small ripples. A shock ran up her arm. She pulled her hand back sharply. Tentatively, she reached out to it again, tracing its outline just above the water. A baby. She felt a flutter in her heart. *It was*

Helen's baby boy. A healthy second child.

She crossed herself furtively even though there was no one to see her. "Jesus-Mary-Joseph," she said, "I am like my mother."

Her breath quickened. She picked up her skirts and ran to Helen's house where she flew up the steps, and pushed the door open. Helen was sitting, her belly round and ripe, kneading bread dough, her swollen feet up on a stool.

"Mary?" Helen couldn't read her friend's bright expression.
Mary still felt out of breath. A moment of doubt made her hesitate. *Maybe I shouldn't say anything.*

Helen pounded the dough.

"Mary?" Helen repeated. She still had so much to do and she knew the baby was coming soon.

Mary took a deep breath. "I had a vision, a premonition: I don't know what to call it," she said. "I just saw your baby. He's healthy." At the word 'he', Helen drew her breath in sharply.

"What?" Helen got up quickly, off-balance. Mary ran to steady her. Helen's hand went to her mouth. "Like your mother…"

"Yes!"

"Truly?"

"Yes! I'm sure."

A soft cry escaped Helen's lips. This was more than she, as a foundling, could have asked for. *A son!*

Helen shut her eyes. "What joy!"

She couldn't contain herself. A boy was sure to be different from her daughter, Emma who had woken up every night, crying, until recently. Exhausted, Helen had hated her during those moments and had been afraid of doing her harm.

"Let's wait until Emma settles down to have any more children," she told her husband, William.

She made William withdraw early during their lovemaking, his warm stickiness ending up on Helen's legs or stomach, anywhere, just as long as it wasn't fertilizing anything. She stirred up a vinegar mixture she kept near at hand, to cleanse herself, just to make sure.

William had waited. He waited for three years. One night, he pinned her down and moving inside her, gasped loudly.

"No!" She pulled away, pushing his weight off her. He rolled to the side and she jumped up. "Why did you do that?" Helen hurried to the cupboard where the vinegar mixture was hidden. The bottle was only a third full, so she topped it up with more vinegar. Helen squatted over the chamber pot, the sharp sting of the mixture inside her making her feel raw and violated.

William turned on his side, away from her.

He sorely missed the comfort of a large family. Despite his overcrowded home and not having enough to eat, he'd always fallen asleep curled up against the warmth of one of his eight siblings. *Emma needed brothers and sisters.*

It happened as Helen feared. But she hadn't told her husband, at first. She tried to rid herself of it: putting salt in her tea to make herself sick, taking scalding hot baths, punching herself in the abdomen, even making herself fall down the stairs. As a last resort, she'd gone to Mary, hoping her friend knew how to get rid of it.

"I can't help you." Mary hadn't been able to look at her friend. "I can't even think that way."

"I have no one else to turn to."

"I just can't." After seeing Helen put her head down on her crossed arms, Mary decided to tell her something nobody knew. Not even Duncan. "Helen, I can't help you because I'm Catholic."

Helen looked up. "Catholic?"

"My mother was Irish Catholic, and even though my father demanded my being baptized as a Presbyterian, she taught me, secretly, to adhere to it as best I could." She paused, letting it sink in. "I don't have to tell you to keep it quiet."

Just that morning, their neighbours had been hotly denouncing the bloody Micks, stirring up trouble in Ireland when all the troops were needed so badly in Europe. No wonder Mary hadn't joined in.

"But I'll help you. Bring Emma here in the mornings and that'll give you time on your own." Mary touched her shoulder. "Go home. Wash your hair, tidy up." Mary hugged her. "Make yourself attractive. If you don't, you'll lose your man."

Helen's second baby turned out to be a healthy boy, named Robert

William James, and William had shown him off at the Goth, the miner's own pub, to all and sundry.

And now, she was pregnant with her third.

***

"Mary!" Helen called her. The women were getting restless. Since the war, the word that Mary was a visionary had spread like wildfire. The women begged her for news, beleaguering her with questions night and day.

"Yes, I know." Irritated by the women's expectations, Mary scrubbed so hard that the skin on her knuckles was rubbed raw.

The women, waiting, chatted, thanking their lucky stars that they had moved here. They loved the washhouse, the fresh scent of soap wiping out the past, no matter how dirty and grimy it was. The facilities were new, the best in the Kingdom of Fife. And there were showers here for the men, so that the women didn't have to fill a bath in the kitchen every day.

Each washhouse had three tubs, a wringer and running water. Glorious running water. Hot too, as long as the women had enough coal to light the boiler at the crack of dawn.

Before the war, the women had relished their time over the tubs. It was a place to catch up on gossip, laughing over the clouds of steam, their faces ruddy and bright. But since January, as they'd realized that the war showed no signs of ending any time soon, the washhouse's atmosphere had become subdued. Familiar faces were disappearing on a regular basis as they received dreadful news from the front, because, to add insult to injury, if they had no one to take their husband's place in the mine, they were given a gracious two weeks to pack up and vacate. "Lest we forget," the women said sadly as they left.

Mary pursed her lips. She had nothing to tell the crowd today. No visions, no desire to make anything up like she sometimes did when nothing presented itself. Knowing the depth of their disappointment if she said nothing, made her feel sick to her stomach. She wiped her hands on her apron.

Mary's green eyes, flecked with gold, were evenly set over lush lips. The shower of light freckles on her thin nose softened her countenance and made her seem younger and somehow glamorous in the greyness of Lochoal. Despite being almost thirty, she still had her figure when most of the other women her age had waistlines that had filled in. The women who were jealous of her figure, called her barren.

The icy wind whipped the women's hair out from under their scarves into their faces. They moved closer together, tucking their hands up inside their sleeves.

Mary couldn't 'see' as well as her mother had. She saw outlines that were sometimes left open for interpretation. The whirlwind of images must have driven her mother mad.

When Mary was young, her mother had tucked her into bed every night, her hair cascading over Mary's face in an aroma of rosemary and lavender, and instead of a bedside story, she would start reciting.

"Little Jimmy next door is going to get his finger caught in a mouse trap… don't worry, he'll be alright but it'll be sore for a few weeks…the wild cat, that lives in the hollow of the old oak, is going to have kittens, six of them…one of you will get a bad scratch… poor Mrs. O'Neill is going to have another baby girl, but the baby won't live long, God rest her soul…"

It fascinated Mary but it also scared her.

The worst time of all, though, was in the morning before a horrible cave-in had happened at the mine where her father worked. Mary's mother had taken to her bed and Mary knew something was terribly wrong.

As the great bell tolled, signaling disaster, she'd finally spoken, "Mary, he's gone."

"Who?" Mary's voice had cracked, knowing all too well from the look on her mother's face.

"Your father."

"Why didn't you try to stop him?" Mary had wailed. "Why didn't you tell me?"

"The visions are a terrible burden." Mary's mother had said to her through her tears. "I'm glad you don't have them."

The visions are a terrible burden.

One of the women in the waiting group was quietly reading a letter, grimy and smudged, aloud. It was from Belgium, where their boys had been stuck in a tug-of-war with the Germans since the beginning of this horror, gaining a few yards, only to lose them the next day. It was a month old but they all listened carefully to its staccato verse, words struck out by the censors. Bringing tears even to the hardest woman's eyes.

"I'm sorry." There was defeat in Mary's voice. She was tired. "It's just soapy water."

Suddenly Mary heard Helen's husband William, clear as a bell. *Duck!* She dropped to her knees. *Duck!* He was shouting. She wondered why all the women were still standing. "Duck!" She screamed at them. "Don't you hear him?"

Then, everything went dark. There was a searing sensation in her head. She gasped.

"Mary!" said Helen. "What's wrong?"

"I don't know." She sounded like she was lost.

Helen helped her to her feet. "You screamed the word 'duck'."

"Did I?" Her knees were sore and she had scraped her elbow. She was trembling.

The women slowly dispersed, looking back at her warily. "No news is good news," somebody commented. "She's pregnant, wait till Duncan hears about it," whispered somebody else nastily.

"You asked us if we'd heard someone," Helen said and then suddenly stopped and moaned.

It took all of Mary's will to focus on Helen. "It's started, hasn't it?"

Helen put a hand under her belly. "I'm losing water."

"Why didn't you tell me?" Mary helped Helen to and then up the steps to her door. From the way Helen was wincing, the contractions weren't far apart.

Robbie was on the floor of the two-room house darning his socks with large, clumsy stitches while 'Emma-bound' when they got there. That's what he called it when he was told to stay home with his bossy sister.

Robbie jumped up. "Can I go out now?"

Helen, her face now pale with pain said, "The baby is coming."

"I don't want a baby," Robbie said. "I want to play."

Suddenly, Helen yelped. Mary put a hand on her abdomen. "Robbie and Emma, I need you to get the birthing bag from my house. It's not heavy," Mary reassured them calmly. "If you come back fast, there's a treat in it for you and then, I promise, you can go out and play."

There were some drops from the valerian root that would help Helen relax. If they hurried. Still feeling shaken from the fall, she was glad she had prepared everything. She'd soaked the instruments in vinegar and then boiled them, like Dr. Lister had shown her.

The children ran as fast as they could down the steps and along the path to the bush that Mary had planted. She had planted it so that Duncan could find his way home from the pub. She'd laughingly told Helen that all the houses looked the same from the outside and she wanted to make sure he wound up in the right bedroom.

Mary's house was clean and tidy. No dirty dishes, no clutter on the floor. It felt like nobody lived there. Emma spotted the birthing bag beside the rocking chair while Robbie looked at the kitchen shelves. Mary always had nice things. *Where are her biscuits and sweets?*

He found a tin of ginger snaps on the table and helped himself to one.

"Come on, Robbie," Emma urged. "We'll get in trouble."

"Here's one for you."

Biting down on the biscuit as he picked up one side of the bag, his tongue got in the way and the sting brought water to his eyes. He ran his finger down the side of his tongue and felt a bump. There was a little blood on his finger and he tasted rust. But soldiers don't cry and he had to be a brave little one just like everyone kept telling him.

The bag was heavy and there were butterflies in Robbie's stomach just thinking about the baby. Having seen and felt the little hands and feet through the stretched skin of his mother's belly, he knew where the baby was.

But how was it going to get out?

Mary went over her instruments in her mind. The scissors she needed to cut the umbilical cord were sharp and there was sea salt solution to clean the baby's eyes. There was a needle and thread, a clean towel and a tiny nightgown, hand-stitched lately on one of her lonely nights.

Helen was bearing up well.

Suddenly, Helen's moan made Emma's birth come back to Mary. Dr. Lister had slapped Helen's face to keep her from fainting. "Helen, keep pushing! Keep going, Helen!" Helen had opened her brown eyes wider, sweat running down her face. She'd given one final great push with a horrific scream. Her body had gone limp. By the time Dr. Lister had managed to get the baby out, she was grey. He'd breathed into the tiny nose and mouth. Finally Emma had sputtered and whimpered. Mary was sure this was the reason why Emma had been so fussy.

"Robbie, you're getting to be such a big boy." Mary squatted and held him by the shoulders. His blue-grey eyes were clear and serious. She wiped the cookie crumbs from around his mouth with her thumb. It was too late for the valerian root. "There are more of those where that came from."

"Now, off you two go."

Mary rolled up her sleeves.

"Go now!" Helen grabbed the sides of the bed as another spasm clenched the muscles in her back.

As the children left, Helen felt a sharp tug in her bowels. "I have to go." She stood up and waved Mary off. "By myself. Please. I'm all right."

Worried, Mary stood at the doorway of Helen's house, watching her make her way to the lavatory, each step planted carefully.

As she grasped the privy door for support, Helen felt the baby bearing down. She cried, "Mary, the baby's coming! Help! The baby's coming!" She crossed her ankles and looked wildly about. Mary came running.

All down the row, doors were flung open.

Robbie pulled on Margie's door but it was stuck. He yelled for his mum. Now he knew how the baby was coming out. *Her stomach is going to burst!*

Margie steered him back to where he'd been playing with Emma and her sons.

She spoke gently, "It's just like when you and your sister were born. Everything turned out with you two, didn't it? It sounds worse than it is." Margie didn't mind telling them this little, white lie.

Outside, Mary and Helen's sister-in-law, Katie, grabbed Helen by the elbows. "Uncross your legs, come on."

"I can't, I can't." The pain was making her eyes roll back in her head.

Not again, not again.

"She'll never make it. Get my bag and a sheet!" Mary said.

23

Helen whimpered. Katie brought back Helen's quilt, and spread it on the ground.

Within fifteen minutes, a baby boy slithered out, red and crying and shaking his fists at them. Mary caught him.

"A boy! He's perfect. Listen to those lungs." Mary wrapped the baby in the apron she still had on from the washhouse. He was sucking on his fist, already looking for his mother's milk. She passed him to Katie. "Bathe him."

As Katie held the crying infant in the tub of lukewarm water, she said, "He's a James boy, alright."

"Thomas," Helen said faintly.

"What, Helen?"

"I want him to be called Thomas."

"William and Iain will like that," Katie said. Thomas James had been William's and Katie's husband Iain's younger brother. The one that had died in the fire-damp explosion. The same one in which Iain had been badly injured.

They helped Helen to her feet. Legs trembling, she made her way into her house, leaning on the women heavily for support.

"It's done," Helen said to herself.

When Robbie and Emma were allowed to see their new brother, Robbie said he mewed like a cat. And then he asked to hold him. Helen placed the still crying newborn in his arms. He sang in a sweet shy voice. Almost immediately the baby settled in his arms. The baby's fist curled around his little finger.

Realizing suddenly that it was dark, a great weariness overcame Mary. Her knees were bruised where she had fallen and her elbow hurt. Helen looked peaceful, the baby wrapped up tightly beside her.

Mary took a second to go outside alone. She gazed at the stars. Looking around to make sure nobody could see her, she crossed herself. *In the name of the Father, the Son and the Holy Ghost.*

Then William's voice came back to her. "Duck!" he'd yelled.

Something terrible has happened.

CHAPTER TWO

William was growing more adept at opening his pouch of tobacco and rolling up a cigarette single-handedly. He rolled them thinly to spread them out more. Every half an hour he lit up when he could, rewarding himself for making it through another thirty minutes of hell.

Hell was the trenches and wasteland between the Germans and The Allies, lumpy with torsos and torn-off limbs, puddles oily with blood. A festering boil of a place where the Devil watched and waited, rubbing his hands. It was brutally, mercilessly cold. And wet, always wet.

Just after 'Hogmanay', which William and the rest of the Scots refused to call New Year's Eve, the joints of William's left hand had frozen into a useless grip, caused, he thought, by the constant dampness and cold. When the coldness began to creep up his left arm towards his heart, like poison, he began to get worried. He hid it in his pocket.

***

Duncan glanced at William leaning against the corner of the reserve trench. They were set back about half a mile from the front where there was some respite from the immediacy of the war. They drank tea, ate the occasional eggs from the locals if they were lucky, talked and walked about freely. They even played 'footie' if the weather allowed and taut muscles were stretched, smiles and laughter cherished for the luxury they had become.

The less athletic played cards, betting the meagre belongings they had.

The look on Duncan's face was decidedly different from the jaunty angle of his cap. A shock of rusty matted hair hung down and then curled up over the tip of his cap, above a worried frown. His uniform was stiffly caked with mud.

"Duncan," William's voice was husky, "I need to see a doctor." His steel-blue stare was fixed on Duncan's face. Duncan looked quickly away from his old friend. He gave him the creeps.

Duncan kept his voice neutral. "It's just nerves. Here, take a swig." He stayed at arm's length and poured some of the gut-rot, government-issue rum into William's mug. Flicking his cigarette with his thumbnail once, twice, Duncan sat back on his haunches. It had rained every day this week and the puddles in the trenches had become cesspools that deepened after every rainfall, the density of the clay earth stopping the water from draining away. It was already knee deep and even lifting one leg out of it required Herculean strength. One more day and they would be up to their hips in the evil slime.

"I can't move my arm."

"Give it another day."

Shut up William.

Duncan reached down to pick up some mud and smeared it on his neck to help protect against the mites.

It is easier to kill when you feel like a pig.

In the reserve trenches, the officers tried their best to make the soldiers pour water into their helmets, lather and scrub their faces with the cabbage-smelling, acidic soap and scrape their whiskers off with their dull razors every twenty four hours. The shorter the hair, the less chance the lice could nest. When they scrubbed their scalp with the soap, it burned. "Good for morale!" said the Lance Corporal. "Good for discipline!" was another line of bullshit.

"For God's sake," William said dejectedly. "You know I wouldn't say anything if it weren't worse."

A green recruit spoke up, "I'm freezing. I can't feel my feet."

Now look what you've started, William.

Duncan sneered, "Freezing? So's my piss."

Then he sighed.

They're just scared. We've got to lighten things up before we go back to the front.

"Lads, my wife has put a spell on me." The boys looked at him.

"Any time I get near a French dame, I get the feeling like two eyes are boring into the back of my head. Like the wife can see me." Duncan flicked his cigarette again and picked tobacco from his lower lip, speaking loudly to make sure all the other soldiers sitting in the trench could hear him.

"So, you know what I do?" The boys waited.

"I put on my cap and pull it down low." He laughed. "I'm getting a reputation as the man who'll do anything with his headdress on." The boys laughed with him.

"Now take William here. His wife has put a spell on him so that he keeps his hands off the French ladies. Show them your rabbit's foot, William." Duncan lit another cigarette from the butt. William took his curled-up hand out of his pocket and the others glanced nervously at each other.

"Duncan's right!" He shook his hand at them. "It's been my good luck charm so far." Then he forced himself to laugh. There was a clearing of throats.

Duncan put on his cap, rolled up a trouser leg to show his calf and then blew them a kiss. Laughing, one of the men hit the butt of his rifle against the ground, another blew an appreciative whistle.

He then took out his cards and shuffled them and they soon had a game going, using cigarettes as the all-important stakes.

The shelling started up again and Duncan felt cold beads of sweat streaming down the middle of his back. Even though they were pretty far back, it sounded worse than the eye of a North Sea storm. The new men flinched.

A few aeroplanes flew over and the random way they were dropping their bombs, they could have belonged to either side. One fell onto a nearby farm and exploded. Within seconds, the barn went up in flames, fueled by the dry hay the army had stored in it for their horses. Even at this distance, they could hear shrill screams and they covered their ears with their hands. No one could tell if the sounds were horses or men.

"You are not to leave your posts," the Lance Corporal said as some of the men got up to help. "We're too far away to do anything, anyway."

As the horrible sounds faded, some men were brought by on stretchers. William and Duncan saw the last of their Kirkcaldy pals, Jamie, getting carried off. He saluted them with a tip of his hat. Their other friends were either dead, 'Missing in Action' or wounded.

The lucky bastard told William and Duncan that he had been saved by his guardian angel yesterday. She'd tripped him at the top of the trench during the nightly foray into no-man's land. He had fallen down, hearing a loud crack as he landed, his foot twisted under him. He'd lain there quietly till morning. None of the others had come back.

"I'll have a pint for you. Maybe three or four!"

Who can blame his grin? Duncan turned away.

He was escaping this hellhole. To a warm, dry bed with only a broken leg. No screaming shells, no mud seeping through the best of boots or thickest socks, no parasites scabbing and scarring scalp and skin. Alive. He had the kind of injury they all wished for.

William said to Duncan, "He's smiling now but once that foot's mended, they'll send him back."

Duncan shouted to Jamie, "McAlister, lucky beggar, we'll keep a warm spot in the trench for you!"

But Jamie didn't hear him; he was already looking north, toward home.

CHAPTER THREE

Their twenty-four hour respite from the front line now over, they had to return, buttoning their caps under their lapels and putting on their helmets. William tried to keep up to Duncan but he was with the two new limeys. They were silent, the constant shelling making conversation difficult. They spread out along the zigzag of the trenches. The Englishmen were around the corner from William and Duncan. There were so few of them.

"Hold your positions," they'd been told "Reinforcements are coming tomorrow."

When there was a lull, William rubbed his left hand with his right, still trying to get his fist to unclench. Duncan opposite, yelled at him. "Stop it. For Christ's sake, stop it. You've been doing that for days. You're driving me mad."

There was a zing as a bullet zipped by them. Duncan laid down his helmet. The weight of it gave him a headache and it was useless anyway against snipers. The first day they had worn them, a soldier had dropped dead in front of them, a hole clean through the middle of it. He peered carefully over the side, standing on a fallen sandbag, to see where the gunfire was coming from. They were so close to the enemy that they caught a whiff of cigarette smoke wafting by.

William turned away, his left side up against the trench as more bullets whizzed by, like angry wasps. He felt a strange, cold chill run up his spine and something made him yell, "Keep your head down, Duncan! Duck! DUCK!" There was a little yelp, like from one of the dogs that sometimes followed them around and something warm struck his neck. There was a thud.

Whirling around, William saw Duncan lying sprawled at the back of the trench, his eyes already lifeless. William cried, "No! Duncan! NO!" The bullet had made a small, perfectly round circle going through his forehead but had blown the back of his head off.

William slumped down beside his friend, sobbing as the sun struggled to break through the clouds. There was a temporary lull. The world felt empty and silent and, he wondered if he were the only man left alive. And then the shelling started again, raining earth on them. William held his one good hand over Duncan's open eyes.

Time passed as he sat there, a few minutes or an hour, he wasn't sure. He took a muddy handkerchief out of Duncan's kit and placed it over Duncan's eyes. Trying to light a cigarette with trembling hands, he dropped the matches into the mud. He needed a smoke. He heard a pop and a whine and another shell burst near him. Then he heard what sounded like return fire coming from around the bend in the trench. He got up to go there, picking his way past the motionless limeys from earlier on and was careful not to step on the limp criss-cross of arms and legs.

In the darkness of the heavy clouds and settling dirt stirred by the shelling, William was drawn to a pinpoint of light.

"Need a light!" William yelled over the fray. A soldier looked through him as he plucked the cigarette from his lips and held it to the end of his. William drew hard to light it.

The new recruits cowered up against the wall as the shelling started again. The Lance Corporal that had been in charge of them lay a few yards to their left in a heap, his kit still slung over his shoulder. It looked like it was packed to the brim. William felt gnawing in his stomach as his thoughts involuntarily turned to the chocolate, fruit cake, biscuits and other pleasures it might contain. It had been so long since he'd eaten anything that tasted good. The officers didn't have the dog-biscuit-like hardtack they had. Duncan had even chipped a tooth on a piece.

He needed the peace of another cigarette more than anything else in the world and recognizing the lad with the cold feet, gestured to his lips. The young man was relieved to see William still alive. Stammering a greeting, he smiled through his tears while passing him a machine-rolled fag from his lips. William wiped his hand on his jacket before taking it and felt the urge to hold the boy, to wipe away his tears, to kiss his forehead like he had Robbie's when telling him everything was going to be all right. He looked no older than sixteen.

Another shell burst and dirt flew into his face.

He wiped his eyes and took a long, deep drag of the cigarette. The stench was unbearable: rot and blood, mud and shit. Everything different shades of brown. He blew the smoke out through his nostrils. It was the only way of masking the smell. He wondered if he would ever be able to rid himself of it.

Saluting the boy, he was strangely calm. A voice whispered to him.

"It's all right, William. You'll make it. Just keep your head down."

Then, something moved at the periphery of William's vision. A dark furtive shape. A rat. He'd better get back to Duncan. They were fast, those dirty filthy beasts.

"Remember, William, keep your head down," the voice repeated.

He nodded and made his way as fast as he could around the corner of the trench. He should have covered Duncan up; that way they couldn't get to him. He could use the magenta bags that some poor misinformed ladies in England had made. A box of the multi-coloured bags to be filled with sand had arrived last week. They'd been made from old dresses or curtains but the men couldn't use them as sandbags.

"We don't want the Fritz to have an easy target," the Lance Corporal what-was-his-name who lay in the other trench, had told them.

William fished in Duncan's pockets for his pocketknife and then, sliced the seam open. He could just imagine the group of woman sitting together, a rainbow of material in their laps, in the safety of their church hall. One woman would have stood up, her chest rising and falling, to tell them to embroider some words of inspiration to the poor lads in the trenches. His had on it, 'Hope and Glory.'

He'd just finished covering Duncan's upper body as the stretcher bearers came around the corner. They pulled the material off Duncan's face. "We'll be back for him, have to check for the living first. Sorry, pal." Seeing Duncan's blood on him and his crippled hand he hadn't hid in his pocket, they stopped. "Are you wounded? What's happened to your hand?" the elder of the two spoke to him.

"I'm not wounded. Sore, just sore, cold and tired."

"You and the whole of the fucking army, mate," the younger one said. "Arsehole Andy" they'd nicknamed him after kicking a ball around with him a couple of weeks back. Andy was a poor loser. William had scored goal after goal on him when Andy was in net. Andy had yelled obscenities at the sun, sworn at the other players and screamed at William that he was offside. That was a lifetime ago.

The cold drizzle had started up again so William moved to get under cover of the slight overhang.

What will I tell Mary? She'll ask me about his last words or what he was like on his last day. She'll want to know if he was thinking of her.

"You bastard," he cursed in Duncan's direction, "Should I tell Mary that you whored around with those French girls?" He drew on his cigarette. "All right, Jesus, Duncan, I know you loved her. Don't worry." Almost out, he lit the next one from the stub. He deserved to chain smoke now. "I won't tell her."

William got up and crossed over to Duncan. As the stretcher bearers came around the corner again, they saw William on his knees looking through the dead soldier's kit and pulling out a bully beef tin.

"What are you doing there? Get your hands off his gear. Don't you have any respect?" Arsehole pushed William away and he fell on his side, the tin still in his hand, his lit cigarette falling from his mouth.

"Just the fags. The fags he won off me playing Crown and Anchor. Let me have them back. Duncan doesn't care anymore." He looked at him suspiciously. Maybe the Arsehole wanted them for himself.

The older stretcher bearer, wearier and greyer than Andy said, "Let him have them for God's sake. It's his dead pal."

As they picked Duncan up, William put the tin on the ground, pushed himself to his knees with his right hand, pulled out a cigarette and asked for a light. Andy put down his side of the stretcher and strode back over to William, Duncan's body sliding down until his feet hit the ground. "I'll give you a light, you shit." He kicked the tin and the cigarettes flew into the mud.

The older bearer yelled, "Andy, what the hell are you doing? Get back over here." Andy glared at William and then turned abruptly. William mouthed, "Arsehole!" Andy tilted his end of the stretcher up, pushing Duncan back onto it and they bore him off.

William, still on his knees, gathered up the cigarettes in a bunch. He sank back on his heels and leant against the wall of the trench, sorting through them. Only a few were dry and he put them in his pocket. He put the sodden rest in the tin, hoping to salvage the tobacco later. The stretcher bearers came back to take the other two bodies.

"Are you sure you're all right?" the older man spoke to him.

William said nothing.

"They should be sending reinforcements soon. Buck up." As they carried the last body away, he said to Andy, "Did you see his hand?"

The Arsehole looked back at him. "Yeah. He's faking it. I know his type."

At that moment, William hated him almost as much as the German who had killed Duncan.

The sky was getting darker and the shelling started again. He pulled himself to his feet wondering which side it was coming from. One hit nearby, sending a sheet of dirt down on top of him. "Shit," he said aloud, "Shit." The barbed wire was usually shelled just before it got dark, before an attack. He picked up his rifle and dropped it again to put his right arm over his head as another sheet of dirt showered him. He pressed his left side into the wall of the trench and covered his other ear with his hand. His face was wet and he wiped it, looking at his hand for blood. It was clear. He must be crying. Then there was a crack as loud as if lightening had struck and a tidal wave of dirt and mud hit him and knocked him onto his back. A ton of clay buried his body, leaving only his face and his right arm above ground. He struggled under the weight, trying to move. With great difficulty, he managed to free one foot and it lay above the earth, looking like it was severed from the rest of him. He was trapped.

Shivering, he yelled, "Help, Help, Somebody, Hey, You Stupid

Limey Bastards. Help Me!" He breathed in through his nose and out through his mouth. No, he thought, it should be the other way. In through his mouth and out through his nose. He coughed and then started to laugh till tears came to his eyes. Blinking the tears away, he yelled again, "Anybody, Anybody, Out There!?"

So, nobody is coming. But they will soon. That cocksure stretcher bearer will be back, if only to taunt me or see if I am dead.

He tried shouting again but the shrill shriek of artillery seemed to coincide with his calls for help.

He would just have to wait. He started to feel drowsy and his eyes closed. He dozed on and off for awhile. He dreamt about fog rolling in over the fields; Duncan and him running toward the enemy, invincible, bullets hitting the ground all around them; jumping into the Germans' trench, his bayonet sharp and ready. The faces turned up at him were round and pink and fat. He woke up with a jerk of his head. He licked his lips. It was starting to get dark. *Why isn't anyone coming?* If he was right and they were on the attack, the Germans would kill him if they found him.

But maybe he could promise them something. Cigarettes, money, secrets? Unless they spoke English, the few words of German the Flemish farmer had taught him wouldn't help. He couldn't say that to a soldier. *Ich liebe dich,* I love you. Duncan had made him practice over and over. "Just in case," Duncan had laughed. "For when we get there."

He thought of Helen, how her legs wrapped around him; the rise and fall of her hips. And then there was Emma, Robbie and little Thomas whom he had never seen. He dozed off again.

There was pale silver light in the trench when he woke from the sound of feet hitting the ground. The clay had become more rigid, tightening around his body. Another thud. And voices. As one of the Germans walked over and kicked William's exposed foot, he closed his eyes. William tried his best to play dead. He thought of the blankness of Duncan's dead face and took slow, quiet breaths.

"Eine Packung Zigaretten! Ich liebe Tommy Zigaretten." Liebe. The German loved English cigarettes. Whose cigarettes had he found?

William heard a match strike. He could smell the smoke and hear the crackle of the cigarettes. How he would love to have one. The shelling started again. Their side, our side? He could hear the Germans trying to scramble up the bank. The falling dirt as they slipped and slid. *"Verdammt!"* A blast. Screams. An avalanche of dirt. William closed his eyes.

Something heavy fell into the trench, very close to him and bits of clay flew into William's face. After blinking the dirt away, he realized his face was close to one of the Germans'. The soldier had fallen on his side, his lips close to William's ear, as though he still had something to say. One of his arms lay across William's chest. An awkward embrace.

What was that? One of the German's eyes stared at him, blue but lifeless in the moonlight. The other was covered in mud. He was sure he heard a low voice. It sounded like *The Lord's Prayer.* The familiar rhythm of the stanzas comforted him. At "Amen", the words began again and again and again until William was reciting it with the Voice. "Our Father."

"Forgive us our trespasses, as we forgive those who trespass against us." *Something like that.* He longed to wipe the dirt away from the German's eye as he knew it must be bothering him and to show he did not blame him, anymore. They were both only doing their duty. He thought back to Christmas when both sides had simultaneously put down their arms and exchanged greetings, the Germans generous with their tobacco and Christmas cake. The memories of candles, cigars and freshly felled pine trees. The German and he were one, both sons of the same God. Benevolence filled his eyes with tears. *Why were they fighting?* The coldness was in his head. He couldn't remember.

The sun rose on a beautiful day, the sky a brilliant blue. William's body was numb, the unbearable pain of lying there twisted for so long, gone. His eyelids fluttered and he mumbled to his only friend left in the world, *"Ich liebe dich. Danke schoen. Auf Wiedersehen."* I love you. Thank you. Goodbye.

He was thirsty, terribly thirsty. As the day grew dark, he began to mumble. The German was a good listener and very quiet. Not like Helen who always interrupted, who always had something to argue about. He avoided talking about Duncan; that would have been impolite under the circumstances.

A soft patter of rain on his face woke him up during the night but it didn't last long. He opened his mouth and it refreshed him: he had never tasted anything so good. The earth softened but he still couldn't move. He heard voices on and off, but they were gruff, guttural. There were grotesque shadows after the clouds were blown away and the sound of rustling made him sure the sprites of his childhood were there to play tricks on him.

CHAPTER FOUR

In the early morning, there were voices: "Wait a minute. This one's alive. He's one of ours. Let's get the poor bastard out of here." They rolled the German away and water was splashed on William's face to revive him, and then a cup was held to his mouth while two others cleared his body of the clay, using the butts of their guns and their helmets.

"Are you alright, fella? Does anything feel broken?" William's arms and legs were moved. "Look at his lip. He's chewed it raw. But all this dried blood on him can't be from that. It must be from the German. I wonder how long he's been lying like that." William lay on the stretcher, thinking he really must be in heaven, his body suddenly feeling lighter than air. "Don't worry, we'll have you out of here in a jiffy."

"Was the German the only one in the trench with you? Just nod or shake your head." The words echoed around him, and he wasn't sure, were they speaking to him? *It didn't matter.*

The Canadian soldiers waited with him until their stretcher bearers carried him to their doctor, who felt his limbs all over for breaks and then helped him get to his feet. William's knees buckled instantly.

"Where did you find him?" he asked the stretcher bearers.

"He was lying in one of the trenches. Buried under a ton of clay and a dead German."

"What regiment are you from? What has happened to the other men, son?"

The doctor, Lieutenant Colonel John McCrae, tenderly wiped his face clean. He stitched the gash in his lip, quickly rinsing it with some clean water and then held some strong liquid to his mouth.

He spoke quietly to him, "You need some rest. And some food." William's eyes were blank. Dr. McCrae looked around for a piece of paper and then tore the only page out of his own personal notebook that had some space on one side. He wrote the word "shellshock" on it and pinned it to him, using William's regiment pin.

"I'm not sure if he can hear us, Harry. Take him over to his own."

William was carried over to the British medical tent and they put him outside on the ground as the morning rush of wounded were brought in.

Andy and his partner noticed William as they were walking by. "What the hell happened to him? Look at his eyes. I've seen that before. They call it 'the thousand yard stare'."

"So he wasn't faking it." The older man frowned at Andy, wishing he could be paired with someone else. The Arsehole shrugged.

The noise of the war escalated again: the pounding of the artillery, the explosion of grenades, the sniper's deadly gunshots. The two men left William, picked up their stretcher and strode back off to their grim task.

CHAPTER FIVE

Robbie glared at his mother's profile from the back seat of Mr. Hunter's motorcar. How he hated her. He didn't want to leave his friends, his home, everything he had ever known, to go and live with his granddad. Her open-mouthed snore resonated in the back of her throat. He unfolded his arms and stared at Mr. Hunter's neck. His scowl softened. He would save it for when his mother woke up. Sandwiched between dozing Emma and Tom, who had been rocked to sleep by the car's motion, Robbie pushed at them until they were right up against the doors.

"All right there, lad?" Mr. Hunter was on the edge of his seat, concentrating so intently on the gravel road that it made Robbie wonder how he noticed what he was doing. He was tempted to fake sleep, but was sure if he did, Mr. Hunter would know he was having him on. He nodded, having vowed, when his mother told him they were leaving, never, ever, to speak again. And so far, he hadn't. Not even when she had yelled at him. He had stuck his fingers in his ears and she had chased him round the room with a broom, until he dove under the table and she gave up.

The seven-year-old was going to miss his friends and surprisingly enough, school. They were doing mental arithmetic and he was getting really good at it. Every time the teacher asked them a question, his arm shot up as if it had a life of its own.

He couldn't even remember his granddad. All he could recall of his trip to Kirkcaldy was the beach where his dad and he had hunted for treasure: stones and shells and things washed up on the shore. His father had picked up a white transparent piece of glass and had held it up in the sunlight where it shone magically. It was still his prize possession.

Mr. Hunter cleared his throat over his mother's snore which had gotten louder and wasn't at all lady-like.

"I said, all right there, son?"

Robbie knew he should answer but he'd crossed his heart and hoped to die, not to say a word. If his mother knew he was acting like this, she'd be angry with him for being rude, especially because Mr. Hunter was a kind man, one of the managers of the mine where his father had worked and was doing them a favour by driving them to Kirkcaldy.

But what should he care? His father didn't work there anymore. He was in the hospital and wasn't going back to the mines. That was why they had to leave.

He'd overheard Johnny say that his father was a coward and Robbie wanted to fly at him and ram those words right down his throat. But there'd been a crowd with Johnny and he was only saying it because he couldn't add up two plus two even if he wrote it down.

When Robbie cornered him later by himself and twisted his arm up hard behind his back like his dad had taught him to, just in case, Johnny said he was sorry. It was a good thing he had practiced the 'iron grip' on Tom and Emma. It'd worked. Johnny wasn't really that big after all. He only had a big mouth.

And then, Robbie apologized too. After all, they had been friends forever, at least two years. Johnny said he really did like Robbie's dad and he wished him good luck.

Robbie went back to staring at the back of Mr. Hunter's neck. He had tried looking out of the window but the blur of things speeding by, was making him feel sick to his stomach. There was a red spot on Mr. Hunter's neck that seemed to be growing as Robbie watched.

All of a sudden, he blurted, "Stop!"

Mr. Hunter, having children of his own, knew that tone and was able to halt immediately. With remarkable agility, he jumped out of the car and wrenched the door handle open as Robbie, one hand over his mouth, threw himself over sleeping Tom and vomited onto the road, splashing Mr. Hunter's polished black shoes.

After that, Mr. Hunter asked Robbie to sit in the front seat so he could keep an eye on him and Robbie dozed for the last few miles with a foul taste in his mouth and a sour smell in his nostrils.

Robbie was jolted awake as they crossed the tram tracks that ran down the middle of the street. His mother took out a tattered envelope to check the address as they pulled up to the house on Links Street.

As Mr. Hunter took the apple boxes with their belongings out of the car's boot, Helen recognized the bleary-eyed, ragged man leaning against the building as her father-in-law, Bill.

There were chunks of stone missing out of the building and there was a musty smell of damp brick. The Wynd that ran beside the building was strewn with fetid garbage. The windows looked fragile and loose.

As he said good-bye, Mr. Hunter gave Helen a thin envelope. "I hope this will help. If there is anything else I can do for you…let me know."

"Thank you." Helen didn't trust herself to say anything more. She was taking in this grey, narrow street which wasn't the day tripper's 'seventh heaven' that William's brother, Iain, had described. Both Iain and his wife, Katie, hadn't mentioned that, to get to the frivolity of the beach, you had to pass the tumbledown houses, the pungent tang of the factory and the dirty barefoot children running wild in the streets. She slipped Mr. Hunter's envelope into her handbag.

Bill had his hands in the pockets of his stained trousers, the brim of his old felt hat turned up. When he spoke he didn't meet her eyes, fixing his gaze on her chin. "Hello, lady. Lovely day." In reply, Helen stammered out a hello, her eyes welling up.

He doesn't know me.

He turned his gaze on the children. "What's your name, little girl?" He reached out to touch Emma's hair. She took a few steps backward. The children stared wide-eyed and frightened at this scarecrow of a man. "Are you three her children?" He pointed a dirty fingernail at Helen. Getting no response, he took his hat off and quickly rotated it, folding the brim down. Then he shrugged.

"Bill. Don't you recognize me? It's Helen," she added, "William's wife." She overcame her revulsion and put a hand on his sleeve.

"Yes. Oh, yes." He nodded but nothing registered in his eyes. "Have you come to help?"

"Of course, Bill. We've come to live here. With you."

Helen was shocked at the change in Bill. When she'd met her parents-in-law at her wedding in Pitlochry, he'd had a spring in his step and a sharp wit. He'd been the life of the party, telling tales with a twinkle in his eye. In the course of a decade, he'd become a stooped old widower, egg bits stuck to his wisp of a beard, each wrinkle deepened into a crease lined with dirt.

He took a deep breath, as bits of his memory churned in his head like coloured glass in a kaleidoscope. "That's nice." He shuffled his feet a little. "Could I bother you for a coin?" Helen dug in her purse and passed one to him. "Thank ye. Much obliged."

Mumbling, Bill then turned away, the coin in his hand putting determination in his step.

The door opened abruptly and William's sister, Agnes, greeted them curtly as she watched her father go down the street. She shook her head. To no one in particular, she asked, "Where's he going?"

Helen started to answer but Agnes had already turned to lead them up the narrow steps.

"How was the trip? Fancy motor car. I've never sat in one myself." Agnes had a complexion the colour and texture of porridge.

"Fine, fine," Helen said. "This is Emma, Robert and Tom."

To the children she said, "This is your father and Uncle Iain's sister, Aunt Agnes."

From the outside, the house looked bigger than their Lochoal home. But when they went up the steps and through the front door, it opened onto a short dingy hallway with three doors. With one straight ahead, one to the right and one to the left, she realized the size was deceptive. It was wide but had no depth. There was no light fixture and something crunched under her foot. There was the sound of something scurrying. She put her hand on the wall and quickly withdrew it. It was sticky. The air was dank, caused by a lack of light and air and being so close to the sea.

Agnes pointed to the door at the end. "The lav's out back. You share it with the two families in the house to the left. That door," she pointed to the left, "is Dad's room." She turned the door handle on the right. "This is yours."

The walls were yellowish, lighter in places where pictures had been. Emma sneezed. Near the rusty oven and sink, there was mould. There was a box bed opposite the oven. The spring sunshine struggled valiantly to get through the greasy film on the windows.

"I live around the corner on Heggis Wynd." They'd passed a lot of the short Wynds, leading east and west. She lived in one of the buildings nearer the Firth. "I haven't had time to clean up in here, today."

Not just today. Helen looked around.

"You'll have to keep an eye on dad. And make his supper."

Helen nodded. *So that's the catch. I'm to play nursemaid.*

Agnes grew bolder. "And, clean his clothes and his room. That should be easy as you have nothing much else to do."

"Yes." But Helen had a question. "How did you manage to get a works flat?"

"That's for me to know." Agnes looked uncomfortable. "Just take care of the old man and you won't need to worry about it."

"Well, I must go." Agnes picked up her shawl from the chair. On her way out she said, "Don't give him any money. When he drinks, he's even more mixed up."

Robbie had been listening carefully. His mother didn't tell Aunt Agnes about the coin she'd given him. He wondered if she'd forgotten.

As the door shut behind Agnes' ample back, Robbie picked up the box and the rolled up clothes and moved them further into the room. Helen rubbed a circle on the window and looked out. She could see a well-kept graveyard across the street. It seemed to be the only green in sight.

Nobody had mentioned anything about taking care of Bill before. She picked up Tom in her arms, and went back out into the hallway and turned the handle of Bill's room. It was gloomy, a grimy sheet filtering the light from the only window. She lifted a corner with two fingers and it floated lazily to the floor, swirling up dust.

She now understood the send-off Katie and Iain had given her and the children. No wonder. They were rid of Helen and her brood and old Bill would be taken care of. *Kill two birds with one stone.*

She'd never liked Iain or her sister-in-law. Of the two brothers, William had inherited the looks of the family. Iain's fire-damaged lungs had given him a waxy complexion, like the oxygen he was able to breathe was all used up before it could get through to his skin.

His wife, Katie, was always jealous. Helen remembered one time when she was picking up a cast-off dress for Emma. Before she could excuse herself, Iain came home. Puffed up like a peacock, Iain had announced he had volunteered to enforce the blackout in Lochoal. It had been imposed on all the communities on both east and west coasts. To do this, he would be out on patrol every night till midnight. The accusations flew. "Who is it?" Katie had demanded, spittle flying. "Who are you seeing?"

He'd surprised Helen by speaking firmly to Katie. "I was not given a chance to serve before." His eyes had grown harsh. "The Zeppelins are making their way north. They've already been spotted. I am going to do my duty whether you like it or not." Helen had left quickly before Katie could continue her tirade.

Helen wrinkled her nose at the strong fug of old man in Bill's room. He must be incontinent. There were dirty clothes scattered on the floor and something nest-like in a corner. Piled up against the back wall right up to the ceiling were old newspapers. Beside which, there were balls of string, pieces of wood and shards of sticky-looking jelly jars. In the corner, there were old flour sacks, wooden apple boxes, empty cigarette boxes, cookie tins. It looked like he'd collected anything he could get his hands on.

She expected she was supposed to clear this out. Helen went quickly back into the other room, slamming the door behind her. This was her future. Tied to a dim-wit father-in-law and three young children. She'd fostered a tiny ray of hope by coming to Kirkcaldy. With Mary out of her life, she'd thought that there would be more support here, living with family. Now there was just one more poor old sod depending on her.

Damn William. A thought shamefully crossed her mind that her husband would be better dead to her than alive. She'd get a widow's pension. She began to cry, holding Tom tightly as he squirmed. There was no chance of escape. The noose was tightening.

Putting Tom down, she went back to the window and looked out. All she had to do was walk out. She could leave with a clear conscience. The children had been delivered to their grandfather with Aunt Agnes close by. And besides Iain and Agnes, William had six more brothers and sisters somewhere. Surely there had to be one warm-hearted member of the family that would take them in.

The only sounds were Tom loudly sucking his thumb, Emma expelling air through her mouth and the squeak of skin on glass as she enlarged the circle on the window above the sink that Helen had started. The children were abnormally quiet, waiting for her next move.

Almost three years since she'd seen William. If it weren't for Robbie, she wouldn't even remember what he looked like. He mirrored his father's sturdy good looks with the same wiry body, soft hair and the family trademark blue eyes.

Helen was weary. It had been so long since she'd felt the touch of her husband. At first, she'd spent furtive moments stroking herself, thinking of him. As her pregnancy with Tom advanced, she'd been content to trace the contours of the baby through the skin of her belly.

Sitting down, she thought back to when she'd received the telegram and had known that the William she loved, had changed forever. A few weeks after Tom's birth, Helen had heard the distinctive rattle of Lochoal's postman's bicycle rims, his tires long punctured and removed, and had looked out of her window in alarm. He'd already delivered the post in the morning and was wearing the black band high on his arm. That meant only one thing. As he passed, curtains all along the Row were pulled aside. The scent of her husband came to Helen in a rush.

The postman stopped in front of her house and hesitated, and as Helen watched, holding her breath, he took a telegram out of his bag. The poor old man had loved his job before the war, being outside, winking at all the young women. He saw Helen at her window. She opened the door before he could knock and took the proffered telegram from him with shaking hands, as he stood there. Sensing bad news, Robbie picked up Tom, who started to cry, his tiny fists curling and uncurling with each wail.

"It's from a hospital, not the War Office," the postman said, wanting desperately to help. She gasped.

Robbie waited for her to speak as she scanned the letter, his fingernails in his mouth. When he saw the relief in her face, he felt an urgent need to pee. "He's in hospital."

"Please, Mrs. James. I need your signature." The postman had another telegram in his hand.

"Who's that for?" Helen felt a cold shiver run through her as she asked this.

"Mrs. Duncan Reid." He read from the envelope.

"Mary!"

"I'm afraid so." He got back on his bicycle and rode the short distance with Helen close behind him.

He reached Mary's door before Helen could catch up and she heard him starting to speak. "My heartfelt condolences, Mrs. Reid…" Mary stopped him by slamming the door in his face. Crestfallen, he stood in front of the closed door, telegram still in his hand and probably thought about retiring; as he'd done every time he'd delivered one of those black messages.

Helen took and signed for Mary's telegram, and then brushed roughly by him, opening the door to a wild-eyed Mary who refused to take the envelope. "They've made a mistake. I would have seen it!" Her voice was shrill.

Suddenly, she put her hand to her mouth. "Oh my God! That's what it was. When I fainted." A moan started in her throat and spilled out over her lips. "Duncan! Duncan! God help me. Duncan!"

It had turned into a dreadful wail, her face contorting and her hands clenched at her sides. "Damn him, damn him to hell!" She'd knocked the table onto its side and a teapot and cup crashed to the floor. Helen had managed to get out of the way of the hot, flying liquid. Picking up the chair, Mary had hurled it at the window but hit the wall, missing it.

Helen was startled out of her reverie by the sound of a chair hitting the floor beside her. Robbie had knocked it over, trying to move it to the window. The children had been quiet, waiting for her to take charge. How her life had changed. She pulled out her hankie and wiped her eyes. The rooms just needed to be cleaned. They'd make do. Helen rolled up her sleeves and flicked her hankie at Robbie.

But as she filled the kettle to make tea, she felt a pang of loss for

Mary, Lochoal and then she longed for her husband until the tears came to her eyes.

She sat down again, drinking her tea after having let the children out to explore. She picked up the weekly that Agnes had left behind. She sighed. The newspapers were always full of victorious battles, in which the Huns were always pushed back. If that were true, she thought, the front would be in Russia by now. She turned the page. Each week another staple was being added to the rations list. Beef, butter, tea and now, margarine were in short supply.

The women's columns were full of tasteless wartime recipes, using nutritious substitutes. Cakes with no sugar. Puddings with no milk. The biggest ads were for resoling your shoes or boots or dying your old coat to make it look new. Changing the collar on a dress would provide a whole new look.

She folded the paper and stood up to look out of the window again while draining the dregs of her tea. Across from them, the church and cemetery fit in neatly between the houses. Tender ivy covered the church, protecting it from the elements. The chimes were gentle, as they rang one, two. Not like the set-your-teeth-on-edge bell in Lochoal that had been installed by the mining company.

The church within a stone's throw. Although it bore another name, she knew it to be William's mother's Church of the Auld Licht, the one that had put the fear of God into William as a child. He'd told her how at every funereal Sunday morning service, the sombre minister always warned his congregation about Satan's work. The Devil never slept, he was always watching and waiting. He'd heard more about the Devil than God.

CHAPTER SIX

After hours of cleaning up, the children were allowed to go outside again. Robbie had seen a mob of kids playing on the street earlier and wanted to join them. But Emma and Tom were shy and so the three stayed close together, kicking a stone back and forth until their mother called them in.

Helen had left almost all the dirty dishes to the last. Judging by the mould, Bill had given up eating off plates a while ago. They were surprisingly good bone china, a little chipped, probably from his wife's family.

There was a plate piled high with bread and a slab of cheese cut into pieces on the table. The rest of the dishes were in the sink. "Robbie, wash the dishes so we can eat. Emma, you dry," she said, not looking at them, nodding toward the kettle, steaming hot. Robbie lifted the rag in the sink. The dishes looked like they were growing green fur. He washed and then rinsed them, the mould sticking to his fingers. Emma, ignoring Robbie's sulk, dried them and put them on the table.

That night, when Bill returned, Helen woke at the sound of the door opening. From the box bed she was sharing with the children, she saw him peer into the room. He stood still, illuminated by the moon, sensing their presence. He took a step forward. She shivered and pulled the bedclothes up to cover her chin. He circled the room slowly and then left, crossing the hallway.

The church clock chimed four. She heard Bill cough and then fall into a deep, rhythmic snore. He had left both doors open.

Helen pulled on a dress and a shawl and tiptoed outside into the early morning. The street that had been so busy with trolleys, automobiles, horses and carriages and playing children during the day, was tranquil. She sat on the graveyard bench just inside the open gate. There was a gentle fragrance in the air. She recognized Lily of the Valley, the scent of an eau de toilette, her husband's wedding gift to her. It brought tears to her eyes as she pulled her shawl tighter, rubbing her arms vigorously. She hadn't been able to get warm since William had left for the war.

But she didn't want to go back in just yet. She was enjoying the solitude. It was half five. She got up and stood facing their new home. The length of the street ran straight in both directions and was a lifeless, cinder grey. If she hadn't seen the multitude of people coming and going the day before with her own eyes, it would have seemed as bleak as the surface of the moon. With a shiver, she went back to the flat, through the dim light.

There was a half bottle of gin near the sink. Bill must have left it there. Just a nip would get rid of the chill. Helen picked up the bottle and wiped off the top with her sleeve. She poured a little into a chipped cup and drank it down in a few gulps. Gasping a little, she then felt heat coursing up from her stomach. She poured some more.

She felt better. She took another large gulp. *What the hell.*

She finished off the bottle, humming to herself. The tenseness in her shoulders was gone. She joined the children in bed and when they got up an hour later, she turned her back to them, telling them to be quiet.

CHAPTER SEVEN

Mary applied her pancake makeup with a damp sponge starting at her chin and working it up to the temples. It was too dark for her complexion and she didn't know how to blend it in, but she wore it anyway, leaving an abrupt line at her jaw. She thought it made her look sensual, exotic. Like one of her new friends at work showed her, she turned up her lipstick in its tube and applied it to the apple of her cheeks, then put a little more onto the middle of her lips and spread it with her finger. Using the scissors that she'd just sharpened, she evened out the wisps of short hair, with the bottom of her ear lobes as a measure.

She cleared up the hair and washed the dishes from her supper. Even though she'd always been a tidy person, she was sharing a room with two girls from the factory, and they all had to be extra careful. There were mice everywhere.

Most of the women wore short hair at work. After the heat of heavy hair tucked up under the cloth cap, it was a blessing to have it short. She took a little of the precious sugar she had left, mixed it with a little water and applied it to the curls in front of her ears.

"Not bad for an old girl," she said aloud, having just celebrated her thirty-second birthday.

Jimmy was taking her to the moving pictures and then for a drink.

She pressed the sponge against her upper lip to blot the beads of perspiration that had formed there. Just thinking about him made the blood rush to her face. He'd been hired as her supervisor at Macready's linen factory six months ago, almost immediately after having been released from the hospital, men being in short supply. There were pock-holes all over his torso where pieces of shrapnel had been embedded and the scars on his face weren't unusual these days. He walked with a limp but the rest of his body worked just fine. Mary had fallen for his kindness and charm.

There was a knock at the door and Mary called, "It's open," as she pulled on the cloche hat he had bought her earlier this week. It was dark blue, like her coat, setting off her eyes nicely and her hair was just long enough to curl out from under it. He was always buying her things, not like Duncan. *Damn it,* Mary thought as she bit her lip. She didn't want to think about Duncan anymore. She was a different person now: her life with him seemed so long ago. She threw her arms around Jimmy's neck so he couldn't see her face.

Jimmy wanted to get married to Mary but needed to get a divorce first. His wife had cheated on him when he was in hospital and had gone off, leaving Jimmy and his family to cope with his children. He knew Mary would be a loving wife and mum to his five, young bairns.

"It is easy for an ex-serviceman to get a divorce these days," he coaxed her.

The more she thought about it, the more it made sense. They weren't youngsters anymore. He was close to thirty-five and, although he was no Duncan, as far as looks went, he was a good man. She loved his children. As he sat at the table, waiting for her to put her shoes and coat on, she plunked a clipping from the Kirkcaldy Free Press down in front of him.

"It looks like you're right, Jimmy. It's about a divorce. The judge was indignant that the woman had fooled around with a civilian while her husband was away fighting. It was granted right away."

"Yeah," he said reading through it, "exactly what I thought."

"Well?" She ruffled his hair. *Nice, thick hair.*

He looked surprised. "I thought you weren't ready."

"I think I am now," she said softly. "Have you changed your mind?"

"Not at all." He got up and pulled her toward him. "Just you try and stop me." They didn't get to the pictures after all, that night.

CHAPTER EIGHT

The summer changed Robbie. He became an adventurer, scavenging for food and coal with a gang of boys in the street who'd befriended him.

He'd made a kind of a bucket out of a cookie tin and shoelaces found in his grandfather's room and, as long as he didn't return with it empty, he was allowed to go off without Tom or Emma. Sometimes he brought home cock o'leekies or winkles, shellfish scraped off the side of one of the docks and they'd have a good meal. He sometimes got coal by following the coal trains and picking up pieces that fell off. They dug for potatoes in local fields, two of the boys acting as lookouts, sharp stones in their pockets in case the farmers let the dogs loose.

Occasionally, he was given an odd errand to do by the butcher or baker in town and was rewarded with a loaf of day old bread or a link of sausages. They said he was still too young to have a job, although he was a real hard worker.

Robbie was proud of his contributions to the family. He was doing his part. But the best thing of all was that while he was foraging, he was free.

Helen bounced between extremes. She would go for days without washing, cleaning, cooking. In fact, Robbie didn't know what she really did all day. Sometimes when he brought his catch of the day home, Helen was sleeping in the rank sheets. He would put the kettle on, clear the mess off the table, while Emma cooked dinner and washed Tom.

He even helped sweep up at the bakery sometimes and would leave with his reward under his arm. Every time he was there, Mr. Lukovski asked his daughter if she had seen the boy's mother.

She shrugged her thin shoulders under her white jacket, looking very much like her mother when she was her age.

"No," she spoke English carefully, wanting to rid herself of the final nuances of her Polish accent. "His sister and his little brother. But his mother, no."

One day, Mrs. MacLeod, the lady who was taking care of the church in her husband's absence, overheard the baker and his daughter as she came into the shop. She understood that they were talking about that woman across the street. The woman with that girl and two boys, one of whom had befriended the stray dog that was always making a mess in the churchyard. She sighed. Another family fallen victim to the war. Maybe the mother was ill. Maybe they didn't have enough money. She'd have to pop over to see if she could help.

***

Helen counted the few coins left in the envelope that Mr. Hunter had given her. She'd have to do something soon. But tonight there was food on the table, courtesy of her almost eight-year-old son. If she could only muster up some energy.

She got up and tugged the window open, fighting back tears. She hadn't heard anything from Mary in quite a while, and William, according to the letter she'd got from the head nurse at the clinic, was still unresponsive. She opened the cupboard and poured herself a thimbleful of gin. She had her back to the children but felt Robbie's eyes burning a hole in the back of her head. The boy was turning into her harshest critic, watching her, judging her. She had to hide the alcohol that had become her warmth, from Bill who would drink it and from Robbie who would hide it.

She let the gin roll around in her mouth, burning her tongue before she swallowed it. She poured another shot, this time a proper one and sat back on the chair. Robbie, with a tight jaw, went outside with Emma and Tom, to play in what was left of the afternoon sunshine.

CHAPTER NINE

As she closed the front door of her country home, Mrs. Cameron placed the palm of her hand on it as if she could feel its pulse. The spring breeze ruffled her hair. She stayed that way for a few minutes while her husband and two daughters waited anxiously for her in their polished sedan. The shoulders that she tried so hard to square, drooped.

When she'd married and moved into this house, she'd been proud and frightened at the same time, proud of becoming part of her husband's established family and afraid that she wouldn't fit in. Her husband, who had always moved in these gentle countryside circles with his parents and sisters, hadn't understood her trepidation. Her fear had passed in time, with his mother requesting her advice on the garden and asking her to co-host festivities.

She'd vowed to stay in this house forever, already planning to plant the new rosebushes that an admirer had named after her.

Years later, at the beginning of the war, when her son came home elated from enlisting, she felt a sharp unease tugging at her heart. Whenever the war was mentioned, she got up and stiffly left the room. She had recognized the heartbreakingly thin line between life and death, so easily erased, that no amount of privilege could thicken.

Then, the day came when they were told their son, their only son, lay mingled with the dirt of a foreign country. She was inconsolable and her husband and daughters, deeply saddened in their own quiet way, grew concerned they had lost her, too. She whispered to her husband, in a hoarse voice unfamiliar to him, "he has disappeared."

Mrs. Cameron swallowed and patted the door goodbye. Parents were not supposed to outlive their children. She would never kiss his cheek, hold his babies, or see his dazzling smile again. But she had to carry on, for the sake of the rest of her family.

She walked slowly away from the house, wobbly on weak knees, towards the running car. The family had agreed to her suggestion to loan the house to the Red Cross for the convalescence of shell-shocked soldiers. The house was too big and quiet for her now, and, these men that no-one wanted, no-one believed in, told to buck up and pull themselves together, could use the fresh, quiet air to heal.

The Camerons went to live in their house in the city, praying that their generosity would be tallied up on their boy's side in heaven, where he now surely was.

***

When Doreen first arrived to get the house ready for the soldiers, she got out of the car at the bottom of the drive. She said she'd wanted to stretch her legs and that was the truth, because the springs had also been coiled hard and tight, right under the thin, cracked leather of the seats, and she'd felt their outline pressed into the back of her thighs the whole ten miles from Edinburgh. She walked up the drive more slowly, rubbing the back of her legs and feeling the crunch of the gravel under her thin-soled shoes.

Standing in the driveway to get a good idea of where she was going to live, she took a long look at the ivy-covered century-and-a-half old building. How lucky they'd been to get this. Something extraordinary was going to happen here, she could feel it. For once, her father had done something good.

After hanging up her coat in the hallway, she'd made her way up the wide staircase to the top floor of the house to make herself familiar with the layout. Two cots were in each of the small rooms on the top floor. There was just enough space for a shared night-table and to be able to change the sheets or lift the patients carefully if they needed assistance. They had been servant's quarters, she thought, with no large windows to encourage idle thoughts.

The grander rooms were on the middle and ground floors. The small, iron cots looked cold and harsh against the pink and mauve floral gentleness of the girls' rooms. She moved on to the magnificent master bedroom, with its French windows leading out onto a balcony. It was still empty. "We could fit at least ten in here," thought Doreen. "And if need be, we could squeeze forty patients into the house."

The only stipulation the Red Cross had given them was not to use the dead son's room. A request from the mourning mother. Mrs. Cameron could not bear to change or remove its contents. It was the only locked door but the key, like the others, was clearly marked on the ring Doreen had been given. She paused in front of it and then opened it, looking around first to make sure no one saw her.

The heavy curtains had only been left slightly open and the stillness of this room felt chilly and damp. Darkly masculine, it had model ships, athletic trophies and a collection of leather-bound books. A white sheet covered the bed and armchair as if the owner were on holiday. She walked over to the chest of drawers and opened the top drawer. Towels, shorts, vests. The next drawer down contained neatly folded, starched white shirts and a pile of handkerchiefs. She ran her hand over them feeling their cool crispness. Hearing the creak of footsteps on the floorboards above, she picked one and shut the drawer. A gold ring flashed as it fell. The footsteps were making their way toward the stairs. She slipped the handkerchief and the ring into her pocket. Finding the key, she turned it in the lock. Not until she was safely on the ground floor did she look at the ring. She traced the engraved 'W' on it with a thoughtful finger. She put it back in her pocket.

Walking from room to room on the ground floor, she noted the thickness of the freshly-oiled, cherry-wood paneling. The movers were almost finished dragging the bed frames into the master bedroom upstairs but the sound was muffled, well-absorbed by these walls.

It was a glorious home even though it had been stripped of anything valuable. The cheap cots, mismatched furniture and the overpowering smell of antiseptic didn't affect its magnificence: whimsical stencils on the walls and marble floors in the bathrooms; shiny faucets, and richly embroidered drapes in all the bedrooms. The kitchen was fully stocked with enormous pots and pans, scoured and waiting.

She opened the doors off the spacious sitting room onto the peaceful garden. It would still be warm enough to sit outside well into October. The small orchard would help shelter them from the elements. She walked out over the terrace to one of the trees and picked an apple, reaching as high as she could. Her father had always said the best ones were at the top. Holding it first up to her nose, she then bit into it. She grimaced. They looked red and ripe and delicious but it was sour.

From the abundance of rich fall colours, she picked some flowers for her night table. Magenta, crimson, gold. Suddenly, a gust of wind stirred up the leaves on the ground. The sweet smell of decay caused a weakness in her knees. She was in the garden at home, her father standing behind her. His breath was hot on her neck. She'd stood completely still.

Dropping the flowers, she turned up her collar and walked back into the house.

***

William James was the first patient to arrive there. To save from going up and down the stairs, he was put into the room near Doreen's.

How fragile his body looked yet only his lip was scarred. Checking his chart, she saw he was one of those who made no sounds except for the nightly, indecipherable nightmares. She was grateful for this house, with its thickly panelled walls, that would draw in his nightly terrors and absorb them. As she looked at the distance in his eyes, she knew his road to recovery wasn't going to be easy on either of them.

Dugald, the only other staff member that had so far arrived, got William's limp body into clean pyjamas while Doreen sorted his things into the chest of drawers. A torn out notebook page, stained with blood and creased, fluttered to the floor. "Shellshock" had been scribbled on one side of it. On the other side, there was a poem written in a close hand. It was called: *"In Flander's Fields."*

In Flanders fields, the poppies blow
Between the crosses, row on row.
That mark our place; and in the sky
The larks still bravely singing, fly
Scarce heard amid the guns below.

There were two more stanzas. When she was finished, she folded the paper and slid it into her pocket as tears welled up for Gregory and the generation of men her age who were being wiped out. It was a terribly sad poem, yet it filled her with hope. Determination and hope. *If our men feel this strongly, we will not lose.*

Dugald was watching her, waiting for instructions. He hoped the rest of the staff were going to be people like him, people who had to work for a living and not upper middle-class, do-gooder types like her. If it weren't for this war, women like her would be spending time at tea parties and church gatherings or whatever they did. She was already crying over the first patient. He left her alone with the poor bag of bones, telling her to call him when she had something useful for him to do.

Doreen covered William's arms and tucked in his sheet. It was cold in the room and she didn't want him to get a chill. Leaving him to rest, she went to her room and put the poem into the drawer of her night-stand for safe-keeping, alongside the handkerchief and the ring.

The unopened letters that had accompanied his things were put there, too.

***

After a few days, others began to turn up, some with mangled bodies as well as souls. She started placing them in rooms from the ground up, the least needy at the top. Most of them were quiet; a few sat in wheelchairs, like William, with their minds still focused on the trenches. Doreen assessed each of the twenty-three men as they arrived.

At the end of a breathless week, just before turning off the lamp in her room, she picked up the picture of Gregory on her nightstand.

It was almost eighteen months since Doreen's mother had told her of Gregory's death, knowing about her daughter and him, even though a relationship had never been mentioned.

It had been a busy day for Doreen's mother, she told her daughter, as she poured the tea. First, attending the church service in her hometown and then, on her way home, stopping by her daughter's nurse's residence. Doreen, wary of the unexpected visit, lit a cigarette, waiting for the reason. Her mother perched her petite frame on the arm of a chair in Doreen's room.

The vicar's sermon had been soothing, especially for all the poor souls who'd lost someone at the front or still had someone overseas. Her mother dabbed her eyes with her handkerchief. Doreen exhaled a long stream of cigarette smoke. "I wish you wouldn't blow that in my direction, dear." Her mother waved the smoke away. "By the way," she continued her hands now fiddling with the clasp on her brooch, "Mrs. Sutherland and her son's fiancé were there, too, dressed in mourning. You knew her son Gregory, didn't you? I think she only had the one?" The cigarette fell from Doreen's fingers.

Her mother gazed down at her hands. Doreen rushed from the room. Her mother picked up the cigarette and crushed it in the ashtray with a twist of her wrist. She noticed a picture frame on the chest of drawers, a dried flower beside it. In it was a newspaper clipping of Gregory.

Sweethearts give their girls real photographs. Why does she always manipulate the truth?

After learning of his death, Doreen had slipped into what her mother called one of her 'states'. Her life had become two-dimensional. Methodically, she had hung up her pretty dresses. Powder, rouge and lipstick had been stowed away. Then she'd taken to her bed. Her mother had been called to take her to her home to Stirling to recuperate. When she'd picked Doreen up, she'd explained to the matron that this was not the first time she'd been like this. She would get over it. Not to worry.

Doreen had stared out of the car window the whole way, to the place she had long stopped calling home.

After a few weeks, Doreen's shipbuilder father, had made one of his rare visits. In spite of his age, his hair a shocking white, he'd been busier than ever, his expertise keenly sought after. While her mother ignored Doreen in her grief, he thought what she needed was good hard work. And so, he elicited, without Doreen's knowledge, the help of a doctor friend to convince his daughter to work in a rehabilitative home with which he was affiliated.

He apologized to the doctor for his daughter. Doreen's melancholy over this boy needed to be put into perspective. From what his wife had told him, Doreen and Gregory had barely been acquainted.

He didn't quite understand it. What had happened to his beautiful long-legged child, her flawless beauty, her sparkling eyes? As he stood looking out over the field at the back of their house, polishing his glasses, he remembered. He remembered the longing for his sweet daughter against which he'd felt powerless.

He was relieved when she accepted the work and left without saying goodbye, not able to set eyes on the woman who had replaced his little girl. On the table in the hallway, he left her a going-away present. When Doreen opened the package, she wasn't surprised.

Well, father, how typical of you.

It contained some reports that he'd requested from a hospital in Devon, written on the treatment of traumatized soldiers.

The doctor came to see her once more before she left. "These men have already been subjected to electric shock treatment, tactile deprivation and solitary confinement," he told her. "But there has never been proof that these methods work." His voice wavered. "We are going to try something different."

He lowered his voice, "A good friend was shot as a deserter. He wandered off during a battle and was picked up trying to make his way home. He didn't know who or where he was." His voice broke. "They didn't believe him."

"Let's try to reach these men with good food, fresh air and peace and quiet," he said.

It was strange that this man and her father were friends. Her father usually did not tolerate weakness.

CHAPTER TEN

The peace and tranquility began to work their magic on the patients, and those who had been curled up tightly, unfurled and those with balled fists, unclenched them.

The staff of five walked or wheeled the patients into the garden and sat them amongst the fallen leaves in the sun. The gardener whistled while he raked and weeded in front of them. Some of the men, after holding the rich, black earth up to their noses and letting it sift through their fingers, began to help plant spring bulbs.

Dr. Andrews, her father's acquaintance, monitored the recovery of the patients once or twice a week. He was satisfied with the way that their skeletal bodies were filling out thanks to the good care and the extra food donations the locals dropped by.

"Your father would be proud," he said, meaning it as a compliment. She didn't respond. Maybe, he thought, she hadn't heard.

***

William and a few others still lagged behind.

Every day, Doreen checked William's temperature and pulse and listened to his heart. Everything seemed fine. He had gained weight. Once a day, they put William's feet over the side of the bed and helped him stand. He could be led by the hand.

This morning, however, when she'd looked in on him, she had noticed spasms in his left arm. She tried massaging his neck, thinking that he'd slept on a nerve. It didn't help. She frowned.

She checked on him every half hour until mid-afternoon with no change. At that time, needing a break, Doreen sat down on the chair in his room, taking off her shoes and rubbing her pinched feet. She'd have to give them a good soak later on. She leant back in the chair, nodding off in the afternoon sunshine that streamed in through the window.

The sudden silence got her attention. She opened her eyes. His arm had stopped its rhythmic twitching on the sheet. And he was looking straight at her.

Clearing his throat, he tried to speak. Doreen got up and poured him a glass of water. She supported his neck so that he could drink.

He cleared his throat again. "Helen?" He spoke hoarsely.

He thinks I am his wife.

"William." She wondered if she looked like her.

"Helen…?" He coughed.

Go slowly. Don't startle him.

She helped him take another drink. "Don't say anything just yet, William."

He was still staring hard at her. His eyes were focused. She touched his hand. "Soldier, you're at a convalescent home near Edinburgh. My name is Doreen, the Matron here."

His voice cracked. "Is the war over?" There was a pause as he caught his breath. He looked at his arms. "What's wrong with me?"

"You were knocked unconscious." She felt his head with a cool palm. "The war isn't over, but you're safe."

"I've got to go back." His accent was thick for an educated man. For a man with the talent he had for writing such sensitive poems.

"Ease up, soldier." She stroked his head as he sank back onto the pillow.

"Where's Duncan?" he gasped.

"Don't worry. I'm sure Duncan is all right."

"The children…Robbie…" He tried to lift himself up but fell back onto the bed, exhausted. The spasms began again. She held his hand in hers, feeling the twitch running through her whole body. There were horizontal ridges on his fingernails from the cuticle to the top. That showed malnourishment. She was surprised he didn't have loose teeth. She checked his pulse. It was fast but not racing. He closed his eyes.

She left the room, butterflies in her stomach. She'd known all along that he'd recover. She hummed a popular tune under her breath.

In the room that had been the study, she reviewed his chart for what seemed like the millionth time to see if there was something she'd missed. Nothing really remarkable on it, health-wise. He was unresponsive to previous treatment. Married with three children, all living with family in Kirkcaldy. The wife, Helen, had been contacted.

Besides his wife, he'd also mentioned Duncan and Robbie. Maybe those were his children.

For supper, Dugald helped William out of bed and they walked for the first time to the dining room. Doreen put his food in front of him. He pushed it away.

"Duncan's dead, isn't he?"

Duncan again.

He lowered his voice. His pupils were dilated. "Everyone is dead." He covered his face with his hands. "I have to go back."

"Not like this you can't. You have to get strong first. Eat something."

"I have to go back. I have to go back." His voice was rising. She placed a hand on his shoulder.

Calmly she said, "I promise you as soon as you can, you will go back. Right now, you'd just endanger your pals." More firmly she said, "You have to eat, William. It's getting cold."

He just stared at her.

"Eat, William. Or you'll never go back."

He managed half a sandwich.

That night, Doreen walked through the garden, elated. She slid the gold ring back and forth on the chain around her neck. Then she stopped with the ring between her fingers.

It was a sign. There is a 'W' on it.

Eventually, when she went back to her room, she picked up the picture of Gregory. Hugging it, she lay down on the bed, thinking about how they had met at her aunt's house in the country. It had seemed like fate then, too.

Her cousin's friends had started off drinking wine punch, eating dainty sandwiches, playing badminton. Doreen's pretty cousin decreed: the boys against the girls. As Gregory and Doreen both won equal numbers of games, they decided to break the tie. She took off her shoes so she would have better footing on the grass.

In the heat, the others went back up to the house to refresh their drinks. After Doreen won a few points and with no spectators to impress, Gregory conceded the game. The sun was blinding him, he said. To cool down, they went to the dock and hung their legs over the side. Doreen reached down and splashed water on her face. The old rowboat, tied to the end of the dock, rocked rhythmically in the gentle waves. Gregory moved closer.

With a furrowed brow, he told her about his art history studies and how they'd been interrupted by the war. Just when things were going well for him, he said. He hoped they wouldn't bomb the hell out of Europe; there was so much he still had to see and do.

Suddenly, he grabbed her hand and brushed his lips against her palm. She felt a rush of pleasure.

"Do you have anyone special?" he asked, not smiling. Doreen looked at him sideways, remembering when she'd met him a few years ago: then he'd been brooding, plump and weak. He hadn't been what she called attractive.

Since then, he'd become a man. Sophisticated, lean and muscular. "No," she said, a little more breathlessly than she wanted to be.

"Kiss me." He turned her head towards him with a finger.

She held her breath and shut her eyes. He pressed his lips against hers. Her lips were tight, anonymous.

"It's hot," he said and stripped off his shirt. The dark hair on his chest tumbled down to below his navel. He helped her up, "Let's go for a boat ride. The others won't miss us." Doreen sat in the bow of the boat, while he inserted the oars, undid the knot and sat down to row. The heat and the creak of the oars made her drowsy.

He rowed along the shoreline until they came to a small, secluded inlet, willow trees dipping into the river as though they were drinking. Using one oar, he steered them into it and dropped the anchor over the side.

"I'm going in for a dip. Nobody will be able to see us here. Coming?" He fumbled with the buttons of his trousers and slipped over the side. Naked. "It's beautiful."

Doreen stared straight ahead. The war had changed everything. Gregory was leaving in a few weeks, perhaps never to return. Right now, anything was possible, everything was allowed.

Perspiration beaded on her upper lip and on the nape of her neck. There were damp spots under her arms. The water looked inviting. Gregory was swimming away from the boat with strong, swift strokes. Quickly she pulled off her blouse and her skirt, her eyes steady on the back of his head to make sure he didn't turn as her underclothes dropped into the boat. She went over the side. It was deliciously refreshing. "Gregory!"

He slowly turned and swam toward her. As he got close, he splashed her and it became a contest between the two, swiping the water with their arms. They were laughing loudly and Doreen momentarily forgot her self-consciousness. A sudden rustle on the bank, though, made her duck deeper into the water.

Almost all Doreen's friends had a sweetheart and the war had accelerated their relationships. There was no time to get to know each other like before. But she felt awkward. It was daylight. They were in the open.

That something with her father when she'd been small; his hands, his fingers, and his mouth came rushing to the surface of her mind.

Gregory dove at her and held her arms behind her back, roughly kissing her neck, bruising it. She struggled and then he let go, his hands sliding up her arms to her shoulders. His lips sought hers. Her response was timid. He pushed his body against hers.

"Come on," he said urgently.

There was nothing to lose. She would have a young man, too. Just like the rest of the girls her age. He led her to the coarse volcanic sand of the beach and lying down, pressed his fingers into her thighs. She wrapped her legs around him as he entered her, so harshly it made her cry out.

Gregory shuddered and then, his stronghold on her relaxed. He rolled off her after a few moments and lay quietly beside her. Her body felt strangely lonely.

After a few minutes, he muttered, "I thought you were a virgin." He threw one arm over his eyes.

"But I am," she whispered. Her father had only used his hands.

Gregory got up and waded into the water and turned on his back and kicked lazily away. Doreen followed him, feeling painfully naked. He reached the boat first and climbed into it then tipping it, helping her to get in. They dressed. As she was buttoning her blouse, he pulled in the anchor.

They rowed back silently. At the dock he helped her out of the boat. For a moment, he held her. "Let's not say anything about this to anyone."

Doreen knew he was afraid because of the war. The stupid war. As she walked behind him, toward the house and the others, she said just out of range, "I'll wait for you. I'll think about you every day. You'll never be alone."

She thought he was going to sit beside her but he sat on the arm of her cousin's chair and laughed and joked with the others. She played with the sleeve of her blouse.

"Why are you so quiet, Doreen?" her cousin asked. "Did he win?"

"It was a tie," Doreen said, looking straight at him.

"That's what you think," he laughed and stood up. "Sorry, pals, I've got to go. You know, spend time with the old girl."

Doreen's eyes followed him and then, she left shortly after, feeling bruised and beaten.

Gregory sent flowers to her aunt's house the next day and the card with them simply said, "Thank you." She felt let down, there being no mention of love, no date to meet again. After a few days, she pressed the flowers, in a book she'd brought with her. She slipped the card under her pillow.

She returned to the nurse's residence and he was shipped off.

When her periods were late she hoped she wouldn't get them. She hugged her body, not caring if they were married or not. She would love their baby, anyway. She asked for his address from her cousin and wrote to him about how happy she was.

She cut his picture out of the local paper where they featured the boys in the region who had gone to war and framed it. She wrote to him to tell him not to worry because she had his picture from the newspaper. She enclosed a photograph of herself.

He didn't reply.

She sent another letter when her periods came, telling him how devastated she was that their baby had been lost. She said not to worry, that she was all right. When he got back, she wrote, they could have another one. She wrote steadily, once a week, hoping a letter would get through to the Front.

She never received one word from him.

Getting up off her bed, she took the picture of Gregory out of the frame and replaced it with the ragged poem.

Doreen decided to put off writing a letter to William's wife. He wasn't all that stable yet and the shock of seeing her might be too exhausting and set him back.

Yes, she would wait.

CHAPTER ELEVEN

It was increasingly difficult to keep Bill clean. His aversion to bathing had begun even before they came to live with him, saying it felt like his skin was being peeled off. Whenever it was Bill's turn to bathe, he baulked, not even wanting to leave his room. "Too cold," he fretted. When Helen tried to help him undress, he leered at her with his watery eyes. She tried to undo his buttons: he tried to undo hers. He called her his sweetheart, his darling girl. She called him a swine, a dirty, filthy pig. He laughed, she sighed. Agnes should be the one doing this, not her.

Late Saturday afternoons, it took Helen, with the help of Robbie, between three and four hours to get the tub ready, heating water in the kettle and every pot they possessed. Then, the children were sent outside and Bill was dispatched to his room. When ready, Helen took the first bath, and it was a heavenly few minutes of peace.

When the water started to cool, she got out and after towelling off, added more hot water. Emma was next. Robbie and Tom bathed together and it was at these times that they looked the most vulnerable and precious to her.

Then Bill. As she finally got him into the tub, coaxing him with the promise of a drink, she listened keenly for the continued sounds of splashing coming from behind a sheet she'd hung, as she combed out the tangles in Emma's hair. It scared her to death, leaving Bill in a tub full of water.

When Helen noticed the rash on Bill's neck that looked very much like The Itch, she gave up. Once the transmittable mites burrowed themselves under the skin, they were very hard to get rid of. She checked herself and the children and so far, they were all right. She washed his clothes in boiling water and put his meals in his room. That became the extent of her contact with him. She had to protect herself and her family.

After an unusually cold day, Agnes, lips white, showed up with her bedraggled father in tow.

"Get out of here for a minute!" Agnes yelled at the children. Emma, who was feeling poorly and lying down, got up and took Tom's hand. Robbie followed.

"Why is he walking around like this?" she yelled at Helen. "I can get you thrown out."

She was loud, much too loud and Helen, alarmed, begged her to be quiet, still not knowing how they were allowed to live on the plant-owned premises.

"Have you seen his leg? Can't you smell it?" she continued, eyes bulging. She lifted his trouser leg. There was an oozing lesion. "How, in the devil's name, did he get like this?" She didn't wait for an answer. "I'm warning you!"

Helen looked at her hands. *Why don't you take care of your own father?*

The smell of him was revolting. Helen was sorry for him, so sorry. But there was no point telling Agnes how unmanageable he had become.

"What kind of daughter-in-law are you?" Agnes folded her formidable arms. "The caretaker's wife, Mrs. MacLeod, has told me she often sees him wandering out late. By himself."

"There's no lock on the door," Helen said, still not looking up.

Bill spoke up, looking at his daughter. "Thank God, you're here. You always turn up just in time."

"It's all right, dad," she said. Helen hated her smug tone.

"Did the children get off the boat?" he said, anguish making his voice rise.

"Which children?" Agnes asked him.

"The children I have to take care of. The crying children." He rubbed his eyes.

Agnes said, "Here we go again. Don't worry, Dad. Nothing's happened."

"They're alone without me. They need me." He looked confusedly at Helen and then at his daughter closely. "Who are you?"

"Dad, just go to your room and take off those clothes. We have to get you cleaned up." He stubbornly stood his ground. "The sooner we get you taken care of, the sooner we can get back to those children."

"Look," she said to Helen as he left the room, "you need to get some sulphur ointment." She jabbed her finger in Helen's direction. "My final warning. Take better care of him, or you're out of here."

Helen called the children back in and while Bill's shirt, then his trousers, simmered in hot water in a pot on the oven, Helen looked out of the open window. The gentleness of spring was in the air. Yesterday had been the first day of real warmth. Her spirits had been lifted by the sound of the innocent play of children, and the twitter of birds.

Today she felt drained. Their very existence was at the mercy of Agnes, the tyrant.

And she had no money for ointment.

She slipped on her soft blue wedding dress. It made her feel even more melancholy, as the material was too loose at her breasts, and strained at the hips. She'd been saving it for William's homecoming, although she often took it out of the tissue wrapping and caressed it, recalling her husband undoing its buttons for the first time.

She opened the door and left without a word, smoothing the dress over her stomach. Although Robbie had seen it before, it was the first time he'd seen her wear it. Before following her, he moved the pot away from the fire. "I'll be back," he said to Emma.

Her ill-fitting shoes made her progress slow and Robbie had no trouble keeping up to her. He wanted to rush up to her and comfort her and lead her back home. But he had a feeling that he wasn't supposed to see her like this and so he shadowed her, helpless. It took her a quarter of an hour to walk to the end of the street which sloped toward the long strand.

She was making her way toward the sea. The north-south streets of Kirkcaldy hugged the curve of the Firth and after living there a year, Robbie knew them like the back of his hand. His nostrils quivered at the smell of salt. She crossed The Esplanade and reached the gritty, black beach as the sun was starting to set behind them.

Holding her head back, she listened to the sound of the sea. The wind whipped her dress against her legs. Robbie watched his mother from within the doorway of a building. He shivered in his hiding spot.

His mother stepped into the icy water and waded in past her knees. Robbie moved out from behind the building, closer to her.

She hesitated when the water lapped at the hem of her dress and stayed, for what seemed to Robbie a long time, facing the open sea. A boat was on the horizon of the Firth in front of her, making its way in the direction of Edinburgh. Robbie shifted from one foot to the other. It was too cold for his mother to be standing in the water. She'd get ill.

Abruptly, Helen turned around and waded back up onto the beach. She took her wet shoes off. And then, as if realizing suddenly that she was cold, she started walking at a brisk pace, her arms hugging her body. She looked anxious and pale. Her chin jutted forward; her shoulders were round. His heart was in his mouth.

Going back another way, first Helen and then her son, passed by the bakery. The smell of fresh bread made his stomach ache from the sheer longing for it. It was getting dark.

By the time she was back near the flat, it was after their usual tea-time. Robbie crossed the street to the churchyard. He didn't want her to know that he'd seen her. That little, yellow bundle of dog was there again, pricking up its ears. As he approached, it rolled over onto its back to have its stomach rubbed.

"Maybe the butcher could give me a bone for you, girl."

His mother called him from the window but he pretended not to hear. He picked up a stick and threw it. She called again.

While the dog ran to retrieve the stick, Helen walked across the street, her nails digging into the palms of her hands. She grabbed Robbie's shirt collar just as the dog dropped the stick at his feet, barking.

"Where've you been?" She had to speak loudly over the dog.

"Here. I've been here. It's all right, girl. This is my mother." Robbie tried to twist out of his mother's grasp. The dog jumped up and down, yapping, its long nails scratching his legs.

"You left Emma and Tom alone. You know Emma's not feeling well. Something could have happened."

"You left them alone, not me."

"Don't you dare talk to me like that!" Helen slapped him. "Get back inside!"

Robbie followed her, dragging his feet, his hand cooling his burning cheek. Helen noticed Mrs. MacLeod at the church window, watching them. Her face quickly withdrew. As they went inside, Robbie looked longingly back at the dog that had seemed to smile at him.

***

The next day, the rain pounded the windows. Emma lay listlessly on the bed while Robbie repeatedly scuffed one of his heels against the floor, scowling, wanting to go out. Two-year-old Tom ran circles round the room on tiny, unsteady legs.

Helen shouted for silence, rubbing her temples. She stirred chunks of a bruised apple into the lumpy, thick porridge she'd made in the morning. She put Bill's portion into his darkening room. He wasn't there.

Let him eat it cold.

That night like the night before, Helen had lain on the edge of the mattress she shared with the children, hands clenched even when she managed to close her eyes, thinking about what had happened to her. She'd little recollection of how she'd got into the water of the Firth. She just remembered the sudden, startling cold and the shock of realizing she was standing in water, staring out at the wild expanse of sea.

A creak of the floorboards in the hallway alerted her to Bill's presence. *How in God's name, does he always find his way back?* His door closed quietly.

She was bone-tired but sleep, blessed sleep, eluded her. Lying there, her thoughts turned to Mary whose friendship she missed even more than that of her husband's. Two years and not a word from her.

The air was stale in the room and she got up to open the window. Lighting a candle stub, Helen rummaged in her handbag. In her change purse, was the piece of paper with Mary's cousin's address on it.

She'd been worried, at first, not hearing from Mary, and then felt miserable and finally betrayed. Her letters remained unanswered. Even if Mary thought she was still in Lochoal, the postman there would have forwarded any letters that had come for her. She had stopped writing.

It was time to forget her pride. Helen made a decision to go to Mary's cousin's in the morning. She had to find her. She let out a deep sigh. Perhaps she could sleep after all. Mary would know what to do.

After making tea in the morning, she patted powder on her nose and put on some lipstick using her little finger to dig some out of the bottom of the tube. She wrapped up her good shoes in a piece of newspaper, stuffed them into her bag and checked her change purse to see how many coins were still there.

Robbie put his shoes on, too. She was wearing her blue dress, again.

"What are you doing?" She tried to keep her voice light. "Robbie, you have to take care of Tom and Emma while I'm gone." Her chest tightened. The momentary peace she'd felt was fading.

"I don't want to." She was in a strange mood. Robbie wanted to follow her. "Besides, aren't I to go to school?" Robbie said, although he didn't have any intention of going.

Helen forced both boys to sit. Emma was in bed, face flushed. "I'm going to find out where Mary is. Robbie is in charge. Do you hear me? I'll be…I'll be as quick as I can."

She cupped a hand under Emma's chin, looking at her red-rimmed eyes. She looked like she'd been awake all night, too. Emma turned away from her mother's hand.

"I really won't be too long, I promise. Robbie, make sure Emma drinks some tea."

She was a little worried about Emma, she was ill too often, but as she walked down the street, she felt years melt away. It was good, to get out of the stifling flat, with a purpose guiding her, without children clamouring around her. At the butcher's at the corner, she asked the pink-skinned woman inside for directions to the address Mary had given her. The woman, hardly looking up, pointed west with a finger that looked unappetizingly like the sausages she was stuffing.

Helen nervously asked a few more times on the way for directions, unfamiliar with this part of town. It was a long walk.

When she finally found the building, she slipped out of her scuffed shoes and put on her good ones, wishing she had the money to buy stockings. The block of houses looked so similar to Links Street; they must have all been built at the same time by the same builder. Flanking the town to the north and the south, grey brick buildings had been erected to house the labourers for the two competing linoleum plants. Kirkcaldy was famous for the floor covering and the overpowering stink of linseed oil, one of the primary ingredients used in making it.

At the top of the stairs, Mary's cousin opened the door. She looked like Mary, tall, the same strong countenance and a thick mane of coarse hair. Yet while Mary had stood sleek and muscular, this mare was broken and swaying. Her frown lines deepened at Mary's name, "Mary doesn't live here anymore." She started to close her door. Helen was surprised: she'd thought Mary was in Glasgow.

"Wait! Please!" Helen pleaded and stepped forward. "I'm a friend from Lochoal. Our husbands were in the same battalion." She held her hand out, running her tongue around lips of a mouth that had suddenly gone dry.

"Mary and I don't speak anymore." She ignored her hand but opened the door a crack wider. "Poor Duncan. A wonderful man."

"Duncan was my husband's best friend. We were all very close before the war. Do you have her address?" Helen was speaking quickly, thinking that if this woman shut her door, she wasn't going to open it again.

"Well," she conceded, raising an eyebrow at Helen's bare legs. "Just a minute."

The door was closed in her face. When it reopened, Mary's cousin passed her a piece of paper with a street name and number written on it. "I don't like what she did. Tell her I said that." A baby began crying and before Helen could thank her or ask for directions, the door was closed again.

Helen leant against the wall of the building to change her shoes, and she wondered what Mary had done. A horse that was pulling a milk cart reared, spilling bottles onto the street. There was the sound of breaking glass. Some children passed by her, clattering up the stairs.

An old, bent street sweeper was working his way towards her, and

Helen turned to him for directions. In a surprisingly young voice, he said, "That's quite a way. Just go straight along here." He pointed with the end of his broom and then switched to another sack, sweeping up the horse manure so that he could sell it.

***

As she walked in the direction she'd been shown, she saw a small tea shop nestled between the worn-out grey buildings. Just what she needed. There was an old woman in it, sitting in a chair facing the door. She was wearing a faded flowered housedress over her skirt and she cocked her head towards the bell that rang as Helen walked in. Men's slippers made it difficult for the old woman to walk. "What would you like, dearie? A cuppa? Black?" she said over her shoulder. "A silly question these days."

"Black is all right." Helen sat down at the table and the woman shuffled back with a tea cup rattling around on the saucer. A light caramel coloured liquid sloshed onto it, and before the woman placed it in front of her, she poured the spilled tea from the saucer into Helen's cup.

"Waste not, want not, I always say, my sweet." She smiled warmly.

Close up, Helen could see the milky growth over her retina. Blind, she must have counted the steps between the table and the counter. She wondered how she hadn't spilled more.

The woman covered Helen's hand with one of her own age-flecked hands.

"Don't worry about him so much. In the end, he'll be alright." The old woman went back to her chair and faced the door.

Helen gave a great sigh and sipped her tea, not caring who she was talking about.

***

After Robbie ripped off a hunk of bread, he opened the door. His grandfather's door opened almost simultaneously, like he had been lying in wait. They stood facing each other in the muted light of the hallway. Bill was dressed and had shaved and combed his hair over the top of his bald head. "Hello, how's my lad?" He was having one of his good days. "It was stormy last night but a fine day today."

"Yes, it is," Robbie said, avoiding his eager eyes. "Granddad, I have to go out. Can you stay with Emma and Tom?" Robbie knew he shouldn't ask but it wouldn't take long; he had to find his mother. Make sure she was all right.

"Who?" He looked puzzled.

"Emma and Tom. My sister and brother."

"Children? The children? Are they crying?" He suddenly looked concerned. "I'll take care of them. Where are they?" He brushed past Robbie as he heard Tom's little voice.

Robbie looked along the street. His mother was at the far end of Links Street, at its curve. She turned and disappeared into the butcher's just before the tram obscured his vision. Tall and thin, it rattled towards him, looking as if it were going to topple. He loved trams. The people riding them were always going somewhere else.

When he reached the butcher's, he looked through the window. There were a few ladies in a queue but no blue dress. He couldn't see her anywhere.

Maybe she was at the water, again.

He swung around the corner to the beach and as he passed the bakery, the smell reminded him of the frightening look on his mother's face when he had followed her just two days ago. He picked up his pace. There were a few dogs sniffing at the dust bins behind the building. Not Yellow, though. He hadn't seen her since that day.

**

It was suppertime and Helen had walked from one end of the town to the other. She was tired and hungry and the address was not to be found. The street existed but not the number. It had either been written down incorrectly or Mary's cousin must be harbouring a bigger grudge than she let on.

Now she had to go back home no further ahead than she was before. Home. She'd not felt at home since she'd lived in Lochoal. Her pace slowed to almost a standstill. She wanted a little more time. On her own. To think.

A placard from the pictures caught her eye. A Charlie Chaplin picture. She reached into her change purse and fingered the coins she had left. She'd never been to the pictures before. So many people raved about the funny little man with his big-shoed, awkward waddle.

Emma would be all right. Robbie would take care of her and Tom. He was a good boy, much older than his nine years. There was bread and drippings for their tea. She looked closer at the placard. This would be frowned upon, a woman going by herself to the pictures…she still had time to get there… it would use up a lot of the money… she deserved it, she never did anything for herself…if she hurried, she might be able to get a good seat… she was desperate for adult company. Before she could change her mind, she hurried to the theatre and bought a single ticket, the woman at the box office not even giving her a second glance.

***

Robbie looked up and down the length of the beach. There were a few figures in the distance but even the furthest one wasn't wearing blue. He raced along the beach and up toward the centre of town. As he reached the road, he bent over from the stitch in his side, realizing he wasn't going to find his mother.

Whenever he made it this far, it always surprised him how the hustle and bustle was so close to the natural beauty of the sea. He liked both. He wandered around some of the main streets, still vaguely looking for her, but was distracted by the window displays of things they couldn't afford. He vowed to himself when he was older, he was going to work very hard so that he could get everything he wanted.

He should go home. He hungrily dragged his feet along High Street toward the duller greyness of Linktown. There was a flash of blue in a window as he walked by. He stopped for a look. It was his mother sitting in a tea shop, drinking a brew. He felt relief and then anger swell inside him. She'd lied. She wasn't trying to find Mary.

He stomped furiously away. She'd left him in charge. To do her job, so that she could have nice things without them. He made his way back down to the beach. He was going to run away. Go to Edinburgh with his friend Angus.

Robbie took his shoes off. The sand was ice-cold. His feet hurt, though, especially after having walked and run so far and he rubbed his toes. They felt bruised and his nails were cracked from banging against the end of his shoes.

He picked up some stones and flicked them at the water, to skip them. Too angry to get them to slant, they sunk with a plop as he thought about going back to the tea-shop to demand a biscuit. But no, she would only be too cross with him for leaving her two angels, as she always called them, alone.

He preferred Kirkcaldy to the town they'd come from. He often went to the sea, when he felt it beckon to him, even when he was supposed to be at school. He felt he could breathe more easily here: it was probably the sea air. He liked to look at the big ships going by, which like the trams, were going somewhere. And he was going somewhere soon, too: he would show her.

His pal, Angus, joined him and told him he hadn't missed anything interesting at school. But Angus always said that. They decided to forage at the tattie field to find something to eat. Robbie had only had a piece of bread and Angus hadn't had anything at all: his father, needing all his strength at work, had taken the last piece in the morning.

***

'The Pally', The Palace Cinema in Whyte's Causeway, was busy, patrons sitting in almost every seat of the picture house. She hadn't realized it was Friday night. There were a lot of women, although it was hard to tell if there were any alone. The man to her right sat with his legs open so that one of his thighs touched her. The heat of his body went through her dress and she slid over, trying to occupy as little space as she could.

The room became quiet as a striking woman entered the room, blond hair pinned up, wearing a vibrant red dress. She sat at the piano, her back upright and hands hovering over the keys until you could hear a pin drop. As she played the opening strains of *"God Save the King,"* everyone stood and sang heartily.

The smell of the waxed wooden floor and the sight of opulence brought back the last estate Helen had worked on before getting married.

There had been warmth and comfort there, if she was careful. She'd never dared to look her employers in the eye; afraid they'd notice her and make her move, like she had so many times before.

Her children didn't know how good they had it. They had her, a home and albeit it nothing special, there was usually food on their table. She had always been alone.

The whirring and clicking from the big projector started and the screen lit up with stuttering black and white images that were so realistic that Helen felt she could reach out and touch them. The woman at the pianoforte burst into a flurry of action, her feet involved in a dance over the pedals. And although she was thoroughly enjoying the moving picture, Helen had to keep reminding herself to watch it rather than the frenetic antics of the pianist.

***

Robbie and Angus were joined by some pals who decided to raid the tattie field near the quarry behind Den Road. There might be some new potatoes already growing there. After scratching through the dirt, they found quite a few very small new ones. They separated them from the pulp of last year's. Filling their pockets, it was a short walk to the burning braes in the abandoned pit, where they put the potatoes amongst the glowing embers of a pile of coal. They left them until they turned black.

Robbie, mouth full, pushed any worries of his brother and sister out of his head. His mother would be home by now. She'd promised. She was probably furious with him, but he didn't care. He blew on another potato, and tossed it from hand to hand until it was cooler to the touch. Drawing his lips back from his teeth, he bit in, deftly using his teeth and his fingers, to peel the burnt skin away.

Finally on his way home, Yellow saw him and bounded up to him, jumping up against his legs, wanting to lick him. He patted her but didn't play. It was time to face the music.

The two rooms were dark. He struck a match against the oven, the sharp smell of sulphur filling the room, and lit a lamp. He began to pace, his footsteps sounding hollow in the emptiness. There hadn't been anyone there for a while. The room was cold.

He got out some kindling and lit a fire, adding some pieces of coal that he had wrapped in leaves and packed into his pocket at the pit. He washed the black dust from his hands.

He nervously tidied the room, making the bed, heating water and washing the dishes in the sink. He paced between the window and the door. She must have been really cross with him to have come home and then disappear with no note. Maybe she was teaching him a lesson.

Cleaning the floor without being asked to - that would put him back into her good books. It took every ounce of his strength to lift the full kettle onto the oven. He ate the rest of the potatoes he had brought home, coating them in the drippings from the pan, as the kettle began to bubble and whistle. He was going to scrub the floor till it shone.

He inched the kettle towards the edge of the oven but it was hot and he couldn't get a grip. Looking around, he took the basin and then, a small footstool to stand on from Granddad Bill's room. He climbed up onto the stool and balanced the basin against his chest. Then he grabbed the kettle. Simple. He would just pour the water into the basin.

As he poured, the water in the basin sloshed from side to side. Suddenly he was off-balance. He tightened his grip on the kettle. It was hot. He let go with a yelp. The kettle dropped backwards. Boiling water spilled out of the basin. Onto his chest. He screamed.

"Mamamamama!" He stumbled out of the flat, down the steps and out onto the street.

Doors opened and neighbours ran out. Mrs. MacLeod was the first to reach him, frantically trying to see what the matter was. She tried to undo the buttons of his shirt, but his shirt was stuck to his skin. He shrieked.

Angus' mother, Mrs. MacNab, made her way through the milling children and took charge. "Mrs. MacLeod, where's his mother?" she said. Together, they carried him back into the house. He had starting shaking uncontrollably. They put him onto the bed and using some cool water, removed his shirt slowly from the burnt area.

"Oh dear. Oh dear," Mrs. MacNab said. "He needs to go to hospital." There was an angry red area of skin on his chest the size of both his hands. Butter or lard should be put on it, they both agreed.

Mrs. MacLeod searched all the cupboards but there was nothing in the room they could use, except for the drippings that were in a pan on the oven. She didn't think that they should use it because it was still warm.

"Does anybody know where the boy's mother is?" The neighbours who had gathered at the door shook their heads and looked at each other.

"He needs to be taken to hospital." Mrs. MacNab shook her head. "Dearie mc. It doesn't look very good." Robbie was trembling violently although Mrs. MacLeod had wrapped him in a blanket.

One of the men volunteered his cart and they took him to the hospital, Mrs. MacLeod cradling his body between her legs, trying to prevent the rattling over the cobblestones from jolting him. Robbie cried piteously at every bump.

CHAPTER TWELVE

After the intermission, Helen found herself positioned between the women. They had changed seats with their men, either very kindly sensing her discomfort or covetous of their husbands' attention.

Helen, twisting her wedding ring on her finger, spoke to the woman on her right who introduced herself as Nancy. She warmed up after finding out that William was a veteran recovering in hospital.

Helen thoroughly enjoyed the show. Nancy chatted throughout the film with her own commentary. Chaplin, did she know, had tried to enlist, but was refused because of his size. It didn't stop him from having a field day with the ladies. While the men were away, Chaplin could play, she snorted.

Nancy told her they went to the pictures every Friday. If she were alone, she was welcome to join them.

Coming out of the pictures, her eyes had to adjust to the blacked-out street. She stepped back into the doorway. Patrons jostled her. As a tall woman passed, Helen heard, "People always stand in the strangest places." She recognized the voice and it took her breath away.

"Mary?" she called. It was her voice, but the back of this woman, with hunched shoulders and short hair, didn't resemble Mary at all. She had her arm slung through the arm of a man who limped.

The woman turned around and they saw each other's faces in the moonlight. "Helen?"

Helen ran to Mary, throwing her arms around her neck. After a moment, she pulled back, wiping her eyes. "I thought I'd never see you again."

Mary introduced her new husband, Jimmy. Helen shook his hand. "What good luck for you."

"What are you doing in Kirkcaldy?"

"William's still in hospital and we were evicted from Lochoal. We're staying in a dirty two-room flat on Links Street with his nutty father. I don't know how much longer I can take it."

But Helen smiled at her friend. Finally something good had happened.

They took a few steps away from the door. Once used to it, the moonlight was quite bright. Mary glanced at Jimmy who was so different from Duncan. Thinning hair brushed close to his head, he looked about fifty.

Mary looked at her husband with pride. "We have five children. I can't believe the luck I've had."

"Five children!"

Mary blushed. "Yes. When Jimmy first got wounded, his wife took off with somebody else," she said somewhat breathlessly. "And you remember how much I wanted a family."

"So they are my children now," Mary continued, eyes shining. "They even call me, mummy."

Helen gave her a hug. "I am so happy for you."

"Speaking of who, we have to get back to them now, but let me give you our address." She gave her another hug. "Come over tomorrow and bring Emma and the boys. We don't have much but I'm sure we could manage to put together some supper." Jimmy flicked the cigarette he had been smoking into the gutter. "Let's have a good chat."

They parted ways, Helen feeling just ever so slightly better.

***

Alan had always been the first fisherman out and the last to come in, but no matter how hard he'd tried, he'd been unable to eke out a living from it. If he'd been on his own, he would have stuck at it but his missus had found him a steady job at the linen factory as a scaffy, picking up scraps as they fell to the floor. He hated it. He told his wife in no uncertain terms: he was going to go fishing whenever he could.

He had about an hour before sunset and there was a fog that hung low around the town, enveloping it in white cold. It didn't concern him. He wasn't going to go far. As he cast off, the waves rocked his little craft but they were by no means dangerous. He tugged hard on the oars, loving the feeling of the wood in his hands. As he pulled away, he noticed a small boat bobbing aimlessly about.

Calling to the boat and getting no response, he expertly manoeuvred alongside it. There was an old man sitting in the prow and a girl lying on the bottom. She was holding a small child to her chest. The old man was unable to help as Alan tied the boats together. With a pull from his strong arms, he landed the boats and moored them.

The fishermen milling about helped the old man onto land. One of the lads picked the girl up; another cradled the little boy, who seemed to be asleep.

Alan shook his head.

What the hell had these three been playing at?

The old fella spoke gibberish. Alan decided it was too late to go out again, so he went back to the warmth of his home.

***

Helen walked home, holding her wee bit of comfort close to her heart. She had found her friend Mary who was the sister she never had. She even managed a smile.

When Helen got to Links Street, she saw a light shining out onto the street from their window. The children were still awake. Surprised, she opened the door to find Agnes, by herself, sitting at the table with her arms crossed and with a look on her face that could kill.

PART TWO

November 11, 1918

CHAPTER ONE

The war to end all wars was over. Ceasefire went into effect at eleven o'clock on the eleventh day of the eleventh month. It is also the date and time that marks the beginning of the *Narren Saison* in Germany, the season for fools.

Two minutes to eleven on November 11, 1918, a German sniper took aim and fired at a young Canadian who had already begun celebrating the end of the war. A hundred and twenty seconds between being a casualty of the war or being murdered. At the shot, the Canuck's comrades who had stayed low in the trenches, mouths dropping open with surprise, checked their watches. At eleven, a cheer rose from the surrounding area, but it was too late for the twenty-one-year-old. Not knowing, his family and friends back in Canada, hip-hip-hurrahed, slapping each other on the back. Everyone toasted the King, Great Britain and Canada, except the dead boy's mother, whose glass of wine unexplainably slipped out of her hand.

Children in Links Street continued to play soldier in the streets, pointing their stick-guns at the imaginary Huns and yelling, "You lose, you bastards!" with Robbie's friend Angus lining the youngest children up against the wall, ordering them to fall over as they were shot.

"Leave your eyes open! Dead men have their eyes open!" Angus demanded. He'd seen the charcoal sketches drawn by his older brother who'd just returned.

Everywhere, people poured into the streets. Helen, feeling lighter than she'd done in months, thought that maybe things would turn out all right.

Mary met Jimmy in front of the plant and they stood close together, holding hands.

Doreen had all her patients taken out into the garden, and they counted down together, throwing hats, crutches, dishes up into the air. She kept her hands on the back of William's chair.

At the Poor House, Robbie and Tom, uncomfortable in the stiff inmate's uniforms in which they were clothed, were allowed to see Emma. She looked so young with her hair sheared short. Granddad Bill looked lost in all the commotion.

Time began to be measured by what people had been doing as the clocks struck the hour of peace and any wild abandonment in people's celebration was excused. It was the beginning of a new age.

Links Street was filled with the peal of church bells. After a short thanksgiving service, most of the churchgoers bolted to the local pubs and the patrons overflowed into the street, bottles and glasses of foaming beer being passed around hand-to-hand. Veterans kissed every woman they could get their hands on, and the drinking, dancing and singing went on well into the night.

Some boys, who made firecrackers from gunpowder and candle-wicks ends, went down into the churchyard to set them off. As they exploded, Mrs. MacLeod came running. She yelled at them to be careful, but had trouble keeping the joy out of her voice. Her husband was coming home.

"Those bad boys," Mrs. MacLeod said, tapping her foot to the pipes someone had started to play.

CHAPTER TWO

Men are so annoyingly shallow.

Doreen was going to go back to wearing the white starched nurse's uniform and cap just to keep the men quiet. There had been leers and lewd comments while she was wearing her civvies. In uniform she was as safe as in a nun's habit when having to look at or touch the forbidden parts of the body.

Yes, men are all the same. Except for a few, like William, who had glared at the ignorant when they were being silly, and she'd appreciated it, thinking that maybe, just maybe, he fancied her.

Before she went into William's room again for his rubdown, she placed the letter he'd written to his wife into the drawer in her room alongside the others that she'd never sent.

Doreen kept Helen's letters to William locked away and hidden from him, because they were desperate. It was her duty to protect him from such a harmful influence. He needed the peace and quiet.

She's just like my mother. Never anything good to say.

Letters to Helen were also never posted for the same reason. If they were sent, the woman might even visit. William was getting better, a lot better. By God, he could speak, Doreen smiled, although he had his ups and downs. Sometimes he froze, occasionally locked in the moment in which he had remained for so long.

She asked him to roll onto his stomach and proceeded to knead a few knots out of his left shoulder.

William kept mostly to himself, and was, for his talent, a man of mysteriously few words. But Doreen surmised that was because he was still traumatized, and the key to healing him lay within his writing. *If only I could get William to start again.*

The poem she'd found on him was brilliant. It would be a sin to waste his gift. But whenever she showed it to spur him on, William shook his head. He didn't recognize it. It wasn't his handwriting. In fact, he said he had never written anything other than letters and postcards.

But shellshock had changed him, Doreen reassured him. Just as it had changed other things like having trouble remembering his children's names or what his wife looked like. Like his conviction that he'd communed with a dead German.

She sighed. If she could get him going, maybe others would join in and they could have a group of poets here and publish a book of poems, like they had done in Devon. She could get father to finance it. What a coup. *That would show my mother.*

His hands gripped the pillow as he lay there. They were not long and dramatic as a writer's hands should be. They were real workers' hands, strong and capable, a few fingers crooked from mining injuries.

Fate is fickle. Inspiring a man who obviously had a natural inclination to write and then snatching it away again. Well, she'd show Fate. She would help him rise above the mundane.

To start with, father can give William an allowance, although they'd have to call it a stipend. William is too proud to accept a handout.

She found a tight knot on the left side of his neck and worked on it, her arms strong after all the massaging she was doing.

Getting money out of her mother and father for this would be easy. *They owe it to me.*

She had been young, maybe six or seven, when her mother had caught her father in her room. He'd started visiting her room late at night, after she'd already fallen asleep. He'd wake her up with his hot breath tickling her ear, his body pressing against hers, his soft murmuring that he loved her.

That had been at first. As his visits became more frequent, his fingers searched, speaking all the while in his comforting father's voice.

Each time the game he said they were playing, was different. One night his hands reached up under her nightgown. The next, he took it off completely. His fingers gently probed and stroked. It was a pleasant sensation. And it made her father happy. He told her not to mention it to her mother, because she would make them stop.

One night he made her get up while he spread a towel on the bed. "Lie on it," he demanded. She obeyed, anxious at the tone. After removing his trousers, he folded them carefully over a chair. He hesitated at the side of the bed, looking down at her small body.

Doreen wondered why his body looked different from hers. He made her lie on her side. He slid one hand between her legs.

That's when it hurt. She cried out loudly for him to stop.

The door slammed open and her mother rushed in. "What's going on?" she cried.

Then her mother picked up a wooden chair and threw it at her husband, screaming at him to get out of the room. She yelled at Doreen to cover herself for God's sake. As her husband stumbled away, she rushed at him and slapped him, her face purple with fury. Doreen cleaned herself with the towel. She was scared at the blood but hid the towel under her bed, out of the sight of her mother.

That night, her father left home.

After he was gone, her mother grabbed her and said, looking her straight in the eye: "Let's not talk of this, ever, to anyone. Promise me, on your grandmother's grave."

It was all her fault that her mother was so upset. "I'm sorry," she said.

A numbing silence descended on the house. Doreen wanted desperately to make it up to her mother, but had been struck dumb by the morbid promise she'd made. Grandmother's ghost would haunt her if she did.

Her father stayed away for weeks. The days went by slowly. Doreen's breakfast and dinner were eaten across the table from her mother's fixed smile. Her days were spent with her tutor, a woman who believed learning was a matter of memorization and drills.

Every night, before she went to sleep, Doreen checked under the bed and closed the closet door.

Within a few months, an appropriate boarding school was found for her. But she knew she was different than the other girls and was lonely; her only friends were the horses.

As she grew older, whenever she went home, she was looked at with distaste, reminding them of an unsavoury incident best forgotten.

"That hurts!" William winced. There were dark, red spots where she'd been massaging. She had bruised him. She switched sides.

Doreen wanted William. She wasn't going to let him, like Gregory, get away. And once she made up her mind, it was easy. She explained to him that she had taken the liberty of writing to his wife to ask her to come and visit.

"I hope you don't mind. I know it upsets you seeing other men's families." She paused innocently. "She wrote back that she doesn't want the children to see their father in such a state."

Quickly, he swung his legs around off the bed and then stood facing her, his shirt hanging limply from his hand.

"I'm sorry, William," Doreen continued. "Sometimes people don't know how to react…they don't understand."

His eyes had gone dark. She thought it best to leave his room, let it sink in.

He continued to write to his wife, but the messages became curt and postcard-like with little tenderness: feeling better, weather's good, feeding me well, hope you and the children are in good health. Those went into the drawer alongside the others.

William stopped speaking about his family.

CHAPTER THREE

Mrs. MacLeod and Mrs. MacNab stood by Robbie until the doctor was ready to see him. He had mercifully lost consciousness.

The young doctor, unkempt and tired-looking, looked at Robbie's chest.

"Thank God you women didn't put any grease on it. Most of the burn patients that are brought here are in a real mess."

The two women looked at each other.

The doctor continued, "We'll just clean it up and put a paraffin soaked bandage on it so it won't stick. They started using them on soldier's burns, you know, so that they wouldn't tear off the scab every time they changed the dressing. I guess the war was good for something."

Mrs. MacLeod thought he was awfully disrespectful about the war, especially for his age.

"Are you his next-of-kin?" he asked them.

"No, doctor. We just heard the poor mite screaming and brought him here straight away. His mother wasn't home."

"This is a serious burn ladies, let's hope it doesn't get septic."

"It's so sad." Mrs. MacNab patted Mrs. MacLeod's hand.

"Do you know how to reach his mother or any other member of the family?" the doctor asked uncomfortably. He hated this part. He could tell by the boy's clothes that they had no money. "We'll need to settle the account."

Money, always money. Mrs. MacLeod said she'd fetch his Aunt Agnes. She lived on Heggis Wynd.

The doctor smiled haggardly. Just as he'd suspected. Linktown. "See to it that she gets here today."

"Please." He hadn't wanted to sound rude.

***

Helen rushed out of the flat without closing the door after her, Agnes' sharp words still stinging her ears. She ran as fast as she could to the clinic, stumbling over cobblestones, falling and scraping a knee, her heart and mind racing, a stitch searing her side.

When she arrived and asked to see her son, the matron, looking her over with disdain, did not permit her. Past visiting hours. Can't disturb the patients.

Helen begged, pleaded.

The nurse looked down at the boy's chart. Brought in by neighbours. The boy's haphazard mother was a mess: sweat marks under the arms of a stained dress, face red, nose running. She knew this type of woman.

After a few minutes of waiting, Helen felt a wave of nausea. She jumped up and ran out the door, barely making it to the bushes where she vomited. The matron looked up as she ran out.

Probably drunk.

When Helen's stomach settled, she came back in and sat in a chair waiting for the doctor. She was so tired and confused about what had happened after arriving home. Agnes had started in on her, yelling about Robbie.

"And where are dad and the other two?" Agnes had looked past her at the door.

"They're not here?! Not in Bill's room? Where have they gone?"

"I thought they were with you!" she'd said with disgust. "Maybe they were scared off by Robbie's accident."

She begrudgingly agreed to wait until Helen came back from the clinic. Her oldest would take care of her other five. "But see to it that you make it snappy!"

This was the icing on the cake. Agnes shook her head, regretting ever having let her meddling sister-in-law Katie persuade her to take Helen and her pack in. What had sounded like the perfect solution had been a problem from the start. *The woman couldn't even take care of her own family, never mind Dad.* She wondered how two of her brothers could have married such awful women.

Good-looking William had been wasted on Helen. Agnes had told him she wouldn't be a good mother from the beginning. *How can an orphan be a good mother?* William and she'd had a falling out over that.

Then take Katie. She's turned Iain into a mound of spineless jelly. It was late. Agnes closed her eyes and tried to nod off.

Sitting in a stiff-backed chair in the waiting room, Helen held her head in her hands. Her temples were throbbing. She knew what Agnes had been thinking as she left. She was a terrible mother. She should have never left them alone.

If only William had been around, this wouldn't have happened. William. She hadn't seen him in so long. Suddenly, it became clear. *He was never coming back. Never.* She began to cry, the tears of the last three years streaming down her face.

The stout matron, as hard as nails as she was, got up from her desk and sat beside her then, taking one of her hands and saying "there, there." Remorse always melted her heart. *The woman is feeling bad for her son.*

The doctor usually took a few minutes break at eleven in which he lay down on a cot to rest, but he consented to see Helen. He ushered her into his tiny office.

"Let me explain your son's situation." He looked so young that Helen thought he couldn't yet be qualified. "I'm afraid this is going to take a few months of recuperation." He didn't believe in mincing words. "If he makes it."

Helen couldn't speak. She just looked at him. This could not be her son. Robbie knew better than to play with fire.

He looked at the wall beyond her. "It is a serious second-degree scald. There's danger of shock or sepsis. The shock is the greater danger right now. We cannot give such a young lad morphine for the pain: it might dangerously affect his respiration. If he survives the shock, infection may set in. There's nothing we can do, except hope and pray."

Helen still didn't speak. She couldn't find her voice. *Should I pray to a God who never listens?* She swayed.

The doctor helped her sit down. "Do you have the necessary funds for the boy's treatment?"

She shook her head.

"Then what I can suggest is that we send him," he cleared his throat, "to the Kirkcaldy-Abbotshall Combination Poor House. It's not too far. He can go to the infirmary there until he's better. I'm afraid that is all I can do."

The doctor spoke with a weariness that usually came with age. He'd seen too many cases like this. He got up and led her by the arm to the matron. "Give this woman a strong cup of tea before she goes on her way, please." He needed to get off his feet.

To Helen, he said: "Come back in the morning and you can see him. Between 9 and 10 in the a.m."

Helen gulped the tea gratefully and somehow summoned the last little bit of strength she had left to get back home.

The Poor House! Life couldn't get any worse.

***

Another letter arrived from his wife and Doreen slit it open. It wasn't the usual nonsense. This time, there was a sense of urgency: Helen needed to tell him about the children, about his father. She had to see him. It sounded almost hysterical. Doreen thought for a moment about giving it to him but then, if it were that important, she wouldn't ask to see him, she would just come. *I would, if he were my husband.*

Taking the bundle of letters out of her desk drawer, Doreen tied it to the pile, locked the drawer and pocketed the key. The letters were becoming fewer and further between. If she could just manage the pretence a little longer, he would be where she wanted him.

CHAPTER FOUR

The infirmary Robbie found himself in was full of moans and groans of distress and discomfort. Under the sharp disinfectant, the smell of rot and feces festered and he was reminded of the lye-laced latrines in Lochoal.

Then he saw Tom quietly playing in the corner, a blanket around his shoulders. "Tom? Tommy?" he said in a quavering voice. He tried to sit up but when he moved, he cried out in pain.

Tom jumped up and ran over, the nurse catching him just in time before he climbed from the chair to the bed Robbie lay on. She held him firmly.

"Where is my mum?" Robbie said, plaintively.

"I'm sorry, laddie, I'm afraid I don't know."

"I want my mother," he said starting, to cry.

"Stop that now. There's no need to do that. You're a big boy. You're going to upset your brother." Out of her sewing bag, she pulled Robbie's special box of bits and bobs. "She's been to visit and left this for you. She said you needed it."

The box of stones and shells and treasure contained the stone his dad had given him, the stone that held light. His most important possession. Sister put the box under his pillow.

She put Tom down on the chair beside Robbie's bed. "Stay off the bed!" she said to Tom. The nurse went to the next bed where an old man was coughing badly. When Robbie turned his head a little more, he saw that it was his granddad. The nurse held a sputum dish for Bill to spit into.

"Where are we?" Robbie managed.

"You've ended up at the Poor House." She returned to Robbie and wiped his eyes. "It's not going to help, you know. Crying never does." She pointed at the next bed. "Your old granddad is here and your sister is in the women's ward."

She told him briefly about how Emma and Tom had been brought to the Poor House. They'd been treated for exposure and scabies. Their clothes had to be burnt.

Did she say rabies?

Emma had recovered quickly and was working in the women's ward. Against regulations, Tom was allowed to stay in the infirmary as he was too young to be in the men's section on his own.

Sister Effie propped Robbie up in bed so that he could drink some tea. His mouth was very dry, and he swallowed the liquid gratefully. She had been stirring, a little laudanum in both Robbie's and the old man's tea, which helped the grandfather sleep and keep Robbie's pain at bay.

"You should have seen your mum when she saw wee Tommy. She went as pale as a ghost; she almost fainted right away with joy."

She smiled at him. "You know, you're a tough little boy. Your temperature was sky-high this whole week. We were worried you wouldn't make it."

Robbie's eyes fluttered and closed, the bad smell and her voice drifting away.

CHAPTER FIVE

Helen had no place to go. After catching wind of the accident, the linoleum company had investigated and sent her packing. As her few sticks of furniture were removed and dumped on the street, Helen saw Agnes watching from a few houses away, amongst the other neighbours, arms folded. The neighbours usually rallied around for an eviction, trying to block the way of the authorities, at least making it difficult for them.

Mrs. MacLeod offered to store Helen's belongings at the church but no one came forward to take her in. Nobody wanted to help a woman who'd abandoned her children.

The day Robbie had entered the Poor House, the supervisor there had informed Helen of her options. She could become an inmate herself to stay with her family; find work and take her family out or surrender them to an orphanage. He was curt with her and unfriendly. The word 'surrender' made her dizzy.

From her blank stare, he knew she hadn't heard everything he'd said. He'd seen cases like this before. The mother, alone, at the end of her rope. The children would be better at The Orphan Homes of Scotland.

"The children can, in any case, only stay another few weeks without one of their parents." Helen nodded. She'd heard that part.

That day, she waited at the relief office for a few hours. The faceless man at the wicket pulled out a card with her name on it. "Your name is James, Helen, nee Bridie? Husband is William?"

"Yes," she said humbly.

"We've just received notice to take your husband off veteran's support."

"What? Why?"

"Yes, it says here that you have two more weeks."

"There must be some mistake." She leaned forward to look at the document. "My husband is in the clinic. He has been laid up, insensible for three years."

He withdrew the card quickly, so she couldn't read it. "I'm sorry. The information is correct." He didn't look up. "Next."

"There's been a mistake!"

"Next, please." He looked up and past her.

"You can't just cut me off like that! How am I supposed to live?"

He looked directly at her before getting up and lighting a cigarette.

"Talk to your husband." He gestured to the next person to come forward. Someone murmured, "Move along, woman. We haven't got all day like you, for heaven's sakes."

There was nothing left to do but leave. Feeling sick to the depths of her soul, Helen went back to the house in Links Street and looked up at the house she had so recently occupied. All her money except the two weeks' allowance was now gone after renting a room for a few days. With the children in the Poor House, she didn't want to spend anymore. It was getting dark. She had no idea where to go.

She looked around and then passed through the gates of the churchyard to sit on the bench there. It was quiet and then she had an idea. She went over to one of the open vaults and looked in. The dead didn't bother her. The vaults offered protection with their three walls. She went in and lay on a flat granite gravestone, turning her back to the church, as she felt God had turned away from her. She closed her eyes. There were no tears left.

As the darkness deepened, she heard the shuffling of feet and low voices. When she got up to relieve herself, she looked for a good-sized stick and kept it close, just in case.

Her words with the supervisor of the Poor House and the relief

100

officer reeled through her mind. *William is well enough to work. Not eligible for relief. Surrender the children.*

It was all a mistake. It must be. The premonition she had of him not returning home came back, suddenly, vividly. She involuntarily let out a sharp little cry.

Toward midnight, the weather was clear and she looked up at the cold brightness of the sky, remembering a time when William and she had first met and had lain in a field looking up at the warmth and the promise of the stars. Now, she wished for a sleep from which she would never wake.

In the early morning, shortly after she finally drifted off, she was startled awake by the poke of a broom and the familiar voice of Mrs. MacLeod. "Off you go. Tramps. No respect for the dead." Then she recognized Helen.

"What have you come to, missus?" Mrs. MacLeod told her to come back if she needed a place to sleep that night. She could hide her in the church a few nights, to help her get back on her feet. The sooner the children were out of that horrible place, the better. The stories she'd heard about the Poor House didn't bear thinking about.

***

Mary was in a good mood. It would be their first wedding anniversary soon and they were going out for the night. Maybe it would warrant buying a new blouse to go with her wedding costume. She was glad she'd spent the extra money on good material for it when she'd bought it. The skirt and jacket still looked new.

A cream coloured blouse would go well with the dark blue. She shrugged. The money her husband made barely paid the bills as it was. Maybe she could just get a new collar.

She almost bumped into a dishevelled woman.

"Excuse me," she said, although it was clearly the other woman's fault for standing there. *I always do that. Excuse myself even when I'm not to blame.*

Then she was taken aback. It was Helen. She looked homeless. She had deep rings under her eyes and her dirty dress hung on her like it belonged to someone else. Mary felt a tug at her conscience.

"Helen?"

Helen's body shook with a rattling cough and Mary hoped she wasn't contagious. She couldn't afford to bring home a grippe.

"Why didn't you come to see me?"

Helen just shrugged. The last of her energy had left her.

Mary led her friend firmly home. It was Jimmy's night with his pals and he wouldn't be around until much later. The children could stay with Jimmy's sister until she collected them. Mary was lucky. Her sister-in-law was a gem.

She made Helen some strong tea and toast, and as Helen perked up, she asked her gentle questions. Mary struggled to keep the horror from showing on her face. Helen's news was bad. The children in the Poor House. Put out on the street in front of the neighbours. Sleeping in the graveyard.

The worst was yet to come. With Mary's kind ear tuned to her troubles, Helen opened up further: "I need help, Mary. I have no one else to turn to. There's been a mistake."

"Go on." Mary glanced at Duncan's pocket watch, the only thing she had left of him.

"The relief office said William had been taken off disability. Yet I haven't received any letters for three years from him. The matron at the clinic wrote to me and told me he was unable to communicate. I think they've made a mistake. He wouldn't leave us, like this." Helen's wide-eyed stare made Mary uncomfortable. "Would he, Mary?"

"No, no. Of course not." She tried to sound convincing.

Mary looked around the crowded room. Two larger beds, one small. A small table, a few chairs. No extra space.

Yet, Mary hated seeing her old friend like this. She put some water on the oven to heat it up. "First things first. You'll feel better if you're clean." She filled a small tub. "Have a wash while I collect the children." She passed her a towel and an old shirt of Jimmy's to sleep in. "I've another skirt and blouse for you to wear but wash yours. Hang them above the sink to dry."

"Now," Mary said, "I've been thinking. You're staying here tonight. Tomorrow, Jimmy's sister will put you up until we find another room. And, Jimmy will put in a word at the linen factory for you."

"One thing. Don't tell Jimmy your children are in the Poor House.

He won't have you here. Just tell him they're with family." Mary was sure of her husband's views on that. Only the worst parents abandoned their children.

Mary picked up her scarf, tied it over her head and wrapped her shawl over her shoulders. "Now, get cracking." She went out to pick up her children.

Helen washed herself, put on the shirt and lay down on the single bed. She drew her coat up to her chin and fell asleep, only rolling over when Mary and her family came home. It was the first deep sleep she'd had since she'd left Lochoal.

CHAPTER SIX

They came to William less frequently now, those pale ghosts, lurching and limping through his nightmares.

But here they are again, surrounded by a green, choking fog, lit up from behind by grinning flame-throwers. There is a gurgle in their throats and there is a loud sucking noise as the drowned stuck in the quicksand-like mud try to pull their limbs out. When the shells start falling all around them, their screams and cries are muffled.

At first, as they approach him, there are tens of them, then hundreds and finally the whole field is moving and swaying as wave upon wave get up from their eternal beds in No-Man's Land. They look at him with hollowed eyes and shake their fists. Coward! Lily-livered bastard!

The shelling is so loud, he can't hear the piper who is leading them.

Hearing William's cries, Doreen rushed into his room. She saw that his eyes were open. Whatever he saw was real to him. Dugald ran in and held him while she administered a sedative.

As the drug took effect, his face relaxed and his eyes finally shut. He slipped into oblivion.

But the spectres were stronger than the drug and, although they were not threatening him anymore, they were still there. Lurking in the background. Watching him. Shaking their heads.

One of them, the Canadian doctor he remembered vaguely from the front, yelled at him with his fist raised. "I told you. *We shall not sleep!*"

***

The pastiness of William's face had been warmed by the afternoon sun. His arms had filled out and grown muscular with the work he was doing in the garden. Even the tattoo he had inked on his bicep was now almost legible as the skin became tauter, although it must have been done with a darning needle and was scarred from infection. It said, Doreen thought, *Flanders.* Part of the name of his poem.

The army doctor had discharged him, reinforcing the original diagnosis of battle-induced shellshock and certified William eligible for retraining that the army provided.

After the doctor left, William refused to come out of his room for supper. Doreen thought they should speak. This time openly.

She went to his room and rapped lightly on the door.

"I've brought you a cup of tea and some biscuits," she called when there was no response. Balancing the plate on top of the mug, she turned the door handle and went in, closing it behind her with a soft kick.

William was lying, fully clothed, on the bed, staring at the ceiling.

"I'm useless." His voice was bitter. "What kind of man am I now? A miner who can't go underground."

"Well," Doreen said. "You heard the doctor. You can get retrained. And you have your writing."

"My writing!" He jumped up off the bed and smacked the tea cup from her hand, smashing it against the floor. "You go on and on about that stupid poem. I told you I don't know where it came from. I never wrote it." He looked at the shards of china on the floor. "Tea? For God's sake, woman, I need a real drink."

Doreen took a step back toward the door.

"You're wrong about me. I can't write." He sat on the bed and held his head in his hands. "I'm sorry, Doreen. I know you're trying to help." He looked at her, his eyes a deeper blue that she'd ever noticed before. "You've been more than just a nurse to me: you've been a true friend." He paused. "I hope I'm not out of line saying that."

It was the first time he'd spoken to her that way.

"I need to work and I can't go back to Lochoal." He stood up and started picking up the pieces of the broken cup. "I have a son I've never seen. My wife hasn't written to me or visited me. And I can't think of any good excuses why she wouldn't. Except, unless, she's found someone else."

Doreen held her tongue, afraid of breaking the spell he seemed to be under.

The door opened and Dugald looked at the shards and the tea on the floor. "Is everything all right?" he asked Doreen.

"Yes, of course," she replied. "I slipped and the cup went flying." Her laugh was nervous. "Don't worry. I'll clean it up."

Dugald pulled an envelope out of his pocket. "This came for you, Jamesie."

William stood stock-still for a moment and then, hand shaking, took the proffered letter.

Doreen struggled with the urge to rip it out of his hands. All was surely lost, now. "Who's it from?" she said, hoping he didn't hear the terror in her voice.

"My sister, Agnes, in Kirkcaldy." He ripped it open. "I haven't heard from her in years."

He read the short letter in silence and then crumpled it and threw it on the floor. "Get the hell out of my room! Get out! Get out!"

"It must be bad news." Dugald shrugged and went out into the garden. Doreen hurried to her room to destroy all the letters she had. *Thank God the letter isn't from his wife. But what bad luck that for once, Dugald had picked up the post.*

CHAPTER SEVEN

The Combination Poor House stood near the shore on a hill a little east of Kinghorn overlooking the Firth of Forth. There was always a chill in the air as the wind whipped up from the churning sea to the buildings, bending the long grass over backwards and stunting the growth of the trees.

They were strong brick buildings, clustered together, made to last an eternity. The rock walls were thick and the windows small. It was as cold and damp as a cave. Wood and coal were scarce. At night, the able-bodied bunched together to keep warm and the infirm lay in bed with their blankets up to their chins, especially on the days when the wind howled through the cracks in the windows and under the thresholds of doors.

The rooms were firmly and irrevocably separated into men's and women's sections and only infants were allowed to stay with their mothers. Personal clothes, if salvageable, were taken and kept for the inmates until, if or when they were able to leave. They were given uniforms to wear.

Unlike prisoners, they were free to leave, although an application to leave had to be made, presented to the supervisor and then their uniforms had to be returned. If they left without returning them, they could be arrested for theft. This was one more worry for Helen. She needed money to buy the children clothes.

The stone walls were a prison to Emma, Robbie and Tom. Emma

was kept with the women and was taught needlework, knitting and ragging from scraps from linen plants in Kirkcaldy. They worked hard, turning out multi-coloured rag rugs which were sold at a local market, generating a much-needed supplement for coal and food.

The boys were kept in the infirmary with Sister Euphemia. Sister 'Effie', as the boys called her, wrapped Robbie's hands in bandages at night, so he couldn't scratch the healing skin, as his dreams were full of crawling insects.

As soon as he was able, Robbie started helping Sister during the day. He made tea for the sick and changed compresses on the brows and on the calves of the ill to bring the fevers down.

Robbie also spent time reading to Tom from some books that had been donated by the rich in the area. When these used books arrived, Robbie devoured them. His favourite, *"Treasure Island"*, he read and reread.

Sister Effie also gave him candle-ends to burn so Robbie could read to Tom, at night.

Robbie tried not to think of his mother between her infrequent visits. He sometimes wished she were dead, especially after the last time when she was wearing new clothes. She'd said: "Just a little longer, I promise. Take care of your brother. Look out for your sister."

Still making me responsible.

Robbie sulked when she was there, missing the boys on Links Street, school and the room they'd called home. Perhaps she could read the scowl on his face. Perhaps that was why her visits were few and far between.

Robbie and Tom were not allowed to see Emma often. Sister Effie fetched her only when they were working in the kitchen garden, pulling weeds or spreading sheep dung. They hugged each other while the sharp wind whipped and stung them, giving Robbie a good excuse for his watering eyes.

More and more, Robbie found himself angry at Tom for no reason. He'd tell him dark, chilling stories, only stopping when Tom cried. At first he prayed like Sister Effie told him to, promising to be a better person if only his mother and father would come back. The days turned into weeks. He gave up.

He told Tom that the island they could see from the garden was called Burntisland, where they burnt people that nobody wanted. "It's not the wind you hear at night. It is their screams as they are pushed into the oven."

"I don't believe you," Tom said, slipping his dirty thumb into his mouth.

"Stop that," Robbie said. "You're filthy dirty. They send sick people there, too." Tom pulled his thumb out of his mouth.

"It's not true!" Tom cried, sitting down in the grass and rubbing his eyes.

"I'm the king of the castle and you're the dirty rascal." Robbie stood over him.

"I'm not!" Tom screamed.

"You are," Robbie sneered at him.

Sister called them in and cuffed Robbie. She was doing it more frequently of late. She was too old to be their nursemaid. And they shouldn't be in the infirmary any more with the sick and dying.

Food was ample in the Poor House but tasteless; the soup thin and the porridge so thick and lumpy they washed it down with ale as the water was unfit to drink.

Sister Effie felt she had to go to the supervisor. The mother of these boys had not kept her promise to get the them out of there. These young boys needed to go to the Orphanage. She was going to advise it.

***

Long after William had settled into sleep, Doreen went back to her room and picked up the framed poem.

We are the Dead. Short days ago
We lived, felt dawn, saw sunset glow,
Loved and were loved, and now we lie
In Flander's Fields.

She held it close to her heart. He had captured the ennui of the trench soldier's war. The demise of his comrades-at-arms. Her tears welled up. William, when writing this, had expected to die.

Take up our quarrel with the foe:
To you from failing hands we throw
The torch; be yours to hold it high.
If ye break faith with us who die
We shall not sleep, though Poppies grow
In Flander's fields.

It was late, about midnight. She wasn't tired in the slightest. She stared outside at how the wind had picked up and was bending the trees over so far that they looked like they were bowing. She was sure some of them would snap. Putting on her hooded cape, she decided to go out anyway, wanting the sticky webs of her conscience to be blown away.

William was hers.

Walking to the edge of the forest beyond the driveway and turning back to look at the house, she felt that they'd all been there for a long, long time. She couldn't imagine ever having been anywhere else.

William was hers.

The rain started and she walked in it, letting it soak through her cape.

CHAPTER EIGHT

Just after breakfast, Doreen went into William's room. She found him dressed and sitting on the edge of his bed, his kit bag packed. He was pale.

"I was waiting for you," he said.

Her heart skipped a beat.

"My sister Agnes wrote to say that my wife has put the children and my dad into the Poor House. I have to go to Kirkcaldy. To see what I can do."

He looked down at his scuffed shoes. "I wish there was a way to thank you for everything you've done."

Doreen sat down beside him. *Now or never.*

He stood up, and picked up his bag, "I'm going down to the road to see if I can find a lift."

"Wait a minute. I can use the motorcar. I have some money saved and this place can do without me for a few days." She stood between him and the door. "You have been very, very ill and I don't want you to have a setback. Let me drive you there."

"I can't ask you to do that."

He hadn't said no. "William," she smiled. "You didn't ask. I offered to go with you. I'm going to throw a few things together."

As Doreen left the room, he caught her scent in the air.

***

Late that afternoon, Sister Effie bade William and Doreen into the supervisor's quarters. She knocked at his door with the side of her foot, while trying to rub the pain out of her hands. Her arthritis was acting up. Soon, very soon she hoped, she would stop working.

"Come in."

"Never a please nor a thank you," Sister Effie muttered.

"Mr. John Stevenson, this is the father of the James children, and Miss Lapointe," she said aloud.

Stevenson nodded slightly in their direction as he stuffed his pipe with tobacco. Effie gestured a bent finger to the hard-back chairs that were in front of the desk and William and Doreen sat down. Puffing on his pipe, Stevenson did not get up or look at them. The room gradually filled with the luxurious scent of plum.

Doreen crossed her legs. *This man looks miserable.* She brushed down her skirt while they waited for him to speak. *He must be a middle brother. No inheritance like the first born and not as loved as the youngest.*

Pictures of pheasants adorned the dark wood wall panels and red velvet drapes flanked the windows. The fire in the grate burnt brightly and there were bottles of delicious-looking amber-coloured liquids in decanters on the sideboard that weren't offered.

Delusions of grandeur. Doreen crossed and uncrossed her legs.

Sister Effie stood near the door, fidgeting with the fraying sleeves of her uniform. All she wanted was to have a nice cup of tea.

Stevenson squinted to push his glasses back up from the tip of his nose. After a few attempts, he gave up and shoved them up with his index finger.

"Mr. James and Miss...?" Stevenson pulled some papers toward him, finally looking at Doreen over his glasses which were once again sliding down.

"Lapointe."

"May I speak frankly in front of her?" he said, continuing to eye the well-dressed woman while speaking to William. *There was something familiar about her name.*

Doreen folded her arms. *He obviously doesn't realize who my father is.*

"Feel free." A sour taste worked its way up from the knot in William's stomach.

"Well, then…," Stevenson sucked on his pipe. "Emma left three nights ago. The local constabulary are keeping an eye out but we are quite sure she can take care of herself. We were just about to place her as a domestic, anyway."

William gripped the arms of the chair, white-knuckled and slid forward. His eyes narrowed. "What are you talking about?!"

"Mr. James, compose yourself." Stevenson kept a level voice. He hadn't expected this reaction from a man who'd been, according to his wife, comatose for the last few years. "Emma ran away. There was no reason."

Sister Effie's knees were now sore, too. She sniffed. *No reason? You never set foot in any other part of the House. You don't know what it's like.*

"This isn't a prison, you know. We don't lock people in," Stevenson said.

William jumped up and slammed his hand down on the desk and then turned toward the door where Sister Effie stood. He wiped his eyes and then his mouth with the back of his hand. Pain from his shoulder shot up his neck to his temple. He barked at Stevenson, "I want to see my father and my boys right now!"

"Mr. James, I will have them brought in when we are finished speaking. Please calm yourself."

William glared at him for a few moments and then abruptly sat down.

"Speak." William said.

"All right, then. No beating around the bush… children are not really allowed to stay here without their parents. We were keeping them here on your wife's promise that she'd pick them up. She hasn't." Stevenson knew he had regained the upper hand. "So, are you here to take them?"

William clenched his fists. The boys. Emma. His dad. He was failing them all. "I need some time." Doreen put a hand on his arm.

"So, you mean, you are not able to take them with you today."

"No. I told you. I need more time."

"Do you know where your wife is?"

"No."

"What kind of injury did you sustain? I must say, you look as fit as a fiddle."

"Battle-induced shellshock," Doreen said.

"Interesting. I heard that at the beginning of the war, they dealt severely with those who wouldn't fight."

Doreen pushed her hair behind her ears. "That's because they didn't understand this type of disability. Thank God that has changed."

Sister Effie leant against the wall. *The poor boys have been waiting outside the door the whole time.*

Doreen continued harshly, "I am the Matron for the Leigh Lane Clinic, Mr. Stevenson, and have helped treat many brave men for this. If you had combat experience yourself, you'd have more compassion."

Stevenson shot up. "I'll have you know that my military record is above question and not up for discussion. Now, once and for all, James, if you can't take your boys with you today, we will send them to the orphanage tomorrow." He gestured to the door. "If you'll excuse me…" Stevenson sat back down and proceeded to shuffle some papers.

"An orphanage?" William swallowed hard.

Mr. Stevenson shook his head, "I will explain as long as there are no interruptions. I am a busy man."

"The Orphan Homes of Scotland's children's village is near Bridge of Weir, just south of Glasgow in the countryside. It is a dignified establishment, set up not only for orphans but for destitute children. Like yours. They have their own school, hospital and church."

"I gave your wife," he continued, "until the end of last week to collect them. I haven't heard from her. So I went ahead and corresponded with the organization's City Home in Glasgow, which is the intake office for the Village. The children are usually registered there. If they meet the requirements, they are taken to the Village by Home staff. I have their train tickets to Glasgow here."

William took a deep breath. "Can't you wait?"

There was a moment's silence. Then Stevenson spoke again, "You can get tickets at the station and go with them if you like. Or shall we continue with the arrangements that have been made?"

"We'll drive them there ourselves," Doreen said. "I have use of a motor car."

William managed to say, "I want to see my boys."

Effie put a hand on the doorknob and Stevenson gave her a nod. He turned back to them, saying quickly. "I think it best not to mention their sister. I don't want any further upset."

Robbie and Tom, who had been waiting in the hall, burst in. "Daddy!" Robbie ran in, tears streaming down his face and threw himself at his father, forgetting about the still sore burn on his chest. Upon contact, he cried out in pain, "Let go. Let go!" William released him as quickly as he'd embraced him, taken aback. Robbie reached for his father's sleeve and held onto it, trying to catch his breath.

His father looked different. His eyes were wrong and there was a scar along his lip.

"Robbie?"

Robbie pulled up his shirt to show his father the red, puckered skin that looked like it had been ironed. William winced. "How did that happen?"

While Robbie was explaining the scald, Stevenson cut in.

"You can talk about everything tomorrow," he said.

"Tomorrow?" Robbie asked. "Are you taking us out of here?"

"Aye." William looked uneasily at his Robbie. Taller, he looked like he'd been stretched, he was so thin. His hair was greasy and there was dirt under his nails. Both of his sons stank and they looked ragged. He didn't have the heart to tell them where they were going.

Disregarding Stevenson, William greeted his second son. "You must be Tom. You look just like your mother." It wasn't so much the colour of his hair or eyes, but more in the way he held his head that brought back Helen's features so long lost to him. He winced.

Doreen coughed.

William bent down and held out his hand. Tom sidled forward to shake it.

"Are you my father, too?"

"Yes, son," William said. Not knowing what else to say, he

straightened. "Look at you, Robbie lad. You're almost a grown man."

"Where's mummy?" Tom asked, snivelling. He wiped his nose on his dirty sleeve.

"I'm afraid I don't know, Tom."

"And who are you?" Robbie asked Doreen.

"She's a nurse from the Leigh Lane clinic where I've been all this time," William said. "I'm so sorry that you've been in this awful place." His head and his heart were throbbing.

"Well, you're here now," Robbie said.

Stevenson interrupted once more, "Mr. James. Sister Effie, take them back."

"No!" said Robbie. "I don't want to go."

Effie rubbed the small of her back.

"I...," William's hand was shaking. He clasped his hands tightly together and turned to Doreen.

Robbie saw and understood in the same moment, even at his tender age, that there was more to their relationship than patient and nurse. There was something personal between them.

Doreen said, "Mr. Stevenson, before we leave, there is still the matter of William's father. I do think we can speak about that without the boys in the room."

"You can't make us go!" Robbie cried, hands and teeth clenched. "Dad?!"

Dots had appeared around the periphery of William's vision. He held up his hand to Robbie to shut him up for a moment while he lit a cigarette. *I need to get out of here, I can't breathe.*

"Dad, don't let them make us go back!" Robbie yelled as Sister Effie held out her hand to Tom to lead him out of the room.

"Don't worry, Robbie." He shook his head and mumbled quietly, "Don't worry, don't worry."

Robbie opened his mouth but his father looked so scary that he turned and followed Tom wordlessly out of the room. As the boys left, William ran a hand through his hair. He was going to disappoint them even more.

Stevenson's fingers were drumming the top of his desk. He wanted a drink. He took his glasses off and stood up, walking toward the door.

"One other thing. They need clothes for tomorrow. They can't leave in the uniforms. Now, what else is it that you want? To see your father? The men's ward is straight down the corridor. Please wait outside and Sister Effie will take you to him."

William cleared his throat. "Then we'll pick the boys up tomorrow to take them to Glasgow. If you hear anything about Emma, my sister Agnes will know where we are. I'll speak to her about dad."

Stevenson shut the door behind them and poured himself a dram.

The poor were really such a nuisance. Always complaining.

He took out his handkerchief and wiped his face.

CHAPTER NINE

Doreen drove the short distance to Kirkcaldy along the shore road to Agnes'. She was the only one who could tell William what had really been going on. The closer they got, the quieter William became.

As they approached Kirkcaldy, there was a sharp smell in the air. A chemical she couldn't place.

"That's the linoleum plant," William said, even though she hadn't asked.

Doreen pulled up at the strand, hoping that the sea air would ease him before the next confrontation. William had told her that, of all his siblings, he liked Agnes least.

It was a warm day for November. Sunny, dry and windless. They got some fresh bread at the baker's, cheese and a few bottles of ale in the shops along the beach and sat on a bench looking out over the expanse of the sea. Seagulls hovered, their beady eyes focused unwaveringly.

The large ships in the distance gently rocked on the waves, anchored in the shelter of the Firth of Forth. Doreen threw some breadcrumbs over the seawall onto the gritty volcanic sand. Within seconds, the birds dove down screeching.

"Don't!" William shouted, almost making Doreen drop her sandwich. He despised the dirty, greedy beggars. He explained to her that seagulls had flown alongside his troop ship on their way to France. "When we got to the beach, they swooped down, like vultures. There were bodies everywhere. And those damn birds were feasting on them." William put his bread away. He had lost his appetite.

With his last sip of ale, William closed his eyes and breathed in deeply. The lapping water, the tangy smell of fish and salt, brought back other, better memories. There was the Lang Toon fair as a child: the penny rides and the sticky candy he'd saved for by doing odd jobs. There was himself as a young man, the thrill of stripping down to swim naked, just out of sight of the day-trippers, in the Sea's frigid water. Stealing into the Raith Rovers' football matches. His last memory of this place was his fondest – bringing Robbie to see the bright lights and hear the hawkers of the fair and afterwards, to the very same beach to collect sand-washed glass and skip stones together.

Doreen had finished her food and was watching a couple who were walking along the beach. The man reminded her of Gregory – the same swagger in his step. They were very different, William and Gregory. Suddenly, she stood up, rubbing her arms. She looked sideways at William, wondering how the meeting between him and his sister would play out. She hoped he was up to it. She wished she'd brought a mirror and comb to fix her hair.

* * *

As William had expected, only seconds after being introduced to Doreen and while stirring boiling water in the teapot to make it brew faster, Agnes started her tirade. "I had it all set up. All Helen had to do was pay a pittance and take care of dad." She poured the tea into the chipped cups. "He's lost it, dad has, you know." She pointed to her head, "Always wandering off, talking nonsense. Dirtying himself."

"I know. I've just seen him." William shook his head. "He didn't know who I was."

"She buggered it up. Imagine leaving that young boy to clean house and take care of the family while she was off gallivanting with God knows who." She tapped the side of her nose with a finger. "I've heard things."

"Do you know where she is now?" William interrupted.

"How in hell should I know? I've got enough on my plate."

Agnes lit a cigarette from the stub of another and continued, embellishing readily, telling the story in her own time, doing her best to leave no question as to who was to blame for Helen's eviction. She told her brother of the filth his family had lived in, the food his children had gone without, the times she, herself, had to pick their father out of the gutter, while Helen squandered money on herself.

"She was watching a moving picture when Robbie had his accident and Emma and Tom were found with dad in a boat and taken to the Poor House half dead from the cold."

William shook his head. *No, no, no, Helen wasn't like that.*

Yet his anger towards Helen was steadily gaining momentum. He looked at Agnes who was squinting at him through the cigarette smoke. *Despite what Agnes is saying, I'm sure she didn't help as much as she lets on.*

But there was no reason for Helen to have left the bairns at that God-awful place.

Maybe he had never really known her at all. He remembered how she hadn't wanted any more children.

After a brief pause, Agnes lit another cigarette. "One thing I want to know from you, William. Helen said you didn't answer any of her letters. Why not?"

He slid forward to the edge of his seat.

Before he could open his mouth, Doreen jumped in, her words running into each other. "William didn't receive any letters from Helen. I would have known. They would have had to come through my office first."

William looked at Doreen in surprise. "I can speak for myself."

"I knew it!" Agnes said, as a string of ashes fell onto the table. "She lied."

William picked up his hat. "I've had enough." He gestured to Doreen. "We're leaving."

"So, that's all the thanks I get? Don't ever expect anything else from me!" Agnes slammed the door behind them.

***

William hurried away, his head aching so badly that he could barely see. Doreen almost had to run to keep up with him. They were walking in the wrong direction, away from the motor car.

Hearing Doreen out of breath, made William stop. "I'm sorry," he said, "but that sister of mine drives me round the bend."

"Helen must have had a hard time with her."

"Nothing should have made her take my children to the Poor House."

"Say," she said as she caught her breath. "Why don't we get the boys the clothes they need for tomorrow."

"I don't have the money."

"You can't take them out of that place naked," Doreen said. "Let me help you."

"You've already done more than enough."

"William, that's what friends do."

William gave in. He really had no other choice. "I'll pay back every penny."

What a perfect woman. Pretty, generous and self-sufficient. Too bad that her fiancé was killed in the war. She deserves to be married and have children of her own.

After shopping, they went for tea at the blind woman's tea shop that William recognized as having been there for years. It was so busy that the bent over old woman didn't even attempt to serve her customers. Everyone helped themselves to tea and buns and left change on the counter. She put wood in the oven and stoked the fire. She filled the kettle with water and as soon as she heard it boil, poured it over the fragrant tea leaves. And then filled it again.

Despite the clinking of china, and low chatter, she overheard them talking and coming close to their table, said she knew where they could get cheap but decent rooms for the night. Doreen was unnerved by the woman's ability to navigate the room without a cane or outstretched hands. As she walked away, the woman turned briefly back to William. "She'll be all right."

"Who?" William asked.

The woman didn't answer.

"Who is she talking about?" Doreen asked William.

"I have no idea."

"Do you know her?"

"Not really."

As William and Doreen left, the woman waved in their direction. He raised his hand to wave back but dropped it, feeling silly.

It only took a few minutes for them to drive to the house that the blind woman had described. William knew the street. Holding his hat in one hand, he rubbed his eyes with the other.

"I'm truly sorry about what happened earlier. I have never been able to stomach Agnes for long." He leant toward her and kissed her on the cheek. She smelled wonderful. "I am grateful for everything."

While she opened the door to her room, Doreen smiled to herself. Her investment was already paying off.

***

In the pink and white bedroom he found himself in, William lay on the bed, fully clothed, with pins and needles shooting up his left arm, again. He couldn't sleep. *If this doesn't stop I could end up in the Poor House myself.*

He got up and lit a cigarette. His mind was working a mile a minute. He supposed it was making up for lost time.

Emma and the boys.

To deal with tomorrow, he needed rest. He took out the vial of laudanum in his jacket pocket, gulped some and then got into bed. Even before the drug took effect, the fact of knowing it was in his system, helped him relax. He drifted, thinking of Doreen, leaning over him with her soft, cool hand on his forehead, the day he woke up in the clinic.

He turned on his side and fell asleep.

CHAPTER TEN

They got an early start in the morning. William checked with the constabulary in Kirkcaldy about his daughter. They had nothing to report. He left his name and the address of the clinic and silently damned Helen again. If he could find her, she'd have hell to pay, no matter what cards the war had dealt her.

Overnight, the weather had turned. There was a scent of snow in the air, and the last few leaves left on the trees rustled as the wind plucked them and flung them to the ground.

When they picked up the boys, William told them they were going to Glasgow for a fresh start. The truth that they were going to be abandoned at an orphanage, was left until later.

Doreen drove as far as Edinburgh. Flurries were beginning to blur her vision and she said she felt more comfortable taking the train to Glasgow, never having driven in snow before.

After buying the tickets, there was about a two hour wait and they went for a walk, getting Edinburgh rock candy for the boys and tea for them all. The city lifted William's spirits. *What a magnificent place this is. This is where I could live. No more small dingy towns for me.* The brisk, fresh wind raced through the streets, chasing the usual dark, oily smell of coal in 'Auld Reekie', Edinburgh's pet name, away.

He helped Doreen on the train. Thanks to her, he was able to spend today with them. He hoped she didn't feel used.

Thank God she thought of buying the boys jackets. It's damn cold today.

There'd been one bad moment when Stevenson demanded money for the cheap, ugly uniform that Emma had been wearing when she fled. He wouldn't bring the boys out to his office till he'd collected. "You've already had enough for free," he said.

William could barely contain himself.

Doreen had opened her change purse and paid Stevenson.

William had put on his hat and pulled at the brim before stuffing his hands in his pockets, embarrassed that Doreen had to, once again, foot the bill.

"William, don't worry," she'd said, loud enough for Robbie to hear. "I'm happy to help."

Robbie was proud of his new clothes but, as he put his jacket on, he kept his head down so that woman couldn't see his smile. He'd never had anything brand new before. Doreen rolled up Tom's lengthy sleeves.

As they were leaving, Robbie asked about Emma.

Seeing William's helplessness, Doreen jumped in again, "Your mum came to collect Emma last night after you two were asleep. She's gone to work with her. "

Robbie looked at his father for confirmation but his father couldn't meet his eyes. *It was a lie.* This woman was lying to them and his father didn't care. Robbie was very quiet after that.

***

When they arrived at Queen Station in Glasgow, they followed Sister Effie's directions to the City Home. On their way, they passed through George Square where crowds of dark-coated men jostled each other. Trying to remain four abreast was impossible. William let go of Robbie's hand and pushed him into the lead with Doreen.

These men had reason and purpose in their faces, something William longed for. His mind had been so muddled since the day of Duncan's death.

He could even sometimes still hear that German, whispering in his ear.

Weariness filled him and he slowed down and then stopped to sit on one of the benches. It was time to tell the boys that they were going to an orphanage. Right up to now he'd avoided it, knowing it would be one of the hardest things he'd have to do in his life. Their queries thus far had been answered with, "You'll see."

The boys were on either side of him. Doreen told them she'd be back in a moment. He took their hands in his. "I know you don't understand right now, but there'll be a day when you know I did the right thing," he said to his sons. "I have to leave you here for a while."

"Here?" Tom looked around at the busy square, his brown eyes large and brimming.

"Not here, Tommy, at the Homes, the Orphanage."

"What's an orphanage?" Tom asked.

"It's a place where children with no parents go," Robbie said in a low voice.

"But we have parents," Tom said, climbing onto his father's lap.

"They don't want us," Robbie said, getting up. He wiped his nose.

William's brow furrowed and his voice was unsteady. "I will be back to get you. I promise. You must believe me."

"That's what mummy said." Tom got up from his father's lap and stood beside Robbie.

"You're lying," Robbie said.

Tom began to cry in earnest. William stood up, knowing he had to get them to the City Home before his heart broke. "It's for the best." He grabbed their hands and pulled them past the great, imposing statues, only some of whom he recognized: Queen Victoria on a horse, Burns and the monument to Scott. The colourless, powerful dead. A reminder to ordinary men of how unimportant they were. Doreen rejoined them.

Tom's little legs couldn't keep up so William carried him and held onto Robbie with his other hand. Robbie felt the urge to suck his thumb, something he hadn't done in a very long time.

They reached the giant grey, five-storey building on James Morrison Street just as a nearby church bell struck the hour of four. Two youths ran by them and opened the door, just hesitating long enough for Doreen to grab it.

To William's relief, they were laughing and looked well-fed and dressed.

The door opened onto a grey tiled hallway. Identical twin girls, about Robbie's age, were sitting on a bench, their hair matted and clothes filthy. Beside them sat a thin woman who was dressed in black, with bulging eyes and a long beak of a nose. She was with a young boy.

"Leaving those boys here?" Without waiting for an answer, she continued, "Then, you might as well sit down to wait your turn."

A door to an office swung open and, even though the girls got up, the woman pushed her way in, steering the boy in front of her. The girls sat back on the bench.

Some minutes later, the door opened again, and the boy was led up the stairs by a young man as the woman hurried out the front door. The girls stood up again, and hesitated, looking at William with pale faces. William gestured for them to go in. *They are used to being pushed around.*

It took all of two minutes before the same young man came hurtling back down, two steps at a time and went into the office. The door opened again and he and the girls went up the stairs. William picked Tom up and grabbed Robbie's hand. Doreen followed.

The room was spotlessly clean and sparsely furnished, with a table serving as a desk and four chairs. The middle-aged man who sat behind the desk had a pained expression on his face but kind eyes. Like the room, he was clean and neat, his fingernails cut short and his eyebrows trimmed. The hair on his head was combed over his bald patch. His suit was well-brushed.

"Good afternoon. My name is MacBride." He stood up and offered his hand.

"I'm Mr. James and this is Miss Lapointe, sir."

"Have a seat."

He picked up his glasses, polished them with a handkerchief and then put them down again. He straightened out the papers on the desk and said, "And you are Robert and Thomas?" smiling at the two boys. He always liked talking directly to the children. If they were going to find Jesus, they needed to know that they would not be deceived here. "You are coming to us from the Poor House?" He picked up his glasses again. "Where's your mother?"

Robbie wasn't used to speaking to kind adults. "I don't know. We haven't seen her for a while. " All of a sudden, Robbie started to cry, rivulets running down the side of his nose. "It's all my fault, because of the accident."

MacBride offered his handkerchief to Robbie. "What accident?"

At that, Robbie blew his nose and then lifted his shirt.

MacBride's eyebrows shot up. "That looks very sore."

Robbie explained what had happened. About the blue dress, the sea, the tea shop. He blew his nose again. "So you see if I hadn't gone out, we'd still be living in Kirkcaldy with mum."

MacBride didn't know what to make of this.

At this point, William spoke up, "I only found out the day before yesterday." He leant forward. "I was in the clinic for…I don't really know how long." He gestured to Doreen. "Miss Lapointe is the head matron there. She can vouch for me."

MacBride said, "Your mother should have never left you alone. So, you see, you shouldn't think it was your fault."

"My mother," Tom cried, "loves us!"

"Yes," MacBride softened, "of course. I'm sorry."

Turning to William, MacBride continued, "Why can't they stay with you?" To William's surprise, it sounded like a genuine question, not an accusation.

"I'm not standing on my own two feet just yet. I need to find work and put a roof over my head."

"Is there no one else to help out? A sister or a brother? Perhaps grandparents? Family that could take the children in till you are able?"

"We lost mother years ago and dad is senile. He's still in the Poor House. My wife is an orphan." He sighed. "The only sister who lives anywhere near has too many children of her own."

"I see," MacBride said, looking at his fingernails.

Robbie spoke up, "I'm old enough to take care of myself."

Tom said, "I want my mum!"

Robbie said, "Don't worry, Tommy. I'll never leave you."

"Lads," Mr. MacBride got up and moved around to the front of the desk. Squatting down so that he was at Tom's level and arching an eyebrow at Robbie as if he were some kind of accomplice. "Would you go with 'Gill' to have some tea? He's waiting just outside the door. You must be famished."

Robbie blew his nose into the handkerchief again. As soon as they'd come into the building he'd smelt something cooking – meat? It'd been a long time since they'd had meat.

He studied Mr. MacBride and felt they could trust him. He put the used hankie on the table. This place was better than the Poor House. And although he missed his mates in Kirkcaldy and that yellow dog and even school just a little, he knew that there was no going back.

Besides, he had to show Tom that everything was going to be all right. He had already let him down once, and was not going to do it again.

Robbie squared his shoulders. "Come on, Tom," he said. "I bet they have sugar."

MacBride, putting his hand gently on Robbie's back, steered them toward the door, where Mungo MacGill, the young man they'd just seen, was waiting.

Gill was an Orphan Homes of Scotland foundling who had been left, swaddled and mewing on the doorstep of the City Home, a spring morning about eighteen years ago. MacBride himself had named him Mungo, after the patron saint of Glasgow. His surname was chosen at random.

He was an enthusiastic youth. A poster boy for the Homes. Dark-haired, ruddy-faced, well built, he'd been asked to work at the City Home after growing up at the OHS Village.

"Can you play football?" said Gill looking over Robbie's slender frame as he took them up the stairs.

"We can play football?"

"Of course! And there's cricket, sprinting and even rugby!"

MacBride smiled at the interchange and shut the door, turning back to William and Doreen. "The boys will be fine here." He picked up the documents, one for each son and handed them to William.

Once the children were away, MacBride felt better. Although he knew that the Homes were a wonderful solution for many children, when a child came through his door with a parent, it made him uncomfortable. He could never get accustomed to the moment when they realized that they were being left behind. It was heart-wrenching every time.

"I just need you to sign these and we'll get them bathed and ready for the night. The doctor will check them tomorrow morning," he said.

"Why can't they stay here?" William asked. "Why do they have to go further away?"

"Only the older boys, who work here in the city, live here. The younger children all live in the Village."

"I'll come back in a minute," said MacBride.

He was satisfied. *In all, there are five today that God has sent to be part of His Village.*

Although MacBride had nothing but compassion for veterans, he wondered what Mr. James suffered from. There were no outward signs of a disability.

No good man could have lived through so much horror not to go mad. God be with him.

On his way out the door, he offered a cigarette to William and Doreen. William lit one with a shaking hand, inhaling deeply.

"Look, Mr. James. I don't judge. There has been an incredible increase in the number of children that have been brought here because of the war."

"Just take your time to fill out and sign the forms."

MacBride closed the door behind him and William picked up the pen and dipped it in the inkwell.

The questions were straightforward and he filled them out to the best of his knowledge. At the top of the third page, he hesitated.

There was some writing. "The father of this child is a disabled war veteran. The mother has lost interest in this child and is not providing the care and attention he needs."

Then, the last part with his name and address and signature had to be filled in. 'I, William James, residing at…'

"What's the address of the clinic?" he asked Doreen.

"You can't use that, you've been discharged," Doreen said. "Why not put down my address in Edinburgh for now. You could always change it, later."

He thought it sound advice. "Good idea. What is it?"

"Nine Brighton Street, Edinburgh. It's my father's building."

Her family must be well off. She has classy clothes, knows how to drive, and her father owns a place in Edinburgh.

He went back to the rest, '…make application to have my son, Robert James, age nine years, received into the above named Homes, with the view of being maintained and educated and thereafter kept at the Homes, emigrated to Canada, or otherwise discharged as the Managers of the Homes may decide. I further agree to leave said child under the care of the Homes until he attains the age of sixteen years.'

"Canada!" he exclaimed. "The boys could be sent to Canada." A blob of ink dripped from the tip of the pen onto Robbie's form as he paused.

"What do you mean?" she asked.

"If I sign, the boys could be immigrated to Canada if the manager of the Homes decides."

"Let me see," Doreen asked. She blotted the still wet ink. "You're right. From what it says here, they could be. Ask Mr. MacBride."

MacBride returned with a tray. There was a teapot, three cups and a little pot of milk. "I thought a spot of tea would…"

William interrupted him, "What is this about Canada?"

"If we're to care for them, we want to do what is proper for the children." MacBride looked at William, who was listening intently. "They can't get enough of our lads over there. Ontario farmers are just crying out for help. Some of the farmers are old Home boys themselves."

"They help out on farms in turn for room and board and earn some money that will be saved for them. If they are younger than fourteen, they will continue to go to school. In Canada, the little immigrants have to reach eighteen, before they are free to follow their hearts. They can come back to Scotland if they so desire. Most stay and we have plenty of success stories: boys who own their own farms, boys who go on to a higher vocation."

"But when I get work, I can take them back, can't I?" William said.

"Yes, of course. That would please us just as much."

"Must I sign these?" William said.

"I'm afraid so." MacBride sat down and poured them a cup of tea. He'd had this conversation before and so few parents came back.

William hesitated and then signed. He stood up, waving off the tea. "Thank you, no. Can I say goodbye to my boys?"

"I'd advise against it. It will be harder on all three of you." He put one hand on William's arm. He nodded to Doreen and then opened the door.

"They will be taken to the Village the day after tomorrow by train from St. Enoch station. It leaves hourly and the Village is just a short carriage ride from the Bridge of Weir station. You can visit them once a month." A note of gentleness entered his voice, "Please don't worry about your boys, Mr. James. They'll be well taken care of."

William walked out of the building with Doreen at his side. He crossed the street, lit a cigarette, and stood staring at the building where he had just left his two sons. He said aloud, "Well, this is the end."

"Or the beginning," Doreen said.

"What should I do? Tinker, Tailor, Soldier, Sailor or Candlestick Maker?" He turned to Doreen, "In any case, whatever I am going to be, I need to start soon." Doreen tucked her arm into the crook of his.

"It's going to be all right, you'll see," she said. He didn't trust his voice to answer. So, for the first time, he pulled her close and kissed her forehead. She was such a good friend.

Unlike Helen. Unless there is a damned good explanation, I never want to see her again.

"Edinburgh is a good place to start," Doreen said. "There's a room in my flat you could use. The War Office can tell you about training and it's a short train trip to see the boys."

William grinned weakly. He was worried about Emma.

CHAPTER ELEVEN

After their tea, the boys were taken to a tiled bathroom where they were scrubbed with carbolic soap. The nurse was very careful around Robbie's wound, but it still stung.

They were provided with nightshirts. When the nurse picked up the new clothes and jackets that they had been given, Robbie tried to wrestle them away from her. They had to be fumigated and they'd get them back the next day, she explained. It was normal procedure. The doctor called over, "Nurse, what's the trouble?"

"Nothing," she said to the doctor.

To Robbie she said, "I'll make sure you get them back." Robbie let go.

"Where's our dad?" he asked her.

"He's gone."

"He didn't say goodbye."

"When's he coming back?" asked Tom.

"Never, Tom." Robbie knew his father was going to pull a stunt like this. *He is really as weak as the lads had said he was.*

This made Tom weep and Robbie put his arms around him to comfort him. "I'm here," he said.

Despite their strange surroundings, and their heartbreak; their fatigue and the rhythmic breathing of a roomful of boys lulled them to sleep quickly.

Early next morning, the sound of rain pattering against the windows woke Robbie up. The room was dark and everyone else was still sleeping. After the initial fright of disorientation, he relaxed. There were no mad, old men who would accidentally climb into his bed, sure it was their own. There was no smell of night soil, as Sister Effie had called it. He drifted back off to sleep and woke up a little while later when the lights were turned on.

After a breakfast of porridge and tea, they were taken to a room adjacent to the bathroom and used specifically for new intakes. They had to undress again and the same nurse made Robbie, Tom and the other boy, wait until it was their turn to be poked and prodded by the white-coated doctor. The nurse hunted for lice with a fine-toothed comb and then checked their elbows and knees for scabies and their necks for scrofulous. The doctor looked into their eyes, ears, nose and throat. "Open your mouth, show me your teeth. Any fever, sore throat, cough, sniffles, chills?" he asked the boys.

The nurse checked off the points the doctor had gone through on their medical report.

Standing up to stretch his back a little, the doctor said to the nurse, "No skin disorders and their eyesight and hearing seem to be in order."

If they asked Tom a question, Robbie answered for him. At the end, they were measured and weighed.

"They seem to be of normal intelligence and I have noticed no peculiarities in disposition. The young boy, Thomas, seems somewhat slow but he is probably just a little reticent because of the situation," said the nurse.

"Thank you, nurse," said the doctor as he picked up the forms and hurried out of the room. He still had the girls to examine.

The boys were asked to get dressed. Tom started skipping round the room but Robbie stopped him. "We don't know if we can stay here yet. Be quiet, be good," he hissed as Tom whimpered. "Look at him." The other small boy was quiet.

They heard Gill singing before they saw him. He knew the boys could hear him and opened the door from the stairwell with a flourish as he sang the last words.

"What's with the long faces?"

"Did we pass?" Robbie said.

"First of all, my pals call me Gill. Short for my last name which means strong one," Gill said. He flexed his bicep. "Did you pass what?"

"The test?"

"What test?"

"The test to stay here."

Gill wanted to laugh but knew from the freshly scrubbed, pale faces that Robbie was serious. "Of course you did. With flying colours. And just wait till you see where you are going to live." He pulled up a chair. "Each one of you will be in a cottage with a mother and father who will take care of you. There's a school, a church, a store, a laundry, a poultry farm, and a playing field. In the spring and the summer, there are flowers everywhere. It's glorious." His excitement was contagious. "You just missed the fairy light lantern parade at Hallowe'en but Christmas and New Year's Day are coming. It's the best time of year! There are two great pine trees," Gill jumped up and spread his arms wide, "set up in the church with presents for everyone."

"What about Emma? Can she come?" said Tom.

"Who's Emma?"

"Our sister. She was at the Poor House with us," Robbie said.

Gill was at a loss and said, "I'll ask Mr. MacBride."

But Robbie knew their mother and sister were lost to them. *They will never find us here. It's so far away.* He felt like crying again but steeled himself. He couldn't let Tom see him cry anymore. *Crying was for little boys.*

Gill reached over and ruffled his hair.

"Time to get a move on. We're going down to the kitchen to help wash up after breakfast and make the soup for lunch. Idle hands are the devil's workshop."

The boys scrubbed dishes and dried and polished them in the enormous kitchen. As Tom was still only five, he was given a blunt knife to butter the bread.

"Spread it very thin, like this."

The older boys chopped potatoes, turnips and carrots. All these good things were put into big kettles of beef broth that had been simmering since yesterday as the cheap beef needed a long, slow cook.

As they moved to the hallway to scrub the floor, Robbie saw the twin girls briefly with their arms full of laundry. Everyone staying in the City Home was given something to do, even if they were only there for a day.

Mungo MacGill watched over them, like a friendly shepherd, making sure they got right into the corners, wiping away all traces of the early morning rain.

CHAPTER TWELVE

The following morning, Gill and the children walked to the St. Enoch railroad station to be taken to the Village. Robbie and Tom were excited. Their first train trip ever, yesterday, was a blur. Robbie decided he was going to enjoy this trip, despite everything.

The train's whistle blew one long and two very short blasts. This, Gill said, was done as a special salute to the Home children. The train jerked and slowly shunted forward, taking them out of the greyness of Glasgow and running inland toward the Bridge of Weir. The sixteen-mile journey followed the valley of the White Cart Water to the Adrossan Canal. As they approached their destination, the Renfrewshire landscape became gentler and more welcoming – even in November, the hills were a mat of green.

They disembarked. It was a two-mile walk to the Village, Gill said, and he set off at a brisk pace. The children had to half run, half walk to keep up to him.

As they passed through the high, black wrought-iron entrance gates, the children stared down the length of Faith Avenue toward the Central building and became quiet. Each child, having come from differing degrees of squalor, couldn't believe that they were going to live in this fairy-tale-like village, the cottages resembling little castles with spires and turrets. Despite the sadness that Robbie had felt since being left at the City Home yesterday, he was bowled over. There was so much space. The lawns in front of and around the cottages were well-manicured and there were shrubs with berries and patches of garden everywhere. Room to run and play on grass, even right in front of each cottage door.

The only thing that was missing was Emma.

There were children everywhere but Robbie saw only one adult, a woman vigorously banging two shoes in front of a shed that was attached to the side of one of the houses. Gill pointed in the direction of the spire of the huge Victorian-style church called Mount Zion, the river Gryffe where they would learn to swim, the sports fields, the school, and the store among other places as they dropped off each girl and boy at different cottages.

"Even though there are about fifteen hundred boys and girls living here," he said, "which amounts to something like thirty to a cottage, we are all one very big family."

Robbie and Tom were the last to be dropped off. They had to cross a little bridge over a rushing brook to Peace Avenue where cottage thirty-seven, the Peddie Alexander house, was. Peddie was one of the furthest from the front gate, on the edge of the Village, and there was a magnificent view of uncluttered green fields, the soil dark and rich. Robbie was comforted at seeing the brook. Having water nearby, reminded him of home. Robbie breathed a huge sigh of relief as both Tom and he were introduced to Mrs. Livet, the cottage mother. He had been really worried that he would be separated from his brother. That would have made a liar out of him, after having promised he wouldn't leave him.

Seeing all the children made him begin to think that them ending up here, wasn't entirely his fault.

It was the war that ruined everything. If I ever get my hands on one of those Germans, I'll knock his block off.

He smiled shyly at Mrs. Livet to make a good first impression, as his mother had once taught him. She had beautiful soft wavy hair and when she smiled back at him in a welcoming way, he was reminded of how his mother used to be before his dad had gone to war. His knees grew weak and he wiped his eyes on his sleeve.

"Oh, you poor little boys," she said. "What have you been through?" She put an arm around each boy's shoulder.

Gill was already on his way off.

"I'll just show you your room." She took them up the stairs to their bedroom. "These two beds are yours."

There were six beds jammed into the room. Robbie claimed the bed right next to the window. "There's a wooden box under the bed for you to put your clothes in." She looked at the small parcels that they were carrying. "If you need a change of clothes, we'll get some tomorrow from the store," she said. "Now, let's go downstairs and I'll show you the sitting room, dining room and cottage altar."

Robbie stashed their meagre belongings, hesitating a moment before walking away.

"No one will touch your things." She walked them back downstairs. "We get up at six, no sleeping in, you do your chores, you get ready, have breakfast and then off you go to school. When you come back you have an hour's free time, and then you must finish your chores before we have supper, say your prayers and go to bed. Follow the rules and there will be no problems between us."

"Now, what would you like to do?" She ruffled Tom's hair. "You have almost an hour of free time. You might want to run over to the sports field. Our boys are playing a football match and have taken the little ones with them to cheer them on. Go back the way you came, past the Central Building, and the school and just before you get to the church, turn right. You'll hear them as you get closer."

She left them and, after a few minutes, Robbie was pulling Tom along. They crossed over the rickety bridge. Tom protested, he was tired and dug his heels in, wanting to walk slower. Robbie could see the church towering over the rest of the Village. As they neared it, they could hear cheering and shouts, the sounds of a lively football match. Annoyed at Tom's stubbornness, Robbie let go of his hand after they rounded the corner to the field.

The sports field was enormous, at least the size of three or four football pitches. And although there was a match going on, there were boys running and playing other games that Robbie didn't recognize. He rushed to the sidelines of the game, in his mind, already playing with them, scoring the winning goal.

The game was tied. The team wearing blue vests intercepted a pass and went with it, running almost a quarter of the field and then kicking it high into the corner. A few minutes later the whistle was blown and the boys on the blue team surrounded the final goal scorer and hurrahed.

It was then that Robbie looked for Tom but, to his dismay, he'd vanished. Robbie ran toward the church, angry that Tom was probably hiding somewhere, to spite him.

Robbie looked down the length of Church Street and in the direction of Love Avenue, but Tom was nowhere to be seen. Robbie stood rooted to the spot, trying to decide what to do. Boys, who had been playing on the sports field, were now streaming off it toward their cottages. All of a sudden, he felt a hand on his arm. It was Gill. He'd seen Robbie standing in the middle of the street, alone.

Robbie was near tears. "I don't know where Tom is."

"Where did you last see him?"

"Around here."

"He can't be far off."

He looked at Gill's face. He was calm, not worried. Robbie followed him into the churchyard.

There was Tom, standing staring up at a statue.

"You little bastard. Don't run away from me ever again," Robbie yelled, still scared.

"Don't use language like that here, Robbie," Gill said sternly.

He asked Tom," Why did you go off like that?"

"I wanted to see what was behind here," he said matter-of-factly.

"Next time I won't bother looking for you," Robbie said.

"This place is for dead people," Tom said.

"And ghosts who get you in the night," Robbie said.

"Boys! This is a place of peace," Gill said, "where souls have been laid to rest."

Their mother had told Robbie once about a boy in their street who had been laid to rest. When he'd asked her what that meant, his mother told him that he had gone to sleep and would wake up in heaven. He'd spent the entire night awake, fighting to keep his eyes open.

"How did all these children die?" he asked uneasily.

"Well, some were really ill when they were brought here and didn't get better. Some got the Spanish flu or something like that."

Tom was already wandering off.

Gill took the boys back to the cottage that was to be their home for the next few years. Mrs. Livet scolded them for being late but then softened, telling them that because it was their first day that they wouldn't be put on Sunday's List.

Sunday's List?

Robbie had trouble falling asleep. Long after the rest of the boys were breathing deeply, he looked out of the window. It was so dark here, so quiet. Being right next to the window, he heard the country night sounds for the first time. It sounded like the scratching and snuffling of something large.

Finally, he dropped off. When he was woken up by all the commotion at six, he felt like he'd just slept ten minutes. It must have been longer, though, because at some point, Tom had climbed into his bed and nestled up against him.

One of the other boys said, "Better not let old Livvie catch you sleeping in the same bed. You'll be on Sunday's List."

Sunday's List again.

When he asked one of the boys what it meant, he just told Robbie to make sure not to get on it before he ran away to do his chores.

Robbie and Tom's chores for the morning included making all the beds, emptying the chamber pots and sweeping and washing the floors. They were slower than the other boys who had completed their tasks quickly, and they had only a few minutes to eat and gulp down their tea before going off to school.

CHAPTER THIRTEEN

The boys left for school together, in a group. The older boys walked fast, leaving the younger ones behind, even though they weren't supposed to. When they got to school, Tom was sent to a first year class and Robbie was put in with boys his own age. Robbie looked around for a friendly face. He hated being new.

One big boy sneered at him and it made Robbie nervous, not wanting any trouble.

At lunchtime, they were let out and sent home for a hot meal. Robbie watched for Tom who he spotted quickly enough. As they walked towards the cottage, he felt someone grab his shoulder and he turned quickly.

"Who were you looking at?" the big boy said, standing an arm's length away.

He had his friends with him.

"Nobody."

The surprising blow hit Robbie hard and he let himself fall to the ground. Looking up and holding his cheek, he saw the boys form a circle around him. It was better to stay down because of his chest. Not many boys would go as far as to hit a boy who was down. He'd learnt that in Kirkcaldy.

"Get up."

Robbie stayed put.

"Breathe a word of this to anyone and you're dead," the big boy said.

He waited until they were gone. Tom helped him up.

Robbie knew as he walked home that he wouldn't tell.

Nobody likes bullies, but everybody hates snitches.

He convinced Tom to be quiet about the whole thing. The boys all had a hot lunch together – lentil soup, bread and semolina and hot tinned apples. Robbie ate slowly, his jaw sore. It was good to have a full stomach.

As they tramped back to school, two of the older boys flanked Robbie and Tom and introduced themselves as Mac and Big Jimmy. They told him not to worry: the 'Peddie' boys took care of their own.

CHAPTER FOURTEEN

The 'Peddie' boys stuck close to Robbie and Tom for the first week. Yet, beyond mere formalities, no one bothered to get to know Robbie. At a football match, he was allowed to play, 'to be fair', explained Big Jimmy to the rest of the team. But, after missing a chance to score, the ball wasn't passed to him again. Subbed out, he had to spend the rest of the game on the sidelines. After the match, Big Jimmy told him to wait until he was older and taller to play again, 'no hard feelings, mind.' Robbie realized that what he had thought was camaraderie was really the Peddie boys showing some muscle.

They met their house father, Mr. Livet, at supper on their third day. He only grunted a hello at them and then sat down to eat. He was a carpenter by trade and had been working long hours at the joinery, finishing some new furniture for the overflowing cottages. Shorter than his wife, he was swarthy and was one of those men who could use his razor twice a day and still never be clean-shaven. He had thick dark hair curling on his arms and his neck; in fact, everywhere except on the top of his head.

Mrs. Livet doled out his stew in a bowl bigger than what the boys were using. He smacked his lips and ignored the serviette his wife placed in front of him, wiping his mouth on the back of his hand. Mrs. Livet, looking down at her hands, waited for him to finish. After he got up, the boys were excused from the table.

On Sunday, the church bells chimed loudly, calling the children to prayer. Mr. Livet stood outside the door and, when the boys were assembled, led them over the bridge. Mrs. Livet brought up the rear. They wanted their cottage to look like it had the most well behaved lads.

Like a river flowing into a bay, over fifteen hundred girls and boys streamed obediently and methodically out of the cottages toward the church. Once inside, the girls settled on the right and the boys were on the left.

Robbie shuffled from one foot to the other. They prayed every day at the cottage altar or at the church. *I'm sick of praying. God hasn't done a damn thing for me.* He felt some satisfaction at swearing at God, even though it was only in his mind. He looked around the church, at the attentive faces and then realized Mr. Livet was frowning at him. He smiled faintly at him. Mr. Livet did not smile back.

A hymn was announced and Robbie helped Tom find the page and then they joined in, Robbie underlining the words with his index finger for Tom. Tom tried to keep up but soon stopped. He couldn't read as fast as they were singing.

The sermon was hard to hear with so many children in the church even though Minister Findlay had a carrying voice, and the room became too stuffy. Tom was already starting to lean against Robbie's shoulder, his eyes shut. The boy beside Robbie jabbed him and he sat up straight wondering what he had missed. He whispered to the boy: "What's up?" Andrew, nicknamed, 'The Fox', as his face was clever and pointed, ignored him.

After the service the children were let out into the fresh air and the Peddie boys returned to their cottage, sombre and in a well-disciplined manner. This time Mr. and Mrs. Livet brought up the rear.

They entered the cottage and squeezed into the sitting room, some on the floor, on chairs and some standing. Not a word was said, not a sound made. The boys looked at the floor. Mrs. Livet followed Mr. Livet into the room and handed him a sheet of paper. He put on his glasses.

"Well, lads, some good news," Mr. Livet said. Some of the boys looked up, surprised. "There are only five names on Sunday's List this week and two are new." He took off his glasses. "Little Jimmy, Andrew, Hugh and Robert and Thomas follow me into the kitchen."

Mrs. Livet placed a chair in the middle of the kitchen. "We'll start with the youngest one first. Thomas, come here." Tom went forward. Robbie had a bad feeling. Mrs. Livet passed Mr. Livet a tawse, a leather strap, about two feet in length. The striking end was divided into three strips. It did more damage than the regular one-piece strap. Robbie's face went scarlet.

"Hold out your left hand." Tom looked at his brother for help but Robbie remained motionless. "Two black marks. One for not singing hymns and one for not paying attention in church today."

"But, I can't...."

"Three...one for talking back." Mr. Livet struck Tom lightly and swiftly and then he was allowed to go to Mrs. Livet. She held a wet cloth to his hand while he cried. Robbie unwound a little. It wasn't as bad as what he'd had at school in Kirkcaldy.

"Robert, step forward. Left hand," Mr. Livet said. "Four black marks...two for speaking after lights out, one for talking in church and the other for not paying attention." Robbie was swiftly dealt with as were The Fox, and Mac.

"Jimmy, you are the worst offender. You know better. Shame on you for taking the Lord's name in vain. Twice. Ten black marks each. Both hands out." This time Livet wound up his arm and swung at Little Jimmy with full force. The three 'tails' wrapped themselves around his wrist like tentacles. The boys winced at each blow. There were a few drops of blood on the floor. Mrs. Livet turned away. Tears flowed freely down Little Jimmy's face.

After Sunday's List had been executed, the boys were allowed outside but were not to play. It was Sabbath – a day to rest. So everyone just stood around and spoke in hushed voices, looking sideways at Little Jimmy who sat alone in the corner of the garden, putting his hands palms down on two large flat stones to cool the welts.

CHAPTER FIFTEEN

As November neared its end, the sky turned into the colour of pale steel. The cold stung their cheeks and bare knees. The River Gryffe began to freeze over and the children were warned about the danger of stepping onto it before it was properly frozen.

A special candle was lit at church to mark the first Advent Sunday. The buzz of excitement began to build as preparations began for Christmas and 'Ne'erday', New Year's Day. The choir practised Christmas carols and parts for the Nativity play had already been auditioned for, allocated and were being rehearsed.

In the middle of December, a letter arrived for Robbie and Tom from their father. Robbie asked Mrs. Livet if they could go to the bedroom alone to read it. It was brief.

"Dear boys," Robbie read the letter aloud to Tom, "I wish you could be here. Auntie Doreen has put me up in a comfortable room in Edinburgh. I have become an apprentice tailor. I am working hard but not making very much money. So, you will have to wait a little longer for me to come and get you. Your sister is working in a nice household with good people. Will come and see you soon."

It was simply signed "Dad." Robbie turned the envelope over in his hand. The address was smudged. He crumpled the letter up and then threw it on the ground.

How can he leave us here? I hate him.

Tom said, "I thought Auntie Doreen said Emma was with mum."

"Don't call her Auntie. They're both liars." Tom flinched at Robbie's tone. "Don't keep your hopes up, Tommy. He's not coming back. Not ever."

Tom cried and Robbie didn't want to comfort him. He left. Tom picked up the letter that Robbie had discarded and smoothed out the wrinkles in the paper on his leg. He put it in his box under his bed.

As they went to bed on Christmas Eve, the flurries started, covering everything with a layer of sparkling white. Robbie lay a long time looking out of the window at the drifting snowflakes and thought he would try to pray again. *Please God. If we could just have our mother and father take us home.*

When they woke up in the morning, they got dressed and ready for church. Filing into the great hall, they saw two great pine trees towering over them, filling the church with a delicious, clean fragrance. When they kneeled, Robbie squeezed his eyes shut, promising God he would go to church every day to praise him. He would even become a pastor if God asked it of him. If only He would let them have their parents back.

The choir sang carols to the overflowing church. The congregation probably numbered over two thousand, including some benefactors and former Home Boys and Girls who lived in the area.

When they got back to the cottage, they were allowed to go through the stockings that they had hung the night before. They were packed with sweets, some nuts and an orange. Robbie held his orange to his nose. He'd never had one before. He helped Tom peel his like the other boys were doing. There was a moment of surprise and delight when biting into the first section as the juice squirted and ran down their chins. They giggled. The aroma filled every room of the cottage as the fruit was devoured before anything else. The smell of orange would forever remind him of the orphanage. "The Garden of Eden story," said Tom, "would be so much better if they had used an orange instead of an apple."

The excitement was palpable. They saw the pine trees daily as they were called to the services. In just a few days' time on Ne'erday, they would be covered in presents. The boys discussed how they would place the gifts so that the trees would not topple.

On "Ne'erday", Robbie and Tom awoke to the *"Ham and Egg Song"*. It had started with just one boy in their room and soon the whole place was singing it as they got dressed.

There is a happy land down at Bridge of Weir,
Where we can have ham and an egg once every year.
Oh how we shout and yell,
When we hear that breakfast bell.
Oh how we shout and yell,
Down at Bridge of Weir.

Breakfast was the most delicious meal they'd ever had and they ate as slowly as they could, trying to savour every bite. After clearing up the breakfast dishes, they marched to the church. Upon entering, there was a collective gasp. The trees were bare.

The Pastor rounded up the service with a prayer of thanksgiving for the end of the war and the new year of peace. Looking down on the misery on the sea of little faces, he added, "Just wait until you come back this afternoon."

Tentative smiles appeared and whispers filled the hall. The cottage mothers and fathers shushed their children. The Pastor, although he had been working here for years, had forgotten how fragile the children were. They had been disappointed so often in their short lives.

And so he added, "There is some kind of magic in the air, children, and a little bird has told me that all is well. Enjoy your dinner and come back this afternoon with full stomachs and overflowing hearts."

Dinner was even better than breakfast. Turkey and plum pudding were devoured and apple cider toasts rang out, remembering the founder Mr. Quarrier and his wife, the health of Miss Quarrier and Mrs. Burges and Pastor and Mrs. Findlay. Then the children were summoned by the bell back to the church. Gasps of astonishment echoed throughout the hall. There were gifts everywhere.

After the Doxology, the children all received a present. Some got practical gifts like warm gloves or a new hat. Some got something to play with: a toy, a doll, a game. When Robbie was called, he received a writing set: a pen, an inkwell and some paper and envelopes. He accepted his gift with thanks. Tom got a soft, cuddly bear.

After the tea which completed their feast for the day, Mrs. Livet asked him how he liked his writing set. She said, "We received a letter from your father wondering why you haven't written. I thought you might be too shy to ask for paper. Now you can write to him as often as you like."

He mumbled his thanks. It was not polite to look a gift horse in the mouth.

When he went to bed, he put the writing set carefully in the box under his bed.

If God is good, I won't need to write.

CHAPTER SIXTEEN

The warm sun and gentle rain brought the unmistakably soothing fragrance of spring. Spring was the season of hope, the Pastor said in his Sunday sermon, and of renewal. This would give them the chance to air all the dark and gloomy thoughts that had collected in their minds in the bleak days of winter.

"Everyone has given up one thing for Lent, and if you manage to keep going, God will reward you." The Pastor's clear strong baritone rang through the church. "Let us pray and be truly thankful."

"Amen," came the chorus of hundreds of voices.

On the way home from the service, eleven-year-old Robbie mulled over the pastor's words.

What I've given up is not enough. Jam and sweets. God wants more proof. I have to give up my treasure. It is the only thing I have that is really mine.

The following day at the river, Robbie, biting his lip, threw in his stones, shells and pieces of broken pottery, one by one, saving the bit of milky-opaque glass for the end. He turned it over in his hand, and a vague memory of that summer day with twinkling lights and raucous noises of a fair came into his mind. His father was holding his hand.

He wound up to throw it as far as the others and then changed his mind. Using the toe of his boot, he cracked the thin ice still covering the shallow water and dropped it beside a rock that was jutting out of the river. He watched it sink down until it hit bottom.

That night, as the others said their prayers, he didn't even ask for blessings. God knew what he wanted and he had done exactly what the pastor had told them to. *Thank you, God. I will try to be patient. Amen.*

As the crocuses, then daffodils and tulips blossomed and the grass became a vibrant green, Robbie waited, thanking God nightly, never asking Him for anything else.

On Maundy Thursday, marking the day of the Last Supper, Mrs. Livet gave Robbie a letter. Tom was out of the house with one of the boys, on an errand.

Robbie's heart beat faster. It was from their dad. His prayers had been heard.

"Dear Robbie and Tom," it read, "I have some news for you." Robbie felt dizzy. "I'm sorry that we haven't been to visit you but I am working long hours. The weather here is still a little chilly but I'm sure over your way, it's a little milder."

The weather?

Robbie felt a sinking sensation. "Your mother and I are now divorced." He read on, "I'm getting married to Auntie Doreen. I'm afraid I don't earn enough money for you to come and live with us yet, but as soon as I do, I'll come and get you." It was signed, "Your father."

Robbie stared at the letter. Reread it twice. There was no mistake. Then, he crumpled it as he had the other and threw it on the floor, stamping on it. Hot tears blinded him as he bolted out of the front door. "Damn you, damn you God," he cried as he ran to the river. When he got to the place where he had left the magic stone, he darted into the water. The shock of the cold took his breath away. He dropped to his knees near the rock. Making wide, sweeping motions with his arms, he searched for it. He felt stone after stone but they weren't his. Sobbing, he stood up, his arms numb. Looking heavenwards he said through chattering teeth, "I trusted you. Now I don't care if I catch cold. I don't care if I die. I hope I die."

But Tom would be alone and he had promised not to leave him. It was so cold. Shivering violently, he turned. But as he tried, his shoe came off, stuck in a crack between two rocks. He fell forwards with a big splash, soaking himself from head to toe in the icy water.

CHAPTER SEVENTEEN

The infirmary's windows let in a lot of light. That, combined with the heat of the stove, was giving Mrs. Livet a headache. "He must be warm enough now," she said to Tom with her arms folded in front of her. "It's so hot in here, you could boil an egg." She fanned herself while Tom twisted the glass eyes of his bear.

Mrs. Livet had sat him down on a chair facing the row of beds and then sat down herself, turning toward Tom. They had to wait while the nurse checked Robbie's temperature and his pulse. Tom hadn't talked since Robbie had been brought to their cottage yesterday, soaking wet, lips blue, his face so white, like all the blood had been drained out of him.

"Stop that," Mrs. Livet told Tom, "You're going to break it." She had so much to do at home.

She smoothed her hair and began to tell Tom a story she called, "The Boy Who Wouldn't Eat His Soup". Tom held his bear close to his body.

She gave up and asked him, "Did Robbie say anything to you about why he did it, Tommy?" There might be an inquiry about the incident. She knew the questions that would be asked.

Then they could faintly hear Robbie's voice.

Tom ran across the room, stopping at Robbie's bed. Mrs. Livet strode to keep up with him.

"I'm sorry, Tommy. Sorry that you were scared," Robbie said, smiling at him and holding a hand out to his brother. "I'm all right." He was covered in blankets. Tom wondered why his hand was still so cold in this warm room.

The eight or nine other boys in the room were either lying very still or were sitting up in the beds with the sheets pulled off, talking. Tom counted them on his fingers. So much space for so few people.

Tom finally spoke. "Is he going to be on Sunday's List?"

"No," she said. "I don't think so. He has been punished enough."

Tom looked around the infirmary. It was a nice room, clean and fresh. It didn't smell like sick. Not like the Poor House had. And the nurse was not like Sister Effie, all stiff and sore and grumpy. Mrs. Livet and the nurse were laughing about something.

"Robbie, are you really going to be all right?"

"Yeah. Don't worry. I'll be back in a few days."

"I had a bad dream last night," Tom snivelled, remembering it. "I dreamt that you were gone too. That germ men had got you." Tom had a picture in his mind of men wrapped in white, like mummies. If they touched you, you would get sick and maybe die. He remembered running as fast as he could but not getting any further away.

"The war is over, Tommy," he said. "Germans are just people."

He had nightmares about Germans, too, though. There was a recurring one he had, in which his mother and father were spies being held. If he told on them, he would be let go, but they would be killed.

Lately, Robbie had been having other dreams too. Strange dreams that made him want to continue where they had left off. They were usually something about being a hero, scoring the winning goal, saving somebody's life. Gill was in his dream, too, wearing his white football shorts, his face flushed with pleasure. In these dreams, he was the same age and height as Gill.

One day last week, before the letter, when he had woken up, his pyjamas and the top sheet had been wet and sticky. He had been frightened, knowing it wasn't pee. It had been like clear blood. Embarrassed, he hadn't known what to do or who to ask. Maybe he was sick.

Nothing had hurt though. He'd changed the top sheet to the bottom so nobody would see. At the end of the week, when they had switched sheets and it was on the pile of dirty laundry, nobody had known it was his. He had folded his pyjamas, hoping they would dry before night.

Tom tugged his arm. "Do you want my bear to keep you company?"

"Thanks, Tommy, but I don't need it."

"Tommy," Robbie said, "I have something to tell you."

"What?" Tom looked frightened.

"Mummy and Dad are divorced."

"What does that mean?"

"It means that I was right. Dad's not coming to get us out of here." Robbie's voice rose and he took on a mean look.

"Oh," said Tom, holding onto his bear tighter.

Mrs. Livet had come back and overheard the last comment. "Come on, Tom. Time to go. Say goodbye to your brother."

Robbie left the clinic Easter Saturday, feeling strong and refreshed. The young nurse had made him feel better; always plumping his pillow, bringing him treats. She had such beautiful, kind eyes and when she had asked him questions, she had really listened to his answers. She was the only person who had taken an interest in him since his Auntie Mary.

The way she perched ramrod straight on the edge of his bed, with her short, curly hair tucked neatly under her cap made him stumble over his words. Her full lips and her long, shapely legs stirred a strange sensation in him. His face felt like it was burning.

The next day, she walked him back to Peddie and right away, Mrs. Livet told him to get off to the store to buy some potatoes for dinner. Smiling at him she said, "No more skiving." She offered the nurse a cup of tea and Nurse Beth sat down gratefully.

They heard the front door bang. As Mrs. Livet poured the tea into two cups, she asked if the nurse had been able to find out what he had been doing in the river.

Nurse Beth rubbed her finger around the rim of her cup.

Robbie retraced his steps back to the house to find the store voucher that had fallen out of his pocket. Worried about getting into trouble for losing it, he opened the door quietly. He saw it on the floor. As he picked it up, he overheard his name and froze.

"I think Robbie threw himself in to get attention," Nurse Beth's cool clear voice said. "He's so full of hate. Do you know how he got that horrible scar on his chest?" She paused, "Lovely cup of tea. I was parched."

"He burnt himself because his mother went away," Mrs. Livet said. "I'm not entirely sure what happened."

"It's the same old story," Mrs. Livet continued. "Tom told me his father is getting married again. Probably a younger woman. Use them up, throw them away." She put down her cup and filled it up again. "Do you want another cuppa?"

"No, thanks." Nurse Beth tilted her head back and finished the cup, "Maybe he should speak to the Pastor, poor little mite." Robbie could hear her chair scrape the floor as she stood up. "I think he might be suicidal."

Mrs. Livet drank her tea noisily. "For heaven's sake, all fifteen hundred bairns here have similar sad stories. I don't know how to..." She stopped, listening. There was a sound of the door closing. Through the window, Nurse Beth saw Robbie running from the house. Mrs. Livet got up from the table and joined her.

"Ach, no," said Nurse Beth. "I didn't want him to hear that. He is such a nice boy."

Robbie ran all the way to the store. On a large rock in front of it, he sat for a moment to regain his composure before going in. Nurse Beth was like every grown up. Not to be trusted.

After a few minutes, he lifted his head. He was going to have to be damn careful.

When he came back from the store, he brought the potatoes to Mrs. Livet. "Do you want me to peel them for you?"
She eyed him carefully.

"Yes, Robbie. That would be very nice."

He sat down and calmly peeled the potatoes and then put them into the pot. She asked him to rest until dinner and he got a book and pretended to read.

Mrs. Livet sighed with relief. *He hadn't heard them after all.*

CHAPTER EIGHTEEN

There was to be no immigration to Canada this year, the Pastor told them in church, because there was no transportation available so soon after the war. It was unfortunate because the demand for their help was great.

The Pastor's voice rose with excitement. The good news was that a very large seaside house with all its furnishings, located between Dunoon and Innellan, had been donated. It had a spectacular view of the Firth and it would afford all the children a twelve-day holiday in the summer in shifts of two hundred at a time. The house was called Torr Aluinn.

Robbie sat with narrowed eyes as he heard this.

I suppose we're going to have to thank the Lord for all his blessings again. It's probably a dump.

When the pastor said, "Let us pray," Robbie closed his eyes tightly and tuned out the Pastor, listening instead to the coughing, sneezing, and foot shuffling of those around him. He could hear the crisp pages of the Pastor's Bible being turned and the creaking of the kneelers as the children shifted their weight. Then he strained to hear outside. Birds were chirping. There was a distant motor.

The Pastor's voice inched its way into his thoughts as they sat back onto the hardness of the pews. His enthusiasm about Torr Aluinn was catching. There were flushed faces all around him.

Spring turned into early summer, and flowers, trees and shrubs around the cottages exploded into lush colours. Every year, there was a garden competition and everyone did their bit: pulling weeds, watering and fertilizing. And, although Robbie loved the feeling of the warm earth between his fingers and his toes, Little Jimmy, who was in charge of Peddie's garden, was impossible to work with. It was surprising that the unlikeable tough had been chosen to do the garden. Little Jimmy watched over everyone with crossed arms and a ready cuff.

One day, Mrs. Livet asked for a volunteer from the boys to help the head gardener who had thrown his back out and needed a worker in the kitchen garden. When he heard that whoever helped him would be released from their other duties, Robbie jumped at the chance.

Every day, when he was finished school, he ran off to Mr. Watson, the gardener, who like him, didn't speak much. As the tiny shoots broke through the soil, he could hardly contain his excitement. He loved picking the weeds from the rich topsoil and lifting handfuls of the life-giving, pungent earth to his nose. His arms grew stronger and his face and upper body tanned in the late spring and summer sun.

Yet Robbie's heart was sore. On the bad days he dragged his feet on the way home.

If I disappeared, nobody in the world would notice. Except for Tom.

At the end of May, in arithmetic class, the church bell began ringing with an urgency.

This is not a drill. Which room is Tom in?

His heart racing, he stood up, as did others. Mr. Goodman roared at them. "Keep your places." Robbie detected panic in his voice. On punishment of caning, he told them not to leave the room as he went to find out what was going on.

The smell of fire seeped in through the open windows. It wasn't the school. Tom was safe. He went to the door and looked out. The halls were empty. Seeing the teacher quickly rounding the corner, he ran back to his seat.

"Killearn cottage is on fire!"

"Killearn!" Sandy Douglas cried. He jumped up. It was his cottage.

"Listen!" Mr. Goodman roared. "The first two rows, follow me." He pointed to the rows Robbie and Sandy were in. "The rest of you go home. Don't let me find out you were somewhere else."

"Right now! Move!"

Killearn was cottage thirty-four, opposite Peddie. They dashed down Church Road, crossed Faith Avenue and as they approached the bridge over the brook, the smoke thickened. Mr. Goodman made them gather in front of Peddie and told them to get a bucket or a pot and meet him back at the bridge.

The fire brigade was already busy pumping water onto the roof. "She's as dry as an old woman's teat!" One of the firemen panted, as he wiped his face with a soot covered hand. Tongues of flames licked the roof and the upper windows. Big, black, greasy flakes floated down onto everything.

A line of boys formed to pass water by hand up from the brook. They were soon passing the water hand over fist, splashing it onto window frames, doors, anything that was wood.

The air was thick with searing smoke. The heat was unbearable. Sparks were flying everywhere and the fireman told them to start dumping water on the shed so it wouldn't spread. Mr. Goodman took the buckets closest to the building. "Keep going, boys. They almost have it under control!"

As the cottage fathers arrived and pitched in, the smoke changed from an impenetrable thickness to a foggy vapour that hissed as the flames were extinguished.

The boys sat down in front of Peddie, their throats and eyes sore. Their faces were all smeared with black.

***

"By the grace of God," the Pastor said the following Sunday, "what could have been disaster, is only an inconvenience. Let us praise the Lord that this fire happened during the day when the boys of Killearn cottage were not in their beds fast asleep." His voice rose. "Let us thank the Lord for his blessings."

Robbie rolled his eyes and said, "Amen" with the others. Once again, they were thanking God for help he hadn't sent. *If God wanted to, He could have made it rain.*

"And there is other news to be thankful for. The building next to Torr Aluinn has been purchased for us by the same donor. Now, we will have two permanent adjacent buildings for holidaying." The Pastor was beaming. "Hoop House, along with Torr Aluinn, will afford us a fine stretch of shore."

Robbie would not get excited, he told himself, although there was one thing he longed for: a body of water vaster than the River Gryffe.

CHAPTER NINETEEN

On July 4th, the same day they were told their American 'cousins' were celebrating Independence Day, school closed and the first two hundred boys were shipped by motor car and then steamer to the newly purchased holiday homes. Robbie and Tom were amongst them.

On the steamer that left from Gourock, for the first time since they had been in the care of the Orphan Homes of Scotland, Robbie felt like a weight had been lifted from him. The day was brilliant, the Firth of Clyde was sparkling in the sun and there was the familiar salty tang in the air.

Finally an adventure! Although Robbie hadn't been able to close his eyes all night, he wasn't in the least tired. The motor vibrated like a live beast under his feet and the wind blew through his hair.

After a short bus ride, they saw the buildings rising up from the beach. There was only a small dirt road running between the two buildings. As the children waited to be let into their rooms, some of them were already running in and out of the water, daring it to wet the bottoms of their shorts.

Sandy took off his shirt and threw it into the air but Robbie would not do the same, self-conscious of his puckered chest. He picked up some flat stones and skipped them across the surface of the water. Some of the boys joined him, wanting him to teach them how it was done.

Their twelve-day holiday was chock full of delightful things that

Robbie had never tried before: rowing the newly purchased boat and playing croquet.

Tom, Robbie and Sandy were staying in Hoop House that had three beautiful greenhouses attached to it.

In the afternoon, Robbie and Sandy visited the greenhouses. Robbie explained to the gardener there how he had been helping with the kitchen garden. They were allowed to sink their teeth into grapes and then, tomatoes. They declared them to be the best things they'd ever eaten. That brought a smile to the gardener's face and they were told to visit whenever they wanted to, with one condition. This was their secret. He didn't want two hundred boys coming in willy-nilly. They left with a fistful of grapes.

After the initial swimming lesson and the boys nudging each other because of his scar, Robbie took like a fish to water. In Kirkcaldy, he had just dog-paddled around.

On Saturday, everyone was given some pocket money to spend at the stores in Dunoon. Two hundred boys descended on the sweet shops to spend their farthings on blackcurrant and liquorice humbugs, acid drops and boiled sweets.

And then there was fishing. Both Robbie and Sandy thought nothing was better than sitting on the dock in the sunshine, swinging their legs and holding real fishing lines, waiting for a bite. There was a pond behind Torr Aluinn where they caught frogs and used them as bait, hooking them through their bellies so that they would swim across the top, luring the fish.

At the end of the day, if they caught something, they cleaned it and then cooked it on a stick over a small fire at the far end of the beach.

It was the best time he and most of the other boys had had in their young lives. All too soon, the trip was over and the boys were sent home, as the next group arrived.

Back at the Village, Robbie sauntered over to find his part of the vegetable garden had been well taken care of and had grown well in his absence. He poked at the soil with his toe. He didn't want to be a gardener anymore: he wanted to be a fisherman.

In his bed the first night back, he realized he hadn't wasted a thought on his parents since he'd been away. It was the first time he could remember being content. Holidays were wonderful.

In the heat of August, there was a Peace Procession. It was the fifth anniversary of the declaration of war. It was an evening celebration and so only the older children were allowed to participate. Eight hundred boys and girls were invited to the grounds of Ducal House in nearby Kilmacolm by Lord Maclay who had lost two of his sons in the Great War.

Greeted at the grounds by pipers, the children marched onto the estate to a spot where there was lemonade and sweet buns. After singing songs about Kings and soldiers, ice-cream was served around a great bonfire. Fireworks completed the evening. Robbie tried not to think about his father and Uncle Duncan.

The days were already getting shorter and September rolled around soon enough and school began. Robbie was eager to get back to his books. On the morning of his birthday, September 8th, Mrs. Livet brought him a special breakfast and the boys applauded him.

That day, he decided to write his father a letter. He got out the writing set and sat down at the kitchen table where he could be alone. After spreading the paper flat, he shook the ink very carefully and then broke the seal. He dipped the pen into the ink and stared at the paper.

"Dear Dad," he finally wrote, "It was my birthday today. Mrs. Livet made me a special breakfast. Tom and I are well. Hope you and your wife are well, too. The last Saturday every month is 'Friend's Day'. That's what they call visitor's day here. Also, please send us our mother's and also Emma's addresses. Thank you. Your son, Robert James." He blotted it and blew on it to make sure it was dry. Then he folded it, slid it in an envelope and wrote the address on it.

CHAPTER TWENTY

The end of September was a celebration of what would have been founder William Quarrier's ninetieth birthday if he were still alive, and was also when the prizes were awarded for the most beautiful cottage garden. The Quarrier clan was there. Lord Maclay was also there to judge. They had spent the previous day walking around the gardens with a group of people who, in their fox furs and waistcoats, observed the children down the length of their noses.

They often had benefactors of the village strolling around making sure that their donations had been well-invested. While they were there, the children had to be on their best behaviour, under strict directives from their cottage parents. Punishment usually involved a thrashing of some sort.

Robbie and the rest of the children squirmed like they were under a microscope.

"Look how happy the children are," was what was usually said as they brushed imaginary dust off their expensive clothes, "What a well-organized place."

The winners of the Best Garden prize were the girls at the Sagittarius cottage who had planted seasonal plants so astutely that the cottage had been constantly surrounded by different colours and fragrances since early spring. They were awarded an afternoon of entertainment at the moving pictures in Glasgow. Robbie was glad Little Jimmy's reign of terror was over.

On Hallowe'en they were rewarded with chilly but sunny weather and as darkness fell, Robbie and Tom walked in the procession. Their swinging lanterns glowed like fairy lights, and in spite of himself, Robbie thought it was one of the most breathtaking sights he'd ever seen. He'd felt foolish trying to cut a silhouette of a fish out of black paper. It looked more like a blob than anything. Then, he'd pasted coloured tissue paper so that the candle would shine through it. Once they were all together and the candles were lit, his individual lantern became part of the colourful mass. It really was quite fun.

Robbie, Tom and Sandy walked back from the parade grounds together. Killearn cottage had been restored and the boys were already settled back in. Sending Tom ahead to Peddie, they stood outside for a moment to discuss ways of harassing the arithmetic teacher without him catching on. Then they parted. Robbie, looking at how the bright moon lit up the fields that rolled away from the village, heard a moaning, coming from behind the shack at the side of Peddie. It sounded like someone was in pain. "Hello?" he called out, "Who's there?"

He heard Little Jimmy's voice. "Stay right there!" Robbie heard loud rustling and Jimmy appeared, his jacket open. He ran up to Robbie and grabbed him by the lapels. He was sweating. "Mind your own business and get the hell out of here, you little spy." He let him go and pushed him back. Robbie noticed an edge of his shirt hanging out of his flies.

Robbie stumbled backward, caught himself and then flew into the cottage. Most of the other boys were already there. A few minutes later, one of the newer boys came in, his eyes downcast and cheeks flushed. Little Jimmy followed him in, glaring. Robbie looked away and pretended like nothing had happened. But he could tell whatever was going on, it was nothing good.

CHAPTER TWENTY-ONE

The excitement of Hallowe'en was hardly over before the preparations for Christmas began. Boys and girls were being recruited for carolling. Robbie would have loved to join them but his voice was cracking and breaking, an octave between the highs and lows. Reddening when spoken to, he answered as briefly as he could - not sure what would come out of his mouth.

A large envelope arrived, addressed to both Robbie and Tom. Something different about the address caught Robbie's eye. It was longer than before. The sender was Mr. William Barrington James.

For some reason, his father had added a middle name. Men don't change their names!

He slit the envelope open with a knife while Tom watched. In it were two four by five sepia photographs of his stern-looking father standing behind his smiling bride. Doreen was wearing a long white gown with lace at the wrists and the high neck. Their father had a hand firmly on his wife's shoulder.

Tom had the envelope in his hands and looked at Robbie with dismay. "Why does he have a different name?" Robbie shrugged and looked over the thin piece of accompanying paper that read, "With love from your father and stepmother. See you soon."

"What does it say?"

Robbie snapped, "It says we have a new mother! It says SHITE!"

As Robbie pounded out of the room, Tom read the note himself, and then put it and the pictures in the box under his bed. From outside, Tom could hear yelling, and he climbed up on Robbie's bed to see what was going on. He saw Robbie pick himself off the ground, his fists flying at Little Jimmy, who wound up and flattened him again. Tom could see a red smear under Robbie's nose, and he took off outside, calling for Mrs. Livet who came running, drying her hands on a tea towel.

"Get off each other," she cried, snapping the towel at Robbie and then Little Jimmy, who turned to her, his lip curled. Robbie ploughed into him, hitting the back of his knees so that they buckled and he fell face first onto the frost-bitten ground. Little Jimmy was on his feet in a minute pounding Robbie.

Enlisting the help of a few boys, Mrs. Livet had them separated. "What is going on?" she said breathlessly. The boys always acted up when Mr. Livet was not around. "You're both going on Sunday's List!"

"He's a nutter. He just rushed at me!"

"You're disgusting! Tell her what you do!" Robbie looked a mess: his nose was bloody, there was dirt and grass stains on his knees and his back.

"What's all this?" she asked.

"Shut up or you'll get your teeth kicked in." Jimmy snarled at Robbie and pushed him.

Robbie pushed him back and they were immediately entangled on the ground again, Little Jimmy on top. Tom saw his chance and with a howl, dove on his back, using his fingers to gouge at Jimmy's eyes. Mrs. Livet got the boys to separate them again.

"That's enough!" She took Robbie and Tom each by the arm and marched them back into the house. Turning back to Little Jimmy, who was rubbing his eyes, "We'll sort this out when Mr. Livet gets home."

Robbie burned with anger even though he didn't even like Frederick, who was all pudgy and soft and wouldn't stand up for himself - Frederick with his feebleness and girl-like blushing. But again, something was wrong, wrong, wrong and he was sure it was because Little Jimmy was a bully.

At supper, everyone seemed to have moved their chair away from

Little Jimmy's as far as they could in wordless support of Robbie. Spoons scraped against bowls, the clock ticked, Mr. Livet sighed, wanting to enjoy the end of his day but knowing he couldn't. When they were all finished and the dishes were carried away, Mr. Livet called Robbie and Jimmy into the kitchen and shut the door.

"Well?" Mr. Livet said wearily.

Neither boy spoke. Jimmy glared at Robbie.

Mr. Livet stood in front of them. Little Jimmy had his arms crossed.

"Put your arms down!"

That's it. Jimmy has to go. We can't do anything more for him here. The real world will sort him out.

Robbie met Mr. Livet's gaze steadily. He liked this boy, but like them all, he needed to be kept in line. Mr. Livet had to keep a straight face. He'd been like that at his age.

"Robbie," he said, "Go into the quiet room for a wee while until you've cooled off." The quiet room was really the pantry, a small room that was off the kitchen where a chair was placed to isolate boys who were unruly. There were no windows in it, the darkness keeping the vegetables longer. Mr. Livet shut the door and Robbie sat on the chair. There was a tang to the air in there, like rotting potatoes. He could see his breath.

"Jimmy," Mr. Livet turned to Little Jimmy, "Pack up your belongings. I'm going to send you to the City Home. You're far too old to tarry here."

The sneer left Jimmy's face. His shoulders hunched. He had lived in the Homes since he was an infant. In a moment, he'd lost his adolescent swagger and become a boy again. His eyes glistened. Mr. Livet scratched the growth on his chin, almost relenting.

"Mr. Livet," Jimmy began and stopped.

"There's nothing else to say," Mr. Livet got up and lit a cigarette and as an afterthought, offered one to Jimmy and they went out of the room together, leaving Robbie in the pantry alone. It was dark and damp.

CHAPTER TWENTY-TWO

As Christmas approached, the children were visited by two Canadian immigration agents. They visited each of the boys' cottages and showed them photographs of the beautifully vast 'New Country' and told them stories of money growing on trees.

The response was overwhelming, as 1920 was the first year in six that boys could be sent to Canada. And so the meeting was held in Mount Zion instead of the Central Building. The orphanage was going to send as many boys as they could, more than ever before. The water routes were clear of danger and new ships were replacing the ones damaged or destroyed.

"We will have no problem placing any boys with a good, solid Ontario family. If you work hard and do as you're told," said the clean-shaven Canadian agent, "the sky's the limit." The man looked at them with his steady grey eyes. He was in his late twenties, muscular and looked like a million.

Canada. Robbie was sorely tempted. This would be a real adventure. A ship, a train and then independence. No more mindless duties, cleaning up after others, taking care of little ones. During the winter, with his garden duties suspended, he was back to chores in the cottage. And, although he'd graduated from the toilets to cleaning the baths, he still resented scrubbing those black rings every night after four or five boys had washed in them. He went on dreaming: he'd have a room by himself, things he could call his own, delicious big slabs of meat. *I can hardly wait.* He turned his shining eyes to Tom. Tom looked up at him.

Robbie's heart sank. Looking at the boys surrounding him, he already knew that Tom couldn't go. There were too many boys older than him, boys who had been waiting for the Great War to be over.

At the end of the information session, the boys who were interested were interviewed. Robbie wanted to know if he would be able to stay together with his brother.

"The farmers are interested in boys between the ages of twelve and fifteen."

"Tom's a hard worker for his age," Robbie said, meeting the agent's eyes.

"You're both too young. They want boys who can carry their own weight," the agent said. "The orphanage has told us they can afford to send about sixty boys this year and we have more than enough."

Robbie looked at Tom. "Will you be back next year?" he asked the agent.

"Yes," said the man, his strange accent sounded like he was stretching his words. "Don't worry. We'll be back every year."

He solemnly offered Robbie his hand and Robbie noticed his clean and clipped fingernails. A sure sign of prosperity.

For the next few months, the selected boys were fussed over by everyone.

Their trunks were made at the joinery and packed with things that they would need: two Sunday suits, two work overalls, work boots, a sewing kit, a bible and a copy of their own *Pilgrim's Progress*. Ties, socks, underwear and collars were added.

Canada was spoken about at the supper table every day as two of the Peddie boys were going. Robbie was sick with jealousy. He wanted to cover his ears with his rough hands.

***

In March, just in time to help with the spring farming, the boys who'd been picked, marched down the children-lined Faith Avenue to the

169

tune of a couple of thousand voices singing: "Don't forget the Orphan Homes of Scotland, don't forget your dear friends here." In his heart, Robbie marched with them. At the gate, they were picked up in a procession of motor cars, lent by nearby well-off Kilmacolm neighbours to take them to the railroad station.

Almost every day, they were told about the journey. The train to Liverpool, boarding the S.S. Scandinavian, picking up mail in Ireland. Robbie imagined the tossing and turning of the open sea and how everyone would think what a natural-born sailor he was. He pictured whales and icebergs and the place where the Titanic had gone down.

When the boys' safe arrival was heralded by the ringing of the Mount Zion bell on April tenth, and a cheer erupted from all the children around the Village, he stuck his hands deep in his pockets, hoping that one day soon it would be for him.

CHAPTER TWENTY-THREE

With the new school year about to start and summer almost over, Robbie and Tom were among the last party of boys going to Torr Aluinn. On their first day there, after they were settled, Mrs. Livet organized a treasure hunt for her boys, telling them whoever brought back the most interesting object would win a prize. It was a dull, cool day and so nobody was in a rush to run into the water.

Stones were too obvious, although Robbie stuck a few odd-shaped ones in his pockets, just in case he didn't find anything else. A shell, a bottle cap, a feather. No, no, no. A worm, maybe something alive? He could just see Livvie's face if he dropped a worm into her apron. He laughed and Tom looked up from where he was under a tree, poking at something with a stick.

Something silver and blue caught his eye in the water and he took off his shoes to wade in and get a closer look. It was a misshapen blue cigarette pack, with barely discernable foreign writing on it. That'd do. It was unusual.

Mrs. Livet called them to come in and Tom had wrapped something in his shirt and was smiling a secret smile.

The boys presented the usual things, just as Robbie had thought. Sand-scoured glass, like his stupid magic stone had been, shells letting off a strong fishy smell, seagull feathers. When Robbie showed his treasure, Mrs. Livet looked at it and said it was an empty pack of French cigarettes,

"Gallwas," she thought you called them. She was surprised to see them here. Robbie thought he'd won.

Tom went last, waiting for everyone to pay attention. He gingerly unwrapped what he had found.

"Ooooh," Mrs. Livet cried, "Get that away from me."

The boys clamoured to see what he'd found. In the pushing that ensued, he dropped the spotted tan-coloured egg that he'd found and it broke completely, spilling the fragile, embryonic bird out onto the sand. Beak and head too large for its body, eyes eaten by an uncaring foe, it looked like a miniature relic of a prehistoric era.

Mrs. Livet went into the house, her appetite spoiled, she said, by what she had seen. No prizes, thanks to Tom. Robbie threw his pack down. The boys looked at the bird for a moment and then followed her in, hungry from the fresh air, Robbie with them. Shrugging, Tom picked up a large rock and placed it on top to bury it. The brittle bones cracked and shattered and he ran inside, shivering at the sounds of mortality.

After supper in the evening, the older boys were busy designing a sandcastle that they were to build in the second week for a contest that the *Daily Mail* was sponsoring.

Robbie opted out of the group after they had voted Little Jimmy's old pal Johnny as the leader. They didn't like each other.

Tom wanted to help build the castle and so, Robbie was alone. He wandered into the greenhouse but there was a new gardener who refused to let any of the boys in.

So Robbie strayed off, pretending he was enjoying the freedom of Canada, not caring if the weather were inclement or not. If he got cold, he would run around and flap his arms against his body.

He found the ruins of a little stone cottage with partial walls. He went back to the house and found a sheet and made a tent, holding it in place by using rusty nails. He fished and ate his catch of the day, cooked over a small fire, augmented with bread and butter taken from the breakfast table. He spent every day there, only returning in time for supper.

One particularly blustery day when he huddled in his makeshift shelter, the waves slapping against the beach and the wind whistling and roaring like a live thing, he vowed to stay there no matter what the coming storm turned into.

I am a survivor.

He had plenty of dry driftwood and he put more wood on the fire. It began to rain: large pellets hit the sheet and when it began to well up, he used a stick to push it up from underneath, causing a torrent of water to spill over. Some of it poured onto the fire, causing it to hiss and sputter.

He shivered and hugged himself closer. He remembered his mum and dad trying to build up the fire in Lochoal during a severe rainfall. The chimney's poor construction allowed the rain to run down inside it onto the coal fire. It had gone out, too.

Mummy. Daddy. What did we do to make you leave us?

Tears welled up and, for the first time in ages, he let himself go.

After a while, he was thoroughly chilled. It was time to stop his stupid, childish game. As he got up, a rush of cold water tipped on top of him.

The boys were finishing their supper, and Mrs. Livet jumped up and grabbed his arm. "Where have you been?"

"Quick now, go and get those wet things off and then get a cup of hot tea into you." Her tone softened.

He nodded and went up the stairs to his room. He towelled himself off and put on his nightshirt. He was suddenly very tired. He lay down on his bed and pulled the covers up and closed his eyes and rolled himself up into a ball. In a few minutes, he was dead to the world.

Mrs. Livet marched up the stairs and into his bedroom. There was still enough daylight to see that he was fast asleep, and she picked up the pile of wet clothes on the floor. She checked to make sure he was covered properly and then heard a sound behind her. It was Tom. "Let's let him sleep."

CHAPTER TWENTY-FOUR

In September, like Robbie, there were five other boys who had birthdays. Johnny, who at sixteen was the oldest boy still in their cottage, nudged him on the way to school. Tom was behind him, walking with the boys his age. "I guess a lot of parents keep each other warm in January."

"What do you mean?" Robbie asked because he knew he was expected to.

"It takes nine months."

"What takes nine months?"

"You don't know?" Johnny laughed.

"Know what?"

"Know what? Know what?" he repeated. "You stupid ass. It took nine months for you to slither out of your mother's body." By the look on Robbie's face, Johnny realized that Robbie had little idea about the birds and the bees. He laughed louder.

"A man sticks his willy up between a woman's legs into her hole and nine months later a baby comes out." He snapped his fingers. "Just like that."

"So if you don't want a baby, you don't do it?" Robbie asked.

"Yeah. Something like that."

"So why did our fathers do it if they didn't want us?"

"Because it feels good." Johnny didn't think this conversation was funny anymore.

"Does it feel that good?"

"You really are stupid." He looked around to see if anyone was listening. "You don't get a baby every time you do it." Johnny wiped his mouth. "Don't you ever do it to yourself? You know, use your hand?"

"How?"

"Like this," he said and made a jerking motion with his fist in front of his crotch. He shrugged, "Forget it. Get lost."

Tom caught up to him and gave him a little push and Robbie, thankful for the about face in mood, pushed him back.

CHAPTER TWENTY-FIVE

Finally, their names were on the list for Canada and Robbie felt like he had been waiting his whole life just for this. It had been six years since they had set foot in the orphanage. He had finished his full Scottish education and had begun an apprenticeship at the joinery with Mr. Livet.

Tom was only eleven, but the Immigration Officers had told them, that starting next year, the minimum age would be fourteen. If they waited, it would be three more years until he was old enough. If they waited, it was highly likely that Robbie would be sent away from the Homes to fend for himself.

Robbie was fond of running his hands along the finished polished wood; he loved the fragrance of the pine they used. To his great pride, his first job there was to cut and sand the boards for the new furniture. They were making it to replace that which had been lost in the recent fire at the Colony of Mercy for Epileptics, part of the compound. When the new beds and dressers were delivered, the look of joy on those fragile girls' faces was worth every moment of hard work.

His last job at the joinery was to finish the immigrant's trunks including his own and Tom's, spending many a long hour making sure that they were shipshape. The boards had to be levelled, sanded, polished, strengthened and the hinges had to be tightened. They were assembled using tiny nails called brads. Then they were stained and varnished. Some of them he was able to line with donated fabric. This was for the pretty girls whom he'd seen on their way to do the laundry and for the first time, were travelling with the boys in the spring, instead of the fall.

As Robbie did his work, he reminisced about his life at the orphanage. They'd been lucky to have been taken in here. There had always been food on the table and they had clean clothes. And there were always those days of delight that had popped up either unexpectedly or with weeks of anticipation.

There had been biweekly magic lantern slide shows that were presented by the missionaries, with exotic animals, savages in loincloths and lush jungles. There had been that riveting first moving picture of the Prince of Wales' holiday in Canada. It had seemed like he really was in the room.

And there was the time they were shown Mary Pickford in, *"Pollyanna"*, which was about how an orphan won over her spinster aunt's heart, who despite a paralyzing accident, always managed to make others happy. Mary Pickford was from Canada, all blond shining curls.

It prompted Tom to ask him to write letters to their mother whose address had been sent to them by Auntie Mary, and their father. "If Pollyanna could overcome all her hardships and be nice to everyone, why can't we?"

Together, they wrote, but there was no response. Tom's resolve didn't last long and they rarely mentioned their parents to each other again.

There had been the visits by the rich and famous, like the old Prime Minister Lloyd George with lots of flag-waving, Janet Maclay's wedding with beautifully sleek motor cars bringing the perfumed and fur-wrapped rich into their church. There had been the holidays at Torr Alluin, where for two weeks every year, they swam and soaked up the sunshine and ate the freshest and best food Robbie had ever had.

Yet, it was time to go. He was ready to start his life out on his own where maybe he could meet a girl.

Two days before they were to leave, a service for the immigrants was held at the church. There was music, and of course their usual hymns, and then a speech from Freddie MacGregor, nicknamed 'Squint' because of the way his eyes creased when he was deep in thought. He talked about how the Orphan Homes of Scotland had saved their souls and now that they were full of the Lord's grace. They were being sent to a rugged, new land where their Faith would be surely be put to the test. "Together with God," Squint said in closing, "we will be strong."

It annoyed Robbie that the service was so melancholy. They should be rejoicing. After all, they were embarking on the greatest trip of their lives.

The day before they were to leave, there was a call from the store that they had a visitor.

They found their mother standing inside holding the hand of a little boy. She was heavier than before and looked older and worn. She looked around the room nervously and her eyes rested upon them for just a moment before she continued looking. She didn't recognize them.

Robbie steered Tom toward her and as they approached, her face lit up. "Robbie, Tom." She held out her arms.

Both boys didn't budge.

"Hello," Robbie said, voice distant and cold.

She moved close to them. "This is your little brother, Ian."

Robbie and Tom looked from their mother to the boy.

"I tried so hard to get you back. I really did. I had a job and lived with Mary's sister-in-law to save every penny. Then I met Ian's father. He said he wanted to get married and I thought we would have a home for you. But it didn't work out." She glanced down at the little boy.

Anger bubbled up inside Robbie. "Why are you here?"

Tom looked from his mother to Robbie. "Did you come to take us with you?"

Robbie glared at Tom. *I'm not going with her.*

Helen looked down. "No, I have barely enough to take care of Ian and myself."

"Well, lucky for you that we're leaving for Canada tomorrow," Robbie said.

"I just wanted to say goodbye and hope you forgive me."

"Goodbye." Robbie strode off and Tom followed, glancing back at her.

"Wait," Tom called to him. He ran back. "One thing I want to know. Why isn't he in an orphanage?" He pointed to the boy who was starting to snivel.

"I know it doesn't look fair to you, Tom. But his father gives me money. Yours didn't."

"At least he wrote to us."

Robbie left the three of them and went to his favourite spot at the River Gryffe for one last time. He threw stones. He was not going to be upset and he had no desire to hear any more excuses. Livvie had been more of a mother to them than his ever was. And that was saying a lot as she had thirty of them to take care of.

***

Finally, on the third day, they got up in the morning, had breakfast and stripped their beds for the last time. Livvie had tears in her eyes when she clutched them briefly to her chest as they left number thirty-seven. Mr. Livet shook their hands and wished them both well. "Just do as you are told and you'll fare fine."

The little immigrants assembled in front of the Central building and then, as every year, were sent off down the children-lined Peace Avenue where hundreds of clear voices rang out with the familiar *"Don't Forget the Orphan Homes of Scotland"* and *"What a Friend You Have in Jesus"*.

It was thrilling to pass through the boys and girls, but he looked straight ahead. He had a lump in his throat and he could barely swallow. All the emigrants were trying to hold their heads high.

There were sixty-four in all: forty-seven boys and seventeen girls.

The older boys looked smart in their new double breasted navy blue coats and caps. The younger ones looked a little lost in their size-too-big clothes. Tom was in breeches and woollen stockings, Robbie and the older boys were in cheap suits. The girls were wearing unflattering long, light grey coats and had hats of all different shapes and sizes perched on their heads.

As they passed the gates of the orphanage, Robbie turned one last time to look back at the pretty, orderly village with the bushes, trees and flowers in full spring blossom. The big bell of Mount Zion was ringing. Tom just stared ahead. He hadn't spoken more than two words since their mother's visit.

After the hubbub of the cheering crowds, stillness descended on the group as they began their two-mile trek to the Bridge of Weir railroad station. The girls were quietly snivelling: the boys were red-faced. To break the gloominess, the superintendent started up with a song to the tune of: *"It's a Long Way to Tipperary"*.

> It's a long way over the ocean,
> It's a long way to go.
> It's a long way over the ocean,
> From the sweetest place I know.
> Good-bye Homes of Scotland,
> Farewell to all who live there.
> It's a long, long way over the ocean,
> But my new life starts there.

There was hardly time to settle on the train when they had to get off again. At Yorkhill Wharf in Glasgow, there was a huge crowd seeing off the fifteen hundred passengers that had already started boarding the one-year-old *S.S. Athenia*. Streamers and confetti were being thrown, and pipers were playing in the midst of the chaos of farewells. Friends, relatives, neighbours kissed and hugged and waved and shouted until all and sundry were on board.

What a beautiful ship. Robbie was in awe of the sleek black hull. The red and white lines going from bow to stern brightened it just enough. Looking up, he saw a single black and white funnel. A large Union Jack flew from one of the two masts.

Going below, Robbie and Tom found their assigned cabin, a room they were to share with four other boys including Squint, Jimmy Robertson, Willy MacLeod and Michael 'Irish' Sullivan in the third class compartment of the ship. It was cramped, but they were used to sleeping in a small space. Third class made up the biggest part of the ship, it having been built specifically for the booming immigrant industry. Their bunks were made up with fresh linen and the nearby toilets and hot showers were spotless. The rooms smelled ever so slightly of fresh paint and varnish. The only thing that Robbie didn't like was the lack of a window.

"Porthole," Tom corrected him in a flat tone. "Don't you know anything?"

After a cursory look, Tom left with Irish and Willy. Robbie was surprised that Tom went with them, as he'd told Robbie before he'd found them to be big stupid louts. He hoped they wouldn't be getting up to no good.

Robbie went to the deck and leant on the rails, heart pounding as the hum of the engines revved up, and the steam was released with a deep, bellowing whoosh. He overheard two sailors speaking, one in stilted English.

"I wish they'd gave her another name. Bad omen."

"What do you mean?" the second sailor said slowly.

"First *Athenia* downed near Ireland." The first sailor pointed to the west.

"Torpedoes?"

"Ya. It gives me a bad feeling."

"Why are you here, then?" the second sailor continued.

"Too many mouths at home," the first sailor said. "Almost every time I go home, my old lady is with baby."

"We have no children," the second sailor said sadly. "Think the wife might be happier when I'm away if she had some."

You don't want any children. They are just trouble. Robbie spit over the side.

The sailors looked in his direction. Then one picked a thick rope and tied a complicated knot. "Better get back to work."

PART THREE

April, 1924

CHAPTER ONE

As they steamed down the calm Firth of Clyde, some of the boys, limited to the crowded third class deck, watched the receding coastline with mixed feelings, and some, like Tom, turned their backs on it. The girls were under the watchful eye of the Canadian superintendent's wife, Mrs. Grimsby, some of them busy cross-stitching. One girl, a real beauty, got up and went to the rail. Robbie had noticed her a few times at the Homes. Today, her eyes sparkled and her colour was high from the fresh, crisp air. Her long and shiny brown hair blew about her.

Robbie wanted badly to talk to her. He made a move forward, but stopped, aware of Mrs. Grimsby's presence. *What am I thinking?* Even if he could slip by the super's wife, he didn't know what to say to a girl. He blushed and went to the other side of the ship as Scotland slipped away.

Their last stop on the Clyde and in Scotland was the town of Greenock, the point where the Firth grew wider and eventually became part of the sea. Some new passengers were taken on, the ship blasted its horn and they were finally really on their way.

Robbie looked for and found Tom who was standing at the stern with a few other boys. "Say goodbye, Tommy." His voice wavered. "Say goodbye."

"Goodbye?" Tom smirked to his friends. "Goodbye to who?" And then suddenly, "Did you see anybody?"

"No, no," Robbie said, wiping his eyes on his sleeve. "I just feel a wee bit sad leaving. Don't you?"

Tom had the glint of a stranger in his eyes. He said loudly. "You're a fucking liar."

"Tommy, don't talk like that," Robbie said.

The other boys looked from one brother to another and moved off. Robbie was tough if he had to be.

Tom said, "It was your idea to go to Canada, not mine."

"What are you on about?" Robbie said, trying to keep the tone down. People were looking. "You said you wanted to. Nobody forced you."

Tom started shouting at him. "It's all your fault."

Robbie tried to be conciliatory. "Tommy, I just wanted us to stay together. We're all we've got."

Tom's voice lowered but he hissed as he spoke. "If you hadn't been so stupid and burned yourself, we would still be with mum.'

"For God's sake, you don't know what you're talking about. You were too small to remember," Robbie said, thinking his brother, the only one of his family that he had left in the world, was turning into someone he didn't like. "We would have ended up in the Poor House anyway." Robbie grabbed his brother's chin roughly and tilted it up so that he would look into his eyes. "They were both happy to be rid of us."

As soon as the words left his mouth, Robbie regretted them. Tom went pale, twisted out of his grip and ran off.

Robbie stared after him but didn't follow. *There was no use.* He looked around for someone to bum a fag off.

***

They left the shelter of the Firth and entered the sea. The icy cold hit him like a wall, but it was the sharp salt air that Robbie loved that made him stay on deck until supper. Tom hadn't resurfaced and he wasn't going to chase him. Alice, for he had found out her name, had long since been herded in. Supper was bland but plentiful. The best thing was the fresh bread that was still warm.

The next day, there was a storm warning and rough waves began to rock the ship. Small hard pellets of frozen rain fell, real stingers.

The uneven rise and fall of the ship made the day miserable. Along with the rest, Robbie hadn't got his sea legs yet but, unlike the others, the queasiness he felt in his stomach was not full blown nausea. It helped to stare at the horizon like one of the sailors told him to do. The others were hanging over the side, 'feeding the fish' or had gone to their cabins, like Tom.

No one ate much. Tom stayed on his bunk, face to the wall.

At night, confined to the cabin, with the repulsive smell of wet wool and vomit, Robbie felt sick again. He had to get out of the stifling room before it got to him. He opened the door stealthily and it clicked shut behind him. He went to the washroom and splashed some cold water on his face.

Up the stairs on the deck, he gulped fresh air. He leant on the rail, feeling weak. He shivered. He was not going back in that room unless someone dragged him. A thin-faced engineer, his overalls stained and worn, on deck smoking, spotted him.

"What are you doing here? Had enough of your fancy accommodations?" He laughed, which brought on a fit of hacking until he spit over the side.

"Can you spare me one?"

"Aye, but see to it that you get back to your cabin after."

"I'd rather go to hell than back there."

"What's that talk? Aren't ya one of the *bible orphans*?" He winked as he left.

Bible orphans!?

He felt wretched. His jacket was too thin; he was exhausted from the nausea and the excitement of the last few days. As for Tom, he could wring his little neck. The only good thing was the cigarette.

He inhaled deeply and glanced up. The storm had cleared and only a few clouds dusted the midnight sky. The beauty was breathtaking, stars sprinkling the heavens with their extraordinary cheerfulness. The moon was large and bright.

Damn, it is cold. He took a drag. *So much light but so cold.*

He smoked the cigarette undisturbed right down to the end, burning his fingers before flicking it over the side. Hearing steps, he hoped to stay unnoticed, although, on the other hand, he wouldn't mind scrounging another smoke.

"All right, young man?" a voice asked.

"Mmmm," Robbie answered, hoping not to be sent back to the stinking cabin.

"Bad down there?" said the man, nodding at the stairs leading to the third class cabins. His skin was burnt to a rough leather, and he was a tough-looking English sailor, straight from the docks of Liverpool or some other raucous port. Yet when he spoke he sounded middle-class.

Robbie nodded and the sailor offered him a cigarette.

"It's beautiful, isn't it?" he said, combing his grey hair back off his forehead with his fingers. "Makes you feel like you are part of something infinite. That's why I love it out here. You don't get the same sensation when you're landlocked."

"Oh…really?" Robbie hoped that the sailor wasn't going to drone on. *Didn't they work?*

"Spend as much time on deck as you can and observe. It's a whole different world. In a few days, you'll probably see porpoises or whales in the path of the ship." He indicated the direction with his thumb.

***

In the morning, the sick buckets were emptied. The dining room filled with wan people, looking for something to fill their drained stomachs. Some were happy just to drink strong tea, others tried toast or a strange crunchy tasteless woven cereal, called shredded wheat. Robbie looked for someone to sit with. Tom was with his hulks. The only person sitting alone was Squint.

He nodded to him and poured warm milk on the cereal. He forced himself to finish it.

Alice resurfaced with the rest of the girls, to take fresh air. This time, Robbie observed her closely. She didn't look as sick as the others. Her head was held high on a long, slender neck. Her dark hair was tied back, and although thin, she looked strong. His body was fully aware of her presence.

Right before they passed the coordinates where the unsinkable

Titanic lay resting deep in the ocean, they saw some icebergs off in the distance, as if on cue. They loomed coldly, looking almost as big as the ship itself. The captain sounded the ship's bell thrice: once for the passengers, once for the crew and once for the *Titanic*. An uncomfortable minute of silence followed.

***

On their sixth day at sea, Robbie was back at his customary place at the bow when he saw something brown and solid extending along the horizon. It stretched as far north and as far south as he could make out. It was land: it was finally Canada.

Suddenly, his knees buckled. He let himself slide down the wall until he sat on the deck, legs crossed underneath him. He cradled his head in his hands and found himself near tears.

I never should have left.

He felt like he was falling, like he had in the hospital after his burn, like in the Poor House when he gave up on his mother coming back, like when his father and that woman had left them at the Homes. Like a dog with its belly exposed.

Out of the blue, he thought of his sister, imagining her as he had last seen her. Her cheery speech, her easy smile. He hoped that she had found someone she could trust. When he had enough money, he would find her and send for her.

Not highly likely.

"Land!" he heard an excited voice cry, and he got up to get out of the way of the rush of people hurrying toward the bow to observe the very thin brown line that he'd spotted a few minutes ago.

Everyone stared at it expectantly, but, after a while, as it didn't seem to be getting any closer, the biting cold wind at the bow drove most people back inside.

A little later another excitement rippled through the ship. "Whales!" someone shouted and there was a rush to the stern. Robbie stayed put. One came up alongside the ship, an enormous, grey mass. It seemed to be moving at the same speed as the ship. A huge tail broke the water and slapped the surface like it was saluting.

In a matter of hours, the atmosphere on the steamship had become all stirred up. There were a lot more people on deck than had been all week, between the whale sightings and the end of the journey approaching.

Robbie began to circle the boat, with his collar turned up, to walk off the anxiety that ensnared him. He looked for Tom but still found no trace of him. He was always looking for Tom; his brother never looked for him. He was probably below deck with his new pals. Robbie went into the dining room and sat with Squint again, eating some powdered, scrambled eggs on toast.

***

In the early morning, before anyone else stirred, Robbie was up and out on deck, scouting the land. Overnight it had taken on definite shape and a rich earthy colour. He even could make out trees. In fact, it looked like the whole coast was a forest, standing up straight and dense, like bristles on a brush.

It was bitingly cold on deck. He pulled his arms in through his sleeves and stuck his hands under his armpits for warmth. He hugged his body. *It was supposed to get warmer nearer the shore, not colder.*

The only other person on the deck, the English sailor, came towards him with binoculars. "Good morning. Would you like to have a gander with these? Bring them back when you're finished." He passed them to Robbie.

Robbie trained the binoculars on the shore, but all he could make out were trees and rocks and rocks and trees. No sign of Indians or tepees or anything else. People were starting to come on deck, and Robbie realized he'd skipped breakfast. At one point Tom sauntered over to see what he was up to.

"Want to try?" Robbie said to him.

Tom just shook his head and went off again.

Robbie had started to look at other things: the clouds, the funnel, and the passengers. When he focused in on them, he felt like he could reach out and touch them. Then he saw Alice standing at the rail. He couldn't take his eyes off her. Her skin was clear and fresh and slightly pink from the cold.

Her hair was tousled. His eyes followed the lines of her neck and her body but there wasn't much to see: she was wearing a thick coat. She started to look in his direction and Robbie quickly trained the binoculars onto the land again. Trees and rocks and rocks and trees.

All of a sudden, there was a change in the hum of the ship. He glanced at the black water and it looked as if they were slowing down. Then back at the shore, he noticed the first buildings. The steamer blasted its horn.

"We're getting close," a female voice said in his ear. It was Alice. "Can I have a look through those?"

"Sure," was all Robbie could manage.

She looked through the binoculars for a moment, focusing expertly. Then she handed them back to him. "Thank you," she said and was gone.

CHAPTER TWO

As immigration to Canada was starting to escalate to pre-war standards, and the facilities at Pier 2 had only been patched together after the Halifax Explosion of 1917, authorities decided to open Pier 21, even though it was not officially slated to be ready for another four years. It only made sense that the collection of brand-spanking-new structures be used, instead of the damaged facilities at the old pier. The new pier housed Immigration and Customs, the Red Cross, a canteen and dining room, a detention centre, dormitories, a nursery and a clinic.

The first two hundred and fifty passengers from the S. S. Athenia, including Robbie's group, were allowed to disembark. The place was abuzz with excitement: children running around, mothers calling for them, destinations being discussed amongst the ongoing sounds of construction. Red Cross workers crisscrossed the area looking for the lost or the sick. Despite the confusion, the wooden floors and benches were fragrant and polished and everything was clean. To Robbie, it really felt like he had arrived in the New World.

They were led into the medical examiners' rooms first. As the doctor brusquely felt and looked at Tom's body, tapping places with two fingers and listening with his stethoscope, he also spoke to the accompanying immigration official in his slow, broad Canadian accent. "The Orphan Homes of Scotland children are always easy to process. They're better quality than the Home Children we usually see."

It sounds like we are livestock. Robbie stood behind Tom, shoulders hunched forward and his left arm crossed protectively over his chest, hand on his right shoulder. He hated taking off his shirt.

When the doctor saw Robbie's chest, he sucked his breath in through his teeth. "I've seen some scars in my time, but that's a nasty looking thing. What happened?"

While he raised his arms out in front of him and to the sides, Robbie told him about the accident. The doctor listened carefully. "It was an accident, wasn't it?" He searched Robbie's eyes.

"Yes, it was my own fault."

"Accidents aren't anyone's fault," the doctor said. "Are you in any pain?"

"No."

"Well, you're lucky. That's quite an area to have a burn," the doctor said running his fingers over the scar. "But I'm satisfied that you're in good health, although you're a little on the thin side. Get dressed." The doctor gestured to Squint who was standing behind him, "Next." He stamped and signed Robbie's documents.

As soon as the children were processed, they proceeded on their way down the ramp that connected Pier 21 to the railroad station, to the train that was already waiting. Just before boarding, Mrs. Grimsby spoke to the conductress who was to accompany them on their next leg of the journey. Alice, Robbie saw, had her hair tied up with a bright blue ribbon. She was standing alone, as usual, a little behind the other girls who were chattering in groups of twos and threes. Mrs. Grimsby was nowhere to be seen. Before he could change his mind, he went over to speak to Alice. As she grasped his hand, he could see that her nails had been bitten to the quick.

"We haven't met. My name is Alice." She looked at him with an intensity that could strip right to the bone.

"Robbie. Nice to meet you."

"Are you going to Brockville, too?" he said and immediately felt foolish.

She didn't smile but he wished she had. To break the ice. "Yes," she said.

"Do you know where you're going after that?"

"Of course, I know. To my auntie's." Then her tone softened, "Do you know where you are going?"

"No. I guess I go where they send me," Robbie swallowed. "I hope it's near my brother Tom."

"You have a brother on board? I haven't seen him with you." Robbie's heart sped up. She had noticed him.

"Tom. He's the one playing the mouth organ."

She finally smiled. "I know who you mean. He's playing it upside down. But it's wonderful learning a musical instrument." She sighed, "I had started learning the piano when my mum died. Dad didn't hold much stock in music." She sighed again. "And then he died, too, of a broken heart. He loved my mother very much."

One of the girls nearest her turned round and said, "Oh, stop it, Alice."

"Mind your own business!" Alice snapped. The girl shrugged, looked Robbie up and down and then turned back to her friends.

After a moment, Alice managed to ask him calmly, "What happened to your parents?"

She was breaking an unspoken rule. Nobody at the Homes asked this question.

"My parents are both dead, too," he said.

Mrs. Grimsby was coming back to join the girls. He took a step away from Alice.

Heads were counted. The conductress who was escorting them, employed by the Immigration Department, was a woman in her late twenties, one of the new breed of no-nonsense working women that had got their start during the war. She shouted, "Welcome to Canada!" and smoothed the skirt of her uniform and squared her shoulders, "Ready?"

She led them down the ramp onto the 'colonist' train, as it was called, a rickety, primitive thing with a coal burning stove at either end of the car. Robbie could tell that the fires had just been lit as the air was still cold. The girls were given the seats near the warmth. Robbie sat down at a window, determined to see as much of his new homeland as he could. Surprisingly,

Tom sat down beside him and fiddled with his mouth organ. Mrs. Grimsby immediately got up to take it off him, proclaiming to have heard 'too much of the screech already today.'

As the train groaned and moved out of Halifax, Robbie stayed riveted to the clean spot he had wiped on the coal-smeared window. A half an hour later he was searching for signs of civilization. In Scotland, in the countryside, you couldn't go more than three miles without seeing a knot of houses.

Tom yawned and stretched and leaned up against him. On the ship, they had barely talked. Maybe he was coming around.

The trees were enormous and some of them had needles that looked as sharp as weapons. Some had just started to bud, the branches like arthritic fingers pointing up at the sky. There was an occasional farm where some of the trees had galvanized buckets hanging on them like giant Christmas ornaments. And once in a while, the landscape was broken up by blasted rocks, wide enough for the train to pass through. The heaviness of coal in the air of their compartment gave him a constant tickle and there was a lot of clearing of throats and coughing. It reminded him of dad and Duncan back in Lochoal, in their rolled up shirtsleeves, drinking ale and laughing so hard till they coughed. Back when things had been good.

He saw quite a few deer, but the clack-clack of the wheels, the billowing of the steam, and the occasional toot of the whistle, scared off any other wildlife. *God knows there is plenty of space to hide in.*

They were served sandwiches and coffee and a vessel of water was passed around. They got their rest on the hard wooden benches, bunched up by the threes, for warmth and comfort. Robbie slept fitfully. The sun rose. The frost sparkled on the trees and on the ground. A pretty picture, except each pull of the wheels took them further inland, further away from the sea, further away from home.

"How will we ever get back to Scotland?" Tom's voice startled Robbie.

Robbie hoped he spoke with conviction. "This is our home now."

"But if we want to…"

"Then we go back the same way," Robbie said.

He needed to get up to use the toilet and his arm was numb from leaning against the window. He extricated himself from Tom who slid over into his place, and, on his way, passed Alice who was dozing beside Mrs. Grimsby near the stove. Her mouth hung open. A slight snore escaped her. He looked away quickly. People were so vulnerable when they slept.

CHAPTER THREE

The train had made a few grudging stops where some people got on and off, but, when they reached Brockville, in Ontario, they were shunted onto another track. This was the end stop for this old basher of a train. As the children disembarked, their trunks were pulled off and none too gently, pushed into a heap. In no time, their luggage took over the platform.

They'd arrived at one o'clock in the morning and the curious onlookers who usually greeted shipments of children from the Orphan Homes of Scotland were fast asleep. The children were sorted into two lines, separating the boys from the girls and they were told to walk quietly. It was an uncomfortable walk. Robbie and the children were exhausted and it was eerie, walking down the high street of a strange town under the cover of darkness as if they were criminals.

After about three quarters of an hour walk, they were taken up the stairs of Fairknowe House, the distribution house for the orphanage, and were quickly shown to their rooms where they went to bed. After the boat and the train ride, all fell asleep within minutes of laying down their heads.

First thing in the morning, before breakfast, they were assembled to have their photograph taken on the steps for the *Narrative of Facts*, the annual newsletter that was sent out to Orphan Homes of Scotland friends, supporters and former Home Children.

They stood there, the boys looking devil-may-care, the girls demure, a front to hide their shaky insides and their fatigue, looking at the camera but also beyond it, trying to catch a glimpse of their future. For the first week of April, it was freezing cold but it was a different kind of cold than they were accustomed to: crisp and fresh, not the get-into-your-bones kind. The sun was shining but the ground was crunchy with frost. Alice looked at Robbie and smiled.

They disassembled and gathered for their last breakfast together.

"In two days, everyone will be at their destinations." Robbie recognized Superintendent Grimsby from his visit the year before. "All the applicant farmers are ready to accept you into their homes. And now let us pray before our breakfast."

After an abundant meal of egg, potatoes, bacon, beans and toast, the children washed up.

Right after breakfast, Robbie and Tom were told to pack up. They were being sent by train to Apple Orchard where they would be picked up by two brothers who had adjoining farms.

This is good news. We are going to be near each other.

Robbie looked for Alice, but Mrs. Grimsby told him she had already gone.

"Do you think that it would be all right if I wrote to her?"

"She's a beautiful little thing, isn't she?" Mrs. Grimsby said. She smiled at him. "Alice is going to work as a domestic at a farm near here."

"What about her auntie in Toronto?"

"Auntie? She has no relatives we know of."

Robbie blushed. *She lied to me.*

"You know, you could write to her," Mrs. Grimsby said gently. "She wrote down Alice's address on a slip of paper."

After passing it to him, Mrs. Grimsby drained her cup of tea. "It might cheer her up. Her entire family was killed in a fire just a year ago."

Robbie's hand involuntarily went to his puckered chest. He shuddered at the thought.

***

Robbie and Tom were taken back to the railroad station to get on the local train to Apple Orchard. It sounded like a pretty place. This train was more comfortable than yesterday's and the next thing he knew, the conductor was gently shaking Robbie's shoulder saying, "Apple Orchard, son." He woke Tom and they got off. Their trunks were plunked down at the end of the station upon which they sat to wait.

The station was small, poorly built and dusty.

"Tommy," Robbie said. "Talk to me."

"What about?" Tom pulled out his mouth organ.

"Are you angry?"

"No."

"Then why won't you talk to me?" Robbie asked.

Tom shut his eyes and strung some notes together into a tune. Robbie felt like slapping the bloody thing out of his hands.

A horse and cart rattled to a stop in front of them, a tall, lanky man steering it with both reins in one hand. When he got down, he did so awkwardly; one hand stayed in his pocket. His thin hair had been brushed straight back from his forehead, bird-like. His ruddy complexion didn't disguise the rings under his eyes. He stepped up onto the platform and sighed.

"You the Home Boys?" he said loudly and slowly as if they were slow.

Home Boys?

Tom said, "Yes."

The farmer sized him up. "Sure you can do the work on a farm? You're pretty small."

Robbie stood up. "We can do whatever you need us to do."

The man turned to him. "You'll hafta speak slowly with that funny accent. Who's Robert?"

"My name's Robert James and this is my brother, Thomas James." Robbie enunciated slowly. He was surprised. They had been taught proper English at the Homes and their accents were pretty clear.

"I'm takin' you. You," he looked at Tom, "are going to my brother."

Robbie looked him over. His dirt-caked overalls were patched, his boots were worn down. Even the horse pulling the cart looked tired. "Are you

Mr. Johnson?"

"Yes, yes. Name's Johnson. Get in."

They loaded their trunks and then got into the rough cart, leaving the station behind. They bumped along the scored and ravaged gravel road, sometimes swerving to miss a pothole, sometimes splashing through one. The cold air found its way through their wool coats and Robbie turned his collar up. With the clip-clop of hooves and the rattle of the cart, it was impossible to carry on any kind of conversation. Tom blew on his mouth organ. Robbie looked up at the sun to discern their direction.

After about an hour, they stopped at a road that was in worse shape than the one they were on. There was dense bush and trees and there were no buildings in sight.

"Damn," Johnson said. "John's not here yet."

Tom swung his legs over the end of the cart.

"Which trunk is yours?" Johnson said to Tom. "Come on. Help me unload it." Robbie jumped down to help.

"You. Get back in."

"What do you mean?" Robbie said, surprised. "I'm not leaving him here alone." He walked over to his brother, arms folded.

"Oh, you wanta cause trouble already, do ya?" Johnson pulled out a cigarette. "I know all about you 'Street Arabs'." Out of his pocket came the stub of a hand.

At their unnerved expressions, he waved it at them, "Plenty of us Canadians didn't come back, saving you lot." He took a drag and then flicked the ash off. His stub went back into his pocket. Robbie looked longingly at the cigarette; he could really use a smoke.

Street Arabs?

"Don't think you can get away with nothing. I'm goin' ta be watching you like a hawk."

They stared at each other. Johnson took another long drag.

Johnson said through thin lips, "I can always leave you both here but my brother will send one of you back. Then you're not goin' ta be anywheres near each other. Up to you."

He pulled on the cigarette that was almost down to the end. He stubbed it out against the side of the cart and then put it into a tin that he'd taken out of his pocket. "I'm goin'."

At this Robbie unfolded his arms. Tom said, "Just go. I'll be all right."

Robbie shook his head. "No, Tom. I can't leave you here."

"Damn it. I'm not a baby," Tom said, his face flushed. "You don't have to worry about me anymore."

Johnson was already on his seat and had picked up the reins.

"Now or never," said Johnson, his eyes on the road ahead.

Before Robbie swung up onto the back of the cart, he put his hand on Tom's shoulder and squeezed. "I'll see you soon," he said to his brother, "at church."

They left him in a cloud of dust playing his mouth organ. The further into the country they went, the more trouble Mr. Johnson had navigating the grooves in the road. Mud flew everywhere and the going was slow.

I could walk faster.

Robbie strained to see his brother, but the tree and bush-lined road curved and, even though the going was slow, he was soon lost from view. Trees, bush, trees. Suddenly there was a gun shot.

"That was my brother." Johnson shouted at Robbie as he swung the cart into a smaller dirt road. "Picking up yours."

CHAPTER FOUR

The farm house was a weary clapboard building coloured the pearly grey that wood gets after years of exposure to harsh weather. It was two stories, with the unsafe remnants of a tiny balcony on the second floor. There had been some attempt made to brighten it up with green paint around the windows and a corridor of grass had been cut from the road to the house. There was a big barn to the left, and to the right another smaller building. All had dull tin roofs. A couple of large yellow mongrels came roaring around the corner of the barn, but a shout from Johnson silenced them. They lay down, put their heads on their paws and watched Robbie, ears cocked.

Johnson gestured to Robbie to get off the cart. The dogs lifted their heads. Robbie took his trunk off the cart, keeping one eye on them. Wordlessly, Johnson led the horse and cart away and then went into the house.

While he stood there, Robbie heard grunts and clucks and the occasional whinny. The air was laced with the fragrance of grass, hay, rain and wet earth. He shook the stiffness out of his legs. A covered well in the front with a pump painted in the same grass-green as the windows, made him long for a drink of fresh water to get the dust out of his throat. The dogs watched his every movement.

The attempts to make the place more inviting had failed. They had wasted their green paint. The whole area was muddy, messy and looked foreign in the breathtaking beauty of the countryside.

Robbie sat down on his trunk.

After a few minutes, Johnson came out, a woman behind him. About the same height as her husband, her greying sandy hair was pulled back painfully from her face into a bun. There were deep worry lines on her forehead. She was wearing a stained apron.

"This is my missus. Take your trunk in. We have to get a move on." He looked up at the sky, shaking his head.

She said to her husband, "He's awful thin."

"Hello," Robbie said. "My name's …"

"Get a move on," Johnson interrupted him, "We're behind with the chores."

Robbie took off his hat and held out his hand, "My name is Robert James." On closer look, she was much younger than her husband, but she was dumpy and plain – not the kind of woman you'd want on your arm. As she moved closer, an odour emanated from her, like rancid butter.

"Follow me." she said.

Robbie picked up his trunk and she led him into the house. "This is the summer kitchen." She passed over a larger doorstep into the 'real house'. There was an oven with chairs around it- a rocking chair for her, a chair with arms for him. It was fairly roomy, but when the table in the summer kitchen was dragged back in, it would be tight. It smelled like soup.

She opened the door of the ground floor room and he carried his trunk in. It was tiny with a roughly hewn bed and a night stand. There was just enough room at the foot of the bed for his trunk and a chair. A faded quilt gave the room some colour. It was musty. He held his breath as Mrs. Johnson brushed by to open the window. "It's been closed since the last boy."

At the door, she turned back to him with her hands on her hips. "Better hurry back out there or he'll give you what for."

"I'm going to change into my work clothes." He closed the door and quickly put his new overalls on. He hung his Sunday clothes carefully onto the hook on the back of the door and then, briefly lay down on the bed, testing it. It had a lumpy mattress and when he turned onto his side, he rolled right back down into the middle of it. The sheets and pillow case had been fashioned out of bleached burlap flour bags.

Johnson was at the pump and working it until a stream poured from it. He bent over, held his head under it and yanked once on the handle, sputtering from the cold water.

"Well?" he said to Robbie, "For Chrissake. Don't you look fancy."

Robbie started at the Lord's name taken in vain. *That would have put me on Sunday's List.*

"That bother you?" Johnson snickered.

Robbie said nothing but inwardly agreed. He had trouble believing in a God who had dealt him so many bad cards. If it were up to him alone, he'd never step into a church again. Yet he had every intention of attending. Church would be the place he could see his brother.

"Cows hafta be milked on Sunday, too." Johnson continued, "There ain't no money growing on trees here like they told ya. There's just hard work. No days off."

Robbie looked down. *I'll be going to church no matter what you say.*

As Robbie followed Johnson to the barn, he wondered if these people bathed. The stench of Johnson was almost visible. He hadn't seen any electricity or running water in the house, only the pump outside.

"Where's the lav?"

"A what?" Johnson said.

"The toilet."

He laughed. "Pick your tree." He went toward the barn.

Robbie, clad in his new overalls and stiff work boots, looked for a private place to relieve himself. The ground was even marshier out in the back, and when he brushed against some tree branches, icy water dropped down on him.

He heard the kitchen door bang open and Johnson say, "Where in hell has he got to?"

His wife mumbled something.

"What have we got ourselves into again?" Johnson didn't try to lower his voice. "He'd better be able to pull his weight. You shoulda seen his brother."

"I don't think he knows nothing about farming," she said, "Just like that other boy we had."

Robbie buttoned his fly and went around to the front of the house to wash his hands at the pump. He splashed cold water over his face and neck. *I'll show them what Scots are made of.*

* * *

Robbie was soaked. The rain had started just after they had reached the part of the fence that needed repairing. At first, the downpour was fast and furious, and within seconds, the already saturated fields reminded him of a moor. It continued on and on and it was difficult to fit the pieces of wet timber together. Yet Johnson worked steadily away, adept even with only one good hand, pausing only now and then to look up at the sky, muttering under his breath.

By the state of things, it'd been raining for a good few days. When Robbie asked him how long, he answered grimly, "Forty days and forty nights. Maybe we should start on an ark."

The day was spent that way, dragging the wood and criss-crossing it. Johnson rarely spoke but that suited Robbie fine. He had time to think about Alice and what he was going to write in his letter to her. He hoped Tom was okay.

Earlier, they had passed the cows huddled together where the ground was drier. They'd seemed peacefully unaware of the power of their bone-crushing bulk, and glanced at him and away again with all the curiosity of a cud-chewing log. Now, they were lowing. They sounded like they were in pain.

Johnson straightened, stretched and said, "Time to milk the cows." He whistled sharply and the dogs who had been waiting under a tree, followed, occasionally stopping to shake the water from their coats.

The cows had already wandered close to the barn, and when Johnson opened the barn door, they waddled in, udders swollen like big, pink balloons.

Robbie, thankful that the hard part of the day was over, started shivering in his wet clothes. Dusk was beginning to set in. He followed Johnson into the barn and almost slipped on a cow pad.

Johnson picked up a three-legged stool and a pail. "You've gotta learn t' milk. Watch me."

Robbie watched him knead and pull. It didn't look so hard. He only had one good hand. The frothy liquid splashed into the pail. He got up and Robbie sat on the stool and began to self-consciously and gently pull on the teats. The cow turned to look at him. "This'll take forever," Johnson said. "I'll get the missus."

Mrs. Johnson milked swiftly and had finished the other cows just as he had finished one. His forearms were aching.

They entered the house through a back door into the summer kitchen and there were towels and dry clothes laid out for them there. Heat flared up in Robbie. *She's been in my trunk.* But it was so good to put on dry clothes, and he was so tired, he soon forgot his anger. He turned his back to Johnson so that he wouldn't see his scar. His wife hung up their wet clothes near the stove.

There was a place set at each end of the table and, as soon as Johnson sat down, his wife placed a plate of steaming meat and potatoes in front of him. "Follow me," she said to Robbie.

She carried his meal into his room and set it on top of his trunk. "The help always eats in his room."

There was a single oil lamp shining in the dark room. Surprised, he followed her and, although the meal was mostly potatoes, there was a beautiful thick gravy covering everything. He devoured it and within minutes, seconds, he was wiping his plate clean.

He opened the door of his room to take the plate out and Johnson and his wife looked up. The house was so quiet, he could hear the clock on the mantelpiece ticking. Mrs. Johnson got up and took his plate from him, poured him a cup of tea and then stood, hand on hip until he'd gone back into his room.

As he propped himself up on the bed and sipped his tea, he heard the scrape of her chair as she sat back down again. He had never been so tired before. Everything hurt, even the muscles in his face. As he finished off the mug, he thought about the strange creatures he'd ended up with. He hoped that Tom and Alice and Squint and all the others had ended up somewhere nice. He'd have to get over to see Tom this week.

He woke up in the blackness of the night, sweating, still fully dressed, tears on his face, a cry on his lips. There'd been steely-eyed Germans taunting him again, threatening to kill Tom and Emma, if he didn't inform on his parents. His body hurt all over from the punches and kicks they'd let fly. He'd blurted out all their secrets. His parents had been brought to a wall in front of him.

Robbie covered his ears. The gunfire didn't stop. It went on and on. He sat up and realized it was the rain pelting the tin roof and he got up, suddenly having to pee.

When he opened the door, a light was wavering down the stairs. His heart was still pounding. It was Mrs. Johnson, fully dressed.

"You're up. Good," she said. "I was just going to bang on your door. Johnson is already in the barn."

He stifled a yawn and went outside. He felt like he hadn't slept at all.

CHAPTER FIVE

Robbie drove the cart up to the cheese factory, pulling back at the reins with all his might. The damn stupid horse. He was sure it didn't like him. No matter what he did, it moved at the same slow pace all the time.

The milk was weighed and tested for its fat content. The empty cans were filled with whey. Then he drove off to his secret place, a place on one of the bends of the Raisin River, and sat against a rock with his feet dangling down to smoke and compose his next letter to Alice.

Two months after sending his first letter to her, she'd replied. He'd almost given up hope. It was only half a page and very polite. She didn't mention her auntie. After that, they exchanged letters once a month. When hers arrived, he carried it, unopened, until he was alone. Then he ripped it open and devoured the meagre contents.

The girls in the area, when he saw any, did not pay him much attention. Although, with his blue eyes and pleasant face and the muscles filling out his shirt, he was whispered about. But, in their minds, he was one of the "Home Boys": undesirable, with a propensity for theft and disease and generally up to no good. Not husband potential.

And it was never so evident than at the United Church, where he went as often as he could on Sundays. The Home Boys sat together in the back pew during the service. When Robbie walked into the church for the first time, he was told to join the mixed, ragged, hungry-looking lot.

Robbie knew now that they had been sent to Canada from Great Britain to break their backs for the benefit of strangers. Their compensation for a seven-day-a-week, sixteen-hour-day, was food and a place to curl up for six or seven hours before starting all over again. They didn't see a penny. The money, if paid at all, went into an account, minus deductions for whatever the farmers thought they could get away with.

Most had just been sent by a do-gooder institution. Their parents or guardians, after signing the Canada Clause, had left their futures up to fate. Without family, and friendless, they saw their only allies, the other Home Boys, once a week.

Of course, there were a few lucky ones: Boys who had found a farmer and his wife to take them in as one of their own.

Robbie looked at them with envy. *We would all work harder for someone who treated us with an ounce of decency.*

The Boys were all different ages, shapes and sizes and mostly came from cities and villages in England and Scotland, although the youngest and the most fragile, Andrew, or 'Tiger' as he was known, was from the Isle of Mann. A real mixed bag.

The Girls sat with their 'owners', but it was obvious who they were by their outfits and their downcast eyes.

None of the others, although from larger families, had any siblings near them. And so, they envied the James brothers.

"What I would give," one or the other would say.

But Robbie and Tom rarely had a heart-to-heart.

"Yes," he'd answer Robbie's questions or "No."

Mattie, from Manchester, was the most good-natured Boy of the lot and the same age as Robbie, but Tom got on his nerves.

"Are you all right?" Mattie asked him one Sunday morning.

"No. I hate it here," said Tom.

"Why? Do they beat you?"

"No. but they are mean. I want to go home."

"If they don't beat you and you get enough to eat and have a warm, dry roof over your head, you've got it made," Mattie said. "And, above all, you're lucky to have your brother nearby."

"What good does that do me?"

After saying this, Tom walked away from the group to sit in the back of his Johnson's cart and he pulled out his mouth organ. Mattie shook his head.

Robbie could tell that Tom was well fed for he was growing fast. He seemed to have landed in the right place. The other Johnson and his wife ran a small market garden. No cows to milk early in the morning and no hay to rake. In September he would start school. Compared to the other Boys, an easy life.

Robbie was ashamed of the way the other Boys moved away from Tom when he came near.

Tiger was the only person Tom talked to. And Tiger was the one who had it the worst. It was a well-known fact. His clothes hung on him like rags on a scarecrow. He had given up wiping his runny nose. There were welts and bruises on Tiger's thin thighs.

Yet Tiger patiently listened to Tom's complaints, nodding whenever Tom paused to breathe.

About mid-June, after two months filled with farmers' anxiety, they were blessed with good weather. The seeding had been finished long ago but the tender shoots were long in developing. Oats, barley, corn, hay and alfalfa all needed the nurturing warmth of the sun. Church that Sunday was filled with smiles. If the weather kept up, they could reap the first batch of hay by the end of the month.

The happy chattering stopped when the congregation saw the darkness gathered on the minister's face. Something had happened. The whispers ran through the church like ripples on a lake.

The end of the pew where Tiger and Tom usually sat, was empty.

The minister, eyebrows drawn together said, "Let us pray for the tortured soul of Andrew Smitherly, who left this world by his own hand, yesterday."

Tiger! Robbie gasped. He looked wildly around for Tom. Where is he?

"Let us pray," came a few timorous responses.

"Almighty God," he continued, "Please find it in your mercy to accept young Andrew into your heavenly flock and absolve him for ending the life that you blessed him with. He was young and did not know what he did. Lord forgive him."

"Lord forgive him," the congregation echoed.

"Also, Lord, please find it in your almighty wisdom, to help your humble servants make sense of this tragedy," he said. "Amen."

"Amen," said the congregation. There were a few sniffles.

After the service, the Boys stood close together smoking.

"How'd he do it?" someone asked. "Like Tom?"

Robbie looked up, startled at the mention of his brother's name.

"Not your Tom, Robbie," Mattie said. "Another Boy named Tom hung himself last year."

"Tiger took Paris Green," said somebody.

That's the unnatural-looking stuff they put on the potato plants to kill the bugs. It's poison.

"Poor little Tiger," Mattie cried. "What a horrible way to go."

"Why was he called Tiger?" Robbie managed to get out.

"I guess because the Isle of Mann is famous for their cats with no tails and we couldn't call him cat," Mattie answered. "He was so meek and mild." He stopped for a moment. "He never said he minded."

"He had bruises all over his thighs," Robbie said loudly.

Nobody said a word.

"Why wasn't something done?" Robbie asked.

"Who listens to us?" Mattie returned hotly.

"What about the inspector?" Robbie answered. "Or the minister?"

"Inspector? What inspector? The outfit that he was sent over with doesn't have inspectors," Mattie spit the words out. "Where's yours?"

"And the minister? He's the one who recommends the farms for the likes of us to go to." Mattie pulled out a hankie and blew his nose. "You know, the homes of good Christians – the ones who put money in the collection box."

"Today, he was more upset about word getting around that a Home Boy had killed himself in his parish than about poor Tiger, I mean Andrew."

"But he's a man of God," someone said weakly.

"Don't be so thick." Robbie had never heard Mattie talk like this. "My Mister Heever wallops me whenever he feels like it. They feed me slop.

They make me stay away from their family, like I have something catching." He blew his nose again. "My father died in the Great War when I was seven and my mother couldn't cope with us five children alone. It broke her heart to send us away but it was better than starving."

"They think we have bad blood," Mattie's voice sounded weary, "but mostly, we've just been unlucky."

The weight of the last sentence hung heavily over their group until they began to drift apart, going to their different carts, waiting to go back to the farms where they worked.

On the way back in the cart, Robbie wondered about the happy letters that he had read from Canada in the *Narrative of Facts*. There was never any hint of misery or discontent.

And the despair reaching into his dreams that night left Robbie pale and exhausted in the morning. When he heard the train whistle off in the distance, a sound that always clutched at his heart, he almost couldn't bear it. And he made up his mind he was going to see Tom that afternoon, Johnson be damned.

CHAPTER SIX

Robbie flicked the sweat off his brow and pulled at the back of his shirt that was sticking to him. He'd put on a clean collar, wanting to make a good impression but he already had spreading circles of dampness. He sat on the steps of Fairknowe House, where he was waiting for his new employer. It was the beginning of July and the dog days of summer had arrived. It was a fierce heat he'd never before experienced. Every action required double the energy.

When he arrived back in Brockville, he went straight to Fairknowe House. He was sent upstairs for a bath and sat in the tub until the water was cold. His upper body, arms and face were a deep brown. The rest of his naked body looked strange, like he was wearing white trousers.

As he dried himself off, he felt cleaner than he had in weeks.

He pulled out clothes from his trunk. When he was sent away from the Johnson farm, he almost left it behind. It would have been much easier going without it. But it held his only possessions, his home. And the thought of Johnson getting everything for nothing, was enough to make his blood boil. So he dragged it behind him most of the way.

When Johnson turned him out, he didn't offer him a lift to the train station. The dogs had followed him for a bit, walking with him, tails down, looking at him with their ears cocked, sensing something was wrong. When they reached their invisible boundary, they sat down and he scratched their heads one last time. In the end, he was sad to leave the dogs and the cows and even the stupid horse. They'd been his comfort.

He thumbed lifts with passing vehicles and slept in barns, or sometimes out in a field. He always told the same story – he had to go to his family in Brockville – they needed his help. If they asked more questions he looked sad, which wasn't hard, and said he didn't want to talk about it.

It wasn't a real lie. The orphanage was the closest thing to a family he had.

One farmer's wife, Mrs. B, she told him to call her, let him chop some firewood into kindling and do other odd jobs in order to put a few coins in his pocket. She fed him heaping portions of mouth-watering meat and potatoes, followed by mixed berry pie. She let him sleep in a real bed and greeted him with a cheerful smile in the morning. "Stay," she said, "my husband needs the help. Our daughters are off on farms of their own and our only son," here she wiped her eyes, "died a few years ago of the Spanish flu." She brightened, "You remind me of him. We would pay you and you could send the money to your mother."

Robbie wanted to, but knew he was bound until he was eighteen. And he didn't have the heart to tell her to apply to Fairknowe House after he telling her an untruth. She'd be so disappointed.

And then there was Tom to think of and still, remotely, Alice, although his memory of her had faded. It was hard to leave Mrs. B, but when he did, she packed him fresh hard-boiled eggs, a beautiful ham sandwich on thick slices of bread, gave him train fare, spending money and a peck on the cheek.

He said he'd visit when he was able to. After arranging for her husband to take him to the station, she said he'd always be welcome. He knew he'd never see her again.

While he was eating alone in the spacious dining room, the Superintendent came in. They'd already found another placement for him and he would be picked up in a few days.

"We need to settle something first," said Mr. Grimsby. "Where's the money?"

"What money?"

"That you took from Mr. Johnson."

"I didn't take anything from him."

"He said you stole from him." He pushed a letter over to Robbie. "Read it."

Robbie skimmed over it. "It's a pack of lies."

"What happened then?"

Robbie looked at him warily. "We found out in church that this other Home Boy in the parish killed himself. I had to go and see if Tom was all right. He was Tom's only friend."

"I did my work in the morning and then left, intending on only being a few hours. I took a shortcut across the fields but it was harder going than I thought."

"When I told him about Tiger, I mean Andrew, poor Tom was gutted. I couldn't leave him until he calmed down."

"By the time I got back, it was dark and Johnson had done the chores by himself. He was furious. He was going to strike me but I told him to just go ahead and see where it got him."

"He told me to get out of his sight and never come back again. He called me a piece of filth."

Mr. Grimsby listened to Robbie's explanation with no expression on his face. "Are you finished?" he said.

"Yes, I am."

"Was it one of our Boys who took his own life?"

"No, he was from the Isle of Mann."

"Good." Grimsby relaxed.

Good?

"In the future, remember this: you are never to leave your workplace unless you have permission. I also knew it was a bad idea right from the beginning to let the two of you stay close to each other. It's better, like the others, to have a clean break. You get over it faster."

Get over having a brother?

"Well, it's your word against his. We'll have to send him the money that he says is gone, even though, I believe you. Be ready on Tuesday to go."

"Did he send any money?" Robbie asked.

"Just for the first month and that's what we'll send back."

Robbie looked down. *The bastard.*

***

The clip-clop of a horse made Robbie look up. A young woman pulled up in front of the building with a click of her tongue. Her hay-coloured hair hung in braids over her ears. Her eyebrows were thick and evenly placed but her blue eyes, nose and mouth were crowded together.

"You are the help?" she asked, shielding her eyes from the sun.

"Yes," Robbie said, knowing now that his name wasn't important.

The girl had a different cadence to her speech. She got out of the cart and lifted one end of the trunk, but he waved her off. Tanned as brown as he was, she was also tall and muscular. As she went back to the driver's seat, Robbie watched her natural swing. She looked good from the back even in the man's clothes she was wearing.

She patted the seat beside her and he swung up onto the cracked leather. *This is different. She's not making me sit in the back.*

"My father is sick." Now that they were heading west, her face had relaxed and she didn't look half bad. "I try to work hard," she said. "But I am not a man."

"What's wrong with your father?" said Robbie, turning his head so that this girl couldn't see him blush. Their thighs were almost touching.

"He has a horrible cough. He spits blood," she said. The horse kept plodding on. "But don't worry," she said. "The doctor told us it is from the fire."

"What fire?"

"Our barn is in flames and I think my father takes in too much smoke."

Oh, oh, that doesn't sound good.

"I'm Robbie," he said.

"My name is Erika Schreiner."

"Where are you from?"

"We are Canadian," she said, keeping her eyes on the road.

"No, I mean, where are you from?" Robbie persisted. She was German. He knew he was right. "Were you born here?"

"No," she said. "Where are you born?" she said, her tone neutral. "In the Home?"

They both kept their thoughts to themselves till they reached the farm, close enough to the town that it would not be difficult to get there in an hour, but secluded enough to have privacy from the townspeople.

The Schreiner's house was smaller than the Johnson's, but it had curtains in the windows and an abundance of colour in the well-tended garden. The clapboard siding was a clean white and there was a stone walkway leading to the front door of the house.

After unhitching the horse, Erika took Robbie round to the summer kitchen door. The steps were swept clean and a delicious aroma of freshly baked bread wafted out of the kitchen. She took off her shoes, Robbie followed suit.

"Have you hunger?" Erika asked him. "My mother is a wonderful cooker."

Mrs. Schreiner, a rotund woman in her late forties came out to meet him and took his hand. "Hungry?" When he nodded she smoothed out the green tablecloth and placed a plate of fresh bread and cheese on it. "Eat now, please. Then we go to your room."

Erika sat down at the table with him. "You know about farming?"

Robbie buttered the bread. He took a bite. The best bread he'd eaten since the steamship. "I've worked on a farm since April."

Suddenly, from upstairs, came a coughing so fierce that Robbie put down his slice of bread. Erika raced up the stairs that led from the kitchen and Mrs. Schreiner poured steaming hot water into a bowl and followed her. Robbie sat at the kitchen table, staring at his hands, wondering what to do. From the sound of it, Erika's father wasn't long for this world.

The coughing slowly subsided, and after a while, Erika came down the stairs. "Finish your bread and then come outside. Hurry. We have to do much work."

I hope I don't have to sleep near the old man.

Robbie stuffed his mouth and washed it down with a glass of milk and followed her. She was already in the field. Looking around, he could see that a lot of work had been left undone and the barn behind the house was charred and looked unsafe. Cold smoke still hung in the air. Various tools and driving implements had been pulled out of the driveshed. They were using it as a makeshift barn.

The girl was struggling with the two workhorses, trying to get them to mow the hay in a straight line. Robbie picked up a rake and glanced at the sky. It was clear and blue and he hoped to hell it would stay that way for four or five days till the hay dried.

Then he noticed the cows near the other crops. Black and white Holsteins. Twelve of them. They were still eating grass but Johnson had bitched about almost losing a cow after it got into the alfalfa patch. The fence had fallen into disrepair. That needed to be tended to first. He rolled up his sleeves. She called his name. And then she called more loudly.

***

It wasn't until after Mr. Schreiner died that the neighbours organized a bee to rebuild the barn. Before that, the mood in the area was against the German-born family, everyone having been touched in one way or another by the Great War. Even young Erika, was the subject of derision. Her father's death changed everything. The community had to help a widow and her young daughter.

In the beginning, Robbie, too, was not happy to be associated with the Germans. Yet Mr. Schreiner, from what Robbie could tell in the brief time that he knew him, was an ordinary man, a far cry from the steely-eyed monsters of Robbie's nightmares. He had told Robbie, in short breathless sentences, of the terror they had lived in. Any dissent had a violent end. He was a short shell of a man with dark brown hair and sunken eyes.

Some days were worse than others. Sometimes the coughing turned into choking. His wife would hold a bucket for him and pat his back and speak to him lovingly as if he were her small child. There, there. There, there. *Lass dich gehen. Lass alles raus.* Let go. Let everything go.

Whenever this happened, Robbie would jump up and leave the house, even if it was in the middle of a sentence. It was too much like the Poor House infirmary.

One day, Schreiner didn't come downstairs at all. Erika got the doctor. After a short examination, the doctor came downstairs and shook his head. He put his hands on Mrs. Schreiner's shoulders, "Prepare for the worst."

The next day, it was all over.

Now that Schreiner was gone, he couldn't tell them what they needed to do. Every morning, while he'd been able, he'd dictated a list. Between Robbie and Erika, they'd managed. As his condition had deteriorated, Erika got bossier. Mrs. Schreiner had left them to themselves, tended her garden, put up preserves and nursed her husband. After he was gone, she looked like a lost child. "*Erika, was sollen wir machen?*" Erika, what shall we do?

It was harvest time. Erika knew some of the things that needed to be done but she wasn't sure, and Robbie had little experience. "You're useless," Erika yelled at him when he asked when to rake in the crops. She said in exasperation, "Why did they send you?"

A neighbour finally stepped forward. He offered to oversee the farm and offered the service of one of his five sons to carry out his instructions. It made sense but Robbie had to go. There was not enough money to pay them both. Mrs. Schreiner gave him the money for the two months he'd been with them and told him to be careful with it. She was sorry, and Robbie knew she meant it.

Erika drove him to the train station. They rode in silence. Robbie was glum. As soon as he'd come to terms with their German background, he'd appreciated the decency with which the Schreiners had treated him. Now, his future was up in the air, again.

He tried to focus on the beautiful foliage around him. Brilliant hues of red, yellow and orange. In Scotland, there'd just been varying shades of yellow. It was a warm day, a throwback to summer. He rolled the sleeves of his jacket up.

In front of the station, Erika stopped the cart, turned to him and blurted, "Don't go!"

"I have to," Robbie said, surprised.

"We can get married." Erika looked wild. Since her father's death, she had gone steadily downhill. She hadn't bathed. Her hair wasn't combed. Her clothes were stained by toil and sweat. She barely slept.

"Married? What are you talking about?"

She bit one of her nails. "If we get married, you don't have to leave

219

and when mother dies, the farm, it is mine."

"Erika, we are too young."

"No, we're not!" She grasped his arm. "Please stay. You always are so nice and work so hard for us. Don't leave me with that other boy. He is rude and stupid."

Aha. That's what this was about: he was the better of her two options.

"But you need him. I'm not a farmer." Robbie removed her hand gently. "I have nothing. I am nobody." As he got down from the cart, he said. "You'll be better off with him."

"Please don't leave." She started sobbing. "I love you!"

"I'm sorry," he said.

He was barely able to get his trunk out of the back before Erika slashed the poor horse with the whip and galloped off in a cloud of dust.

She'd have had me at her beck and call for the rest of my life.

In the waiting room, he bit into the sandwich that Mrs. Schreiner had made.

He heard the train whistle blow and the chug of the engine. It was pulling into the station. He wrapped up the remainder of the sandwich for later. As he wiped his mouth, he felt someone watching him. A dark-haired, sultry young woman was staring at him. He got up and picked up his trunk. He felt her eyes follow him and as he passed her, she spoke.

"It wouldn't have worked, you know."

"Excuse me?"

"It wouldn't have worked between you and her." She got up and straightened her skirt. "I know. I can read the future."

Like Auntie Mary, so many years ago.

"Sorry. Not interested."

She followed him to the platform. With a piercing squeal of the brakes, the train stopped and the fireman let out the steam, like a great sigh of relief.

Robbie looked at the beautiful black and gold beast. It was a lovely sight. He never got over the excitement of taking a train. Not since the trip to Bridge of Weir. He should learn to be a driver. He smiled. *What a life that would be.* The woman stood beside him.

"Oh no!" the young woman said, dropping her valise. "How terrible!" She turned to him with wide eyes.

"What's wrong?" Robbie gripped her arm to steady her.

"Someone close to you." He let her arm go.

"What's wrong?" Robbie repeated. "Is Tom all right?"

She shook her head. "I need a minute. Let me sit down, first."

They boarded and the young woman sat down carefully, smoothing her dress. She leant over to speak confidentially to Robbie. "I don't have a ticket," she whispered.

"What?" Robbie said.

"All aboard!" the conductor yelled.

"I suppose I still have time to get off," she said and stood up.

"But what about Tom?" Robbie said. "You have to tell me about my brother."

"I'd like to but…" she picked up her valise. With a jolt, the train's wheels started to turn.

"Wait. Sit down," Robbie said. "I have some money."

Her eyes were framed with long lashes and her coffee-brown hair was held back loosely with a ribbon. The little wisps that framed her face were intentional. But up close, Robbie could see that her collar and cuffs were grimy and there was a slight metallic odour about her.

"Thank you," she said. "I can see by your aura, that you are a friend of the spirit world." She sat down again and Robbie heard the jingling of metal. She was wearing a multitude of bangles.

What on earth was an aura?

"Is Tom in trouble?"

When I held my newborn brother in my arms so many years ago, I promised him he could always count on me.

"Do you have someone close to you that has passed? Someone who can help us see?"

Robbie thought carefully. "Uncle Duncan. He wasn't really my uncle, but he was like one. He never met Tom."

"I'm sure he'll help us. Now, please be quiet while I commune with Duncan's spirit. Hold my hand." She held one hand to him and the other up and shut her eyes. The woman's voice became husky. "Tom's very sad that you're apart."

A line of perspiration formed on Robbie's upper lip. But before she could say anymore, the conductor tapped him on the shoulder to collect his fare. Robbie paid to Brockville.

"Single to Toronto, please," said the girl.

With a sinking feeling, Robbie put away the fifty cents he had left after paying for her.

After the conductor moved on, she took his hand again. She was quieter. "I hope I can get Uncle Duncan back. Didn't you feel his presence?"

"Tell me what was so terrible?" He glanced around. People were not interested in them. "Does Tom need me? Should I go there?"

"Sssh." They stayed that way, hands joined until Robbie could no longer stand it. He drew away. She opened her eyes. "Uncle Duncan says Tom needs to stay where he is for now. If he leaves, a terrible thing will happen." She shuddered. "So terrible I can't tell you what it is."

"What do you mean – will he die?" Robbie asked.

"No, worse."

"What could be worse?" Robbie stammered. "Tell me more. Tell me what you saw."

"I can't. For if you leave him alone, you need not worry." She sighed and closed her eyes.

"That's it?"

She opened her eyes again and glared at him.

"Don't you understand? That is the message. Leave him where he is. Leave him alone." She wiped her hands on her skirt. "And now, if you don't mind, I need to rest." Within minutes she was breathing deeply.

CHAPTER SEVEN

Robbie quit the day he turned eighteen. On the eighth of September, without warning the farmer he was working for, he got up, milked the cows, had breakfast and then looked him in the eye, and said that, unless he paid him regular hired hand wages, he was leaving for Toronto, where the streets were paved with gold and not with cow shit.

Robbie said, "I'm old enough to be treated like everyone else now."

The farmer hadn't expected this. It had been his first time hiring someone from the Fairknowe distribution house, and although there had been a few warnings from neighbours to make sure he nailed down everything that moved, Robbie had been a valuable asset at about the third of the cost. The farmer, who was a middle-aged, balding man, knew Robbie had him over a barrel. The threshing bees were starting and he'd promised to show up at his neighbours with help. If he didn't, there might be a problem getting his farm done on time. It was a dirty trick to ask for more money at this point in the season.

Robbie folded his hands on the table. Except for paying him what he deserved, the man had treated him well. He'd had a real room of his own and the food was good. But he wanted to earn more than the dry bread and water wages he'd been getting.

He was itching to spend. He wanted to be able to play cards with the

223

men if he felt like it and buy new clothes and go out on the town. But most of all, he wanted to try his hand at something else.

The farmer reluctantly agreed to up Robbie's pay if he stayed on till the end of September. In his mind, though, he was going to figure out a way to get back at him.

They spent the last two weeks of September going from farm to farm to help. For the rural community, this was the most exciting time of the year. Outside of the church socials or the occasional barn raising, it was the only time of the year that neighbours got together. The farmer's wives tried to outdo each other at mealtimes and each spread would be progressively better. The men would devour mountains of food while sizing up the cherry-cheeked farm girls who served them.

Robbie's farmer kept a constant eye on the sky, hoping it would stay blue until they got to his farm. It was a farmer's curse: half of their lives were spent looking up at the sky, always worrying about too much rain or not enough sun or too much sun and not enough rain. The other half was spent looking down – at the earth and the growing plants and how they were developing, watching for the insects that could suck the life out of all their dreams.

Robbie always saved a lot of room for dessert. His favourite was sour cherry pie, and if allowed, he could eat an entire one himself. After the food, there were the drinks and sometimes, someone had a fiddle or an accordion and there'd be music and dance.

The Home Boys from the different farms huddled together, drinking away the fact that the local girls avoided them like the plague. Their daddies all watched their daughters carefully around the 'waifs and strays'. Robbie drank until all he wanted to do was fight or curl up in a corner and sleep.

At the very last threshing party, somebody pulled out a mouth organ and started to play. Robbie felt like he'd been punched in the belly. The last time he'd seen his brother was over a year ago.

When Robbie had returned to Fairknowe House between placements, after having been sent back because of a free-for-all, Mr. Grimsby had told him Tom had been expelled from school. He had also complained to their father about working on the Sabbath. Their father, in turn, had written to Miss Quarrier, who had taken over after her father's death, in Scotland. She had sent a terse note to Brockville demanding an answer.

Two things surprised Robbie. One was that their father had actually taken the time to write a letter on Tom's behalf and the other was that something was actually being done about it.

Mr. Grimsby soon squelched that though. He wrote back that the family where Tom was working, were reputable citizens as far as their minister was concerned. He saw no reason to investigate further. All farms required some work on Sunday.

The farmer had been outraged and had sent Tom packing. Luckily, the Boys were always in demand and so, Tom ended up at an older couple's farm doing gardening.

"You boys are getting a bad reputation," Grimsby said while he was putting the papers away. "Tom's been returned three times and you've been sent back four times. I could write to your father or Miss Quarrier and tell them that."

Robbie kept his mouth shut. *There is no sense arguing with him. Grimsby was a born Canadian and had no idea how bad things could be. Just that morning there was another Home Boy suicide.*

He wanted to see how Tom was doing with his own eyes. He asked for some of his money.

"We hold everyone's pay on account until the age of consent is reached," Mr. Grimsby said. "Otherwise, it'd all be gone."

"And by the way," he added, "Tom is not under your care, so you shouldn't go meddling."

It was a beautiful day and Robbie sat on the steps, smoking until Grimsby went out. The door to his office was open and Robbie went in, closing it behind him. He rifled through the files until he found theirs. All he wanted was Tom's address but couldn't help reading a little. He snorted. He, Robbie, had a difficult temperament, so Grimsby had said and Tom was a liar. He put the files back exactly as he had found them, went out the door and made his way to the King's Highway.

The first truck that came along picked him up. He sat in the back with some crates of chickens.

Why did Tom write to our father? I'd rather be struck down dead by lightening than ask him for help.

It took him two days to get to where Tom was. He'd been given lifts on the backs of trucks, in carts and had walked or rather limped. He had blisters the size of two-bit pieces on the bottoms of his feet. Finally, he'd arrived at the Buckley's, near Lansdowne, tired, hungry and grubby, yet overjoyed at being able to see his brother again.

When they saw each other, Tom's whole face lit up. But it grew dark so quickly that Robbie wondered if he'd been mistaken. They were now almost the same size.

"Hi brother. You look like hell."

"Hi Tommy, it's good to see you, too."

The Buckleys were a nice old couple and gave them some time to talk alone in the kitchen with a ham sandwich and a glass of milk. While Robbie chewed, he looked around at the homey room. There were embroidered proverbs on the walls and a collection of pipes on a pipe rack. The red gingham tablecloth matched the curtains. An expensive Radiola, that you could listen to without earphones, sat polished and waiting on a small table surrounded by comfortable chairs. They had no children. Tom was in the money.

"I hate school and I'm not going back," Tom said. "They can't make me."

"Go to school, Tom, it's only one more year. It beats working."

"They call me 'Stray Dog'," Tom said, picking his nails. "Or 'Street Arab'. They make jokes about my accent. Nobody wants to make friends with me."

"Let it roll off your back, Tom," said Robbie, although he himself didn't practise what he preached.

"Yeah," Tom said. "As soon as I'm eighteen, I'm going back to Scotland. Dad told me he could land me a job."

"Really?" Robbie said sarcastically, "Doing what?"

"Don't know. Something good, though."

Tom isn't looking me in the eye. What's he hiding?

"Stick it out here, Tom. You've got it made."

"Dad's changed his name, you know," Tom said and laughed awkwardly.

"Again?"

"He's changed his name to his wife's." Tom laughed again. "Isn't that funny? Our father has a different last name than us, now."

"What?" Robbie pulled out a cigarette and lit one. He didn't offer one to Tom but Tom grabbed the packet off the table and stuck one in the side of his mouth like a pro. Robbie lit it. *What the hell.*

"He told me to address my next letter the same way as the return address on the envelope."

"What did it say?"

"It said William Barrington James Lapointe, Brighton Street Nine, Edinburgh." Tom enunciated each word clearly and carefully.

"Is she up the duff?"

"No." Tom's glance told him he hadn't thought about that. "They're too old."

"No, they aren't," Robbie laughed nastily. "You know why he did it, don't you Tom?" Robbie flicked his cigarette.

"Her father's a big shipbuilder. He probably made dad change it, just in case they do have any brats. Then we won't be in the way."

"He writes to me. He's going to help me when I go back."

"Tom. Don't you think that if he'd wanted to help us, he already would have?"

"Well…" Tom's features tightened even more. He bent over to retie his shoelaces.

If Tom doesn't let go of the father he never knew, he'll never be happy.

"Dad has sold us out." Robbie took a deep drag and stubbed out the butt. He said more coolly than he felt, "He'll never do anything for you."

Tom jumped up, knocking over the chair. "Get out of here!"

Robbie looked at him startled. "Come on, Tommy. You know I'm right."

"Get the hell out of here. You think you know everything."

"Tommy!" Robbie said, "I didn't want to argue with you. I only wanted to see if you were all right."

"Leave me alone," Tom said. "You always spoil everything." And he turned and left Robbie sitting alone in the Buckley's kitchen.

Mrs. Buckley came in from the garden, wiping her hands on a cloth.

She must have been listening. "Is anything wrong?"

Robbie went to the door and called Tom's name a few times but he didn't come back.

Mrs. Buckley said, "He gets like this sometimes. He doesn't really mean it."

Robbie looked at her for a moment. He knew she meant well. But goddamn it, this stranger was telling him about his little brother. The brother he had always protected. *He is an ungrateful little bastard.* He raised his voice, hoping Tom would hear him. "Seeing as you know him better than me, he's all yours."

He limped down the road to the King's Highway, his heart sore.

***

Threshing was over and Robbie asked the farmer for his wages. He was given an envelope with some figures on it. He fingered it. It was thinner than expected.

"This is all I get?"

"It's your pay, minus room and board, minus the oil that you used in your lamp. Minus the laundry and the stitching my wife did to your clothes." The farmer was counting on his fingers. "You're lucky to get that much."

Robbie took the money and let the crumpled envelope drop to the floor. He was tired of fighting everyone for everything. It was enough money to get to Toronto and would cover his expenses for a couple of weeks. If he got lifts then he'd be able to spread it out more. By then, he would have a job and be better off. No more getting up at five o'clock to milk the cows, no more working a fourteen, fifteen, sixteen hour day, seven days a week.

He packed his cardboard suitcase, his heavy trunk long gone. The weather was a bit chilly in the mornings and late evenings but there was no frost yet and he figured it would only take a few days to get to Toronto. He was excited to see the big Lake, a lake as big as a sea, he'd been told. Just before he left, he took the lamp out of his room and poured the oil all over the rosebush near the front door. If he had to pay for it, then nobody else was going to use it. He hoped that the roses died.

The rides that he got that day were short. People going a few miles here and there and he didn't get very far at all. As the sun started to set, he needed to find a place to lie down. He snuck into a barn, and although a dog ran out to bark at him, it was old and soon gave up. He found himself an-out-of-the way corner, fluffed up some hay and lay down.

CHAPTER EIGHT

Robbie arrived in Toronto on the passenger seat of a Model T, asleep. He'd nodded off in his fatigue, in spite of his excitement, missing the transition from country to city. When he opened his eyes, he saw a confusion of red brick buildings spreading around him. The squeal of the trolley cars pierced his ears. The crisscross of electric wires marred the sky. He loved it.

Robbie laughed, feeling free for the first time since he'd arrived in Canada. The doctor, in the driver's seat, blinked over at him through his thick glasses.

Robbie didn't care. The doctor had been drinking out of a flask the whole time they'd been on the road. He leant back into the car's heady fragrance of oil, gas and new leather and thought: *my life starts now.*

***

Up to the point where the doctor had picked him up, he'd again been making his way on foot, in plodding horse-drawn carts or in the backs of trucks amongst hay and animals and tools. When the doctor had stopped, Robbie had hesitated, aware that he emanated a tang: grease, barn and sweat. He was damned if he knew why the doctor had stopped his luxury motor car.

"You! Can you drive?" the doctor had called over the rumble of the engine.

Robbie's fingertips had rested lightly on the black, shiny newness of the chassis until he saw the dirt under his nails. He leant into the window. *Please*. "Yes, sir," he lied. He'd only been in an automobile twice before, in the ride from Lochoal to Kirkcaldy and once with his father and the witch.

"I am going to Toronto and I might need some help driving. Where are you going?"

"Toronto, too." Robbie waited for a frozen moment as the doctor sized him up.

The doctor saw the bright, blue ambition in Robbie's eyes.

Please take me.

Nothing happened.

Too long. Robbie squared his shoulders and took a step away from the automobile. *What a shame.*

"Get in." The doctor opened the door from inside the car.

Robbie, startled, hesitated and then got in.

As soon as Robbie sat down, he noticed a strong reek of alcohol. Over it, the doctor would not be able to smell his unwashed self. He needn't be so embarrassed.

Otherwise, the doctor was nondescript. He was taller than Robbie, but his shoulders were small and round. His head, covered by an older navy fedora, was perched on a long, thin neck. His skin had an unhealthy hue. His small eyes were hidden behind unfashionable frames. His light coloured hair looked longer than it should be and he had a day's growth on his face.

He sat forward, on the edge of the seat and gripped the steering wheel tightly, only to let go when taking a swig from his flask. His buttoned-up serge suit was visible under a like-coloured overcoat.

"I'm Dr. Bruce."

"Robert James, sir."

"Talk to me while I drive so that I don't drop off. I need to get used to this new car."

Robbie stifled a yawn. He was very, very tired. But he had to keep awake or the doctor might go off the road.

He didn't know what to say. He'd never had much practice at casual conversation. In Canada, the farmers he'd worked for, were a silent breed.

They talked to animals better than to people. It took a lot of good food and especially good drink to get them going. The only banter he'd had was with other Home Boys, whose brief encounters had been more like meetings of a secret society.

And so, he waited, wary, for the doctor to start speaking. He would follow his lead.

After a few long minutes, the doctor broke the silence. "So, you're from the old country?"

"Yes, from Scotland."

"Loch Lomond. My mother's people were from around there."

"I'm from a small town just south of Glasgow, from the...." Robbie stopped. He had almost said from the Orphan Homes of Scotland.

No. I am damn well not going to be called Home Boy anymore. Never again. Nobody needs to know.

"...the Highlands?"

Robbie wanted to correct him but didn't want to offend, "Near enough."

"I'm thinking of going over myself one day. Tell me, what should I see?"

"Edinburgh is the place to go. It's the most beautiful city in the world. My father is a tailor there."

Be careful, be careful.

"You don't look very old. When did you come over?"

"I'm eighteen. I came over with my brother three years ago."

"That must have been hard for your parents to lose two sons. How much older is your brother?"

"There are five years between Tom and I." Robbie took another nervous breath.

He hated lying although, really, he was merely leaving out part of the facts. It made him feel sick. He swallowed past the lump in his throat.

"So, you've been here since you were fifteen. What have you and your brother been doing?"

"Farm work."

"And I take it that you've figured out that you're not cut out for it. That's why you ran off." The doctor looked him over. This boy would do for what he had in mind.

"Excuse me, sir, I didn't run off." Robbie kept his tone polite. "I just wanted to come to the city."

"What did your brother say?"

"He told me to do whatever I want."

"So you are here all alone?" Dr. Bruce glanced at him with a deep, odd look. He licked his dry lips.

"Yes, sir, I am."

"But you didn't leave each other on bad terms, did you?" The doctor turned very quickly back to the road. He spoke in a flat tone. "Your family are the only ones you can truly depend on."

Robbie just said, "My brother understands." *If he only knew.*

"I see," Dr. Bruce said. He nodded toward the window. "Look at the colours. They're exceptionally brilliant this year because we had such a hot summer."

Robbie's eyes were closing. The lack of sleep in the past few days was taking its toll. He breathed in deeply and hugged himself. Even though fall was his favourite time of year and the cool crisp air was welcome after the heavy heat of summer, he was cold.

He looked out. The gift of colour that nature gave them was like one last hurrah before the lights of summer went out. It was breathtaking. Yet, there was that underlying taint of rot that forewarned of winter. *Another one of God's tricks.* Robbie rubbed his arms to get warm.

"Cold?" Dr. Bruce asked. "Have some of this." He passed the flask.

It was pretty early in the morning for a drink but Robbie took a swig and made a face. The liquid burned a hole down his gullet to his boots. He took another and passed it back. The doctor took a long draught and slipped it inside his coat.

Robbie yawned again.

"It's all right," said the doctor, pursing his lips. "I'll call you if I need you."

***

Robbie pushed his foot down on the clutch with all his might and then shifted gears. The taxi jolted forward and then reared up like a horse being reined in during a false start in a race. "NO!" said the Irish cabbie. "Ease it out! If you do that again, it's going to cost you your balls!" He was a big man, the buttons on his vest bursting over his belly. He had meat hooks for hands and a nose that had obviously been mended a few times. He was about mid-forty and lit each cigarette from the stub of the one before. Robbie glanced at him sideways. As the smoke curled and twisted elaborately on its way out of his mouth, he wheezed. "Look at the road, not at me, Jock."

At those words, Robbie stepped on the accelerator and they sprang forward. Paddy looked like a hard guy but Robbie knew if he had to, he could dance circles around him. Paddy was a fat, old man.

"Take it easy, Jock." He rolled his cigarette around in his stained teeth.

Forget him. Concentrate. Robbie went over the steps in his mind. Clutch, gear, gas. "Ok, Paddy."

"That was better," said the cabbie. "You have to treat an automobile like a woman. Handle her gently, but let her know who's boss."

These driving lessons were costing Robbie an arm and a leg but he had no one else to turn to.

"Ease it out, ease it out. Ease It Out!"

If he says that one more time....

At first Paddy, the cabbie, had shown him how to crank the car. "Even if it's got a starter, you still might have to crank it on cold days. Get out of the way right quick or it'll break your arm."

So, the morning was spent learning to start the car and brake. After lunch, he got the gist of changing the gears, although it still wasn't smooth sailing. The Irishman sat with his hands under his belly, grimacing at every jerk.

The damn clutch.

Around lunchtime, just when Robbie was starting to feel more comfortable, a drunk suddenly lurched in front of the car. Robbie swerved to miss him.

"Stupid Indian," Paddy swore. "They're all drunks and smugglers."

Robbie had never knowingly seen an Indian before. He stopped and looked back at the man. He looked like everyone else. He wasn't wearing fur nor did he have red skin or long hair.

And as far as drunks went, he was in the taxi with one and his respectable new boss was another.

By the end of the day, Robbie began to enjoy himself. The automobile was easier to steer and more reliable than a horse. It went where and when he wanted it to go.

"Just like a pro. C'mon Jock. Let's go down the pub to celebrate," said Paddy after Robbie paid him. He slapped him on the back. "My treat."

His jibes aside, Paddy was turning out to be quite affable.

"We'll go after I get my licence."

"I'll drive you down to the police, then." He tapped his nose. "I have friends in the right places."

"How much is it going to cost me?"

"How much do you have?"

"Not much."

"A couple of dollars should do it. C'mon me boy, after all this, I'm as thirsty as a dried-out dromedary."

The superintendent in the newly-built precinct issued the driver's licence without even checking to see if Robbie could drive. "If Paddy says you can drive, you can." He held out his hand. Robbie shoved a few dollars in it. He stamped the document. "What do you want it for anyway?"

"I've got a job as a driver for a doctor."

"When do you start?"

"Tomorrow."

He laughed. "Nothing like leaving it to the last minute."

***

Toronto wasn't at all like the well-established Edinburgh or Glasgow, of which the buildings themselves were deeply rooted in the history of the country. Almost everything was new in comparison – most of the structures were less than fifty years old. Fifty! Robbie remembered that the new part of Edinburgh was almost triple that age.

They arrived at the doctor's, which was in East Toronto, a community just amalgamated into the city. Most buildings in the direct vicinity had just sprung up in the last few years.

The doctor's home, which was also his office, had a large front veranda with two wicker chairs upon which the doctor and his sister sat when the unbearable sticky heat waves made being inside impossible. The front door swung open onto an enclosed hallway where patients could hang their coats. From there they went into a small waiting room that was outfitted with three straight-backed wooden chairs. The other door opened onto the tiny doctor's office, only big enough for Dr. Bruce's oak chair and desk, his cabinet and two more chairs for a patient and companion. From this room, one went further back into the actual treatment room.

It was a beautiful brick house with a lane beside it, where the horses used to drive through to the ten-yard away carriage house. Not a mansion but solid. It backed out onto a small but charming park.

Behind the doctor's office, there was the small sitting room, dining room and the kitchen. The bedrooms, all four of them, were upstairs. One of them had been converted into a study. The bathroom separated the two guest rooms.

The rooms were similarly set up with good quality, yet drab furnishings, as if everything had been bought in a hurry, all at once, probably at the T. Eaton's department store, downtown. There were no knick knacks, just books and publications stacked about the rooms. The curtains and the pictures on the walls seemed like they were an afterthought. They were pastel impressionist paintings and looked out of place in the masculine environment. The armchairs and the settee in the sitting room were still stiff in their newness and the walls were unmarred by soot. It all looked uncomfortable and unlived in.

When they arrived, the doctor introduced Robbie to his unmarried sister, who kept house for him. The doctor and his sister were very unalike in appearance except for the fact that they were both thin. She was petite, with short, naturally wavy, salt and pepper hair framing her face. She wore browns and greys and made no attempt to brighten herself up and so looked her age, or older, which was around thirty-five.

At one time, she had to have been pretty, perhaps even beautiful. She had large eyes, framed evenly by long lashes; her nose was perfectly straight and her cheekbones were high, giving her a chiselled look. But the bloom had been drained from her features.

"I hope he will replace Sam," the doctor said to his sister as he poured himself a drink. She watched her brother gulp with disapproval. He continued, "He is not coming back." Sam, he told Robbie, was returning to his family.

The doctor explained to Robbie that he needed someone to help with the winter driving which he found nerve-wracking. He also was experiencing arthritic pain in his wrists and needed help, not only with cranking the damn car but with lifting and carrying immobile patients and perhaps with the preparation of injections and bandaging. It sounded appealing. There were other odd jobs, like shovelling snow, cutting grass, raking leaves. It sounded like a walk in the park.

Miss Bruce showed Robbie to a room above the carriage house, which, although it hadn't seen a horse for a few years, still smelled like a stable. It now housed the shiny new automobile.

It was a small room, but was furnished with a pine bed, night table, armchair and electric light. There was a book shelf filled with books. It looked sparse, yet neat and clean. The first real place of his own. It was too good to be true. Robbie picked up a magazine from the shelf. It was a recent copy of the *Family Herald*.

Miss Bruce turned to Robbie and suggested a bath and a change of clothes after his long trip, as if he were an invited guest.

As they passed the sitting room on the way upstairs to the bathroom, she said, when real winter hit, he would be wise to move to the guest room in the house. There was no way of heating the carriage house.

The doctor looked up from the *Telegram* and peered at him over his glasses, in a way that doctors have, and said quite seriously, "Wouldn't want to amputate any digits because of frostbite, would we?"

It was Friday and Robbie needed to learn how to drive by Monday, which was when he would start his new job. He excused himself under the pretence of stretching his legs.

They were situated near Woodbine and Kingston Road, near the cemetery. He walked over to Woodbine and then towards the lake. From this point, it looked like the lake was higher than his vantage point.

He walked further south until he reached the vast body of fresh water. The sound of the waves rushing onto the shore reminded him of the North Sea on its benign days.

If there had been salt in the air, he could have almost imagined himself back in Scotland.

But then again he was fooling himself. The North Sea was wild and it could entice people like his mother to disappear in its depths or bewilder his grandfather with an unearthly racket that sounded very much like the voices of ghostly children.

He stood for a while, looking out at the lake with his hands in his pockets, wondering what to do. Then he turned and walked back up Woodbine and stood on the corner looking at the Fire Hall. A car pulled up in front of it and a big Irish voice boomed, "Looking for a taxi?"

***

As well as afternoons, when the patients came to the house and the doctor's sister assisted him, Robbie was occasionally allowed to take evenings off, if there were no house calls. After getting an advance from his first pay, he familiarized himself with the area.

Paddy, his friend, the cabbie, invited him to frequent the Legion as his guest. He usually nursed a ginger ale and Paddy would add a drop of rye from his hip flask. It was surprising how many men slipped their drinks under the table for a quick spike. Robbie wondered how they dealt with their wives when they got home. He had heard that the Ladies' Temperance Movement was very strong in the East End and if they got wind of it, they'd be after the police to raid the place.

Paddy, known to all, taught him to play darts and he found he had a natural affinity for shuffleboard.

Robbie was happy there. He was accepted as one of Paddy's friends. As well as Canadians, there were Limeys, Micks and Jocks like him. Funny thing, away from the homeland, there was no animosity between the groups.

He hadn't realized how much he had missed the busy hum of a community. He never wanted to live in the country again. But late at night, just before sleep, there was that emptiness that was still in his heart and his soul.

***

He caught the end of the season at the Woodbine Race Track and the excitement of the horse races. The men who bet on them, shouted and swore at the top of their lungs, bets clutched in their hands. The horses rushed by, heads held high, nostrils flaring, muscles rippling under their polished coats. "Go! Goddamn it! Go number five, Go!"

Where he was, in the cheap seats, there were mostly other men. But he managed to glimpse the young ladies who had taken to betting, too. They were fashionable, daring girls and he spotted one group of three he couldn't take his eyes off. One of them, was obviously telling a funny story, gesturing with her racing card, her mink fur collar flatteringly turned up. All three of them had legs to die for. Robbie knew he didn't stand a chance with them. They were girls who went with men in top hats. But there was no harm in looking.

He, himself, was loathe to bet his wages on something so chancy. He saw how men, with thin, brown, hand-rolled cigarettes hanging out of their mouths, squinted in the smoke as they scratched calculations with the stubs of pencils, going through triumph and defeat: both emotions sometimes registering on the same face within minutes.

Occasionally, he rode the Toronto Transit Commission streetcars, staring out of the windows at the city that he was making his own. As they rumbled down Kingston Road or along Queen Street, he noted the stores, the banks, the pawnshops, the greasy spoons.

Ahhh, downtown is more like it. There was always a vibrant congestion of cars, and people, now dressed in seasonal colours. There were tall buildings like the ten-storey Temple building, the International Order of Forester's building and behind them down at Bay and Richmond, Sterling Tower was being finished. It was going to be twenty storeys. He loved to sit in front of City Hall and look down Bay at the empire of commerce. He could go places in this city.

Once, he thought he saw Alice, but when he called out her name, a girl turned, a beautiful girl, but it wasn't her.

Alice's letters had been returned to him, both at her last address and at Fairknowe House. There was no forwarding address.

Tom sent back curt answers to his letters. Robbie felt like he was pestering him.

As a driver for the doctor, he spent the mornings and some evenings doing house calls. He always attended the patients with the doctor. As time went on, the doctor called on him more frequently, as his alcohol-driven hands were unsteady, to use tweezers to extract a deeply imbedded splinter or to help bandage or prepare a syringe.

Robbie wondered where the doctor got the whiskey. He seemed to have an endless supply and it was good quality stuff, not the homemade rot-gut that had been available in the country. Most of the time, the doctor didn't drink before the business of the day was finished but, after dinner, he would sit stiffly in his chair with his glass and his *Telegram*.

Miss Bruce wasn't a full out temperance lady but she still disapproved. She would sit with him, doing her needlework and sipping a tonic that the doctor mixed to help her sleep.

Every now and again, the doctor would be incensed by what he read and his ire, fuelled by whiskey, would overflow. "For God's sake!" At the beginning of his rants, his sister always gathered her sewing things together and got ready to leave the room. "They should leave Dr. Hastings alone."

"The man has done so much for health in this city and they dare to question his spending? If it weren't for his relentless pursuit of hygiene, we'd still be living in the dark ages!" Dr. Bruce's face was darkened by an unflattering flush. "How many children would still be dying of typhoid from contaminated milk and water?"

His sister said with just a slight touch of impatience, "Why do you read the *Telegram*? It always gets you upset."

"It's the people's paper. You have to read it to understand the people." He threw it on the floor.

When his sister left the room, shaking her head, he put on a gramophone record and slid out the lever on the machine until it was as loud as it could go.

People didn't know about his drinking habit, but Robbie suspected he would have been welcomed into the area anyway. Doctors were scarce after having their ranks depleted during the war and as a result of the pandemic Spanish flu.

***

Robbie had become their boy for all seasons. Besides performing some first aid, he raked the leaves, swept the sidewalk, cleaned the windows, the eaves and he knew he would have to shovel the snow. People greeted him with a smile and a nod and sometimes, even stopped to speak to him.

Their meals were cooked by the doctor's sister, who was also her brother's nurse during office hours, and the three of them sat together in the wood-paneled dining room. They were like an old, married couple with nothing left to say. At supper time, this suited Robbie, as he'd rather eat than talk. He ate carefully, adopting the table manners he'd had drilled into him at the Homes.

Afterward, he would slip out to his room, to read, he told them, but more to get away from the same odd look in Miss Bruce's eyes that he'd seen before in the doctor's. Something had happened to them, something that couldn't be forgotten, yet was not spoken about. It was giving him the creeps.

The house was cozy, having been built twenty years earlier than the others around it. The developer, who had planned the subdivision, had lived there. And, before he saw all of his beloved golf course disappear, even though it was by his own hand, he left for good. The street was called Golfview to the puzzlement of generations to come.

***

The first house, into which Robbie accompanied the doctor, was that of an elderly woman who had been living in her house for twenty years, below Queen Street, near the lake. She'd been alone the last five years.

Mrs. Bracken was rail-thin and was sitting in an armchair in her front room, a handkerchief clutched in her right hand. She had a pain that came from her stomach, she said, and was too dizzy and weak to move. To examine her, Dr. Bruce had Robbie carry her to the bedroom. She was light enough and when Robbie took her to the made side of the double bed, she stiffened and became agitated. "That's Jack's side. I can't lie on Jack's side."

Her voice was as brittle as thin ice.

The doctor gently pinched a flap of skin on her stomach between his fingers. A test for dehydration, he said to Robbie. Then, using his stethoscope, he listened to her heart and her stomach. He tapped her abdomen. Mrs. Bracken stared at Robbie. "Jack?" she said.

"No, Mrs. Bracken. This is Robbie."

"Where's Jack?"

"Mrs. Bracken, you're not eating and drinking enough," Dr. Bruce said firmly, looking at her over his glasses. "You need to keep your strength up. Flu season is coming."

"I keep asking that woman to make more but she doesn't. I have to give Jack half of mine." Mrs. Bracken looked at them through watery blue eyes. "It's Jack you should be looking at, not me. I am worried about him. He doesn't eat at all."

"Robbie, make a cup of tea for Mrs. Bracken and put plenty of milk and sugar in it. And make some toast. And while you're at it, throw an extra log on the fire."

When they left her, she was feeling better and she was sitting at the fire with another cup of steaming tea. The doctor said he would look in on her next week.

"Senility. She's got no family. She's lucky her neighbour looks in on her," Dr. Bruce said to Robbie after they pulled away from the cottage. "I'm surprised she's lasted so long." The doctor sat back in the seat and closed his eyes. "It will get worse. Eventually the simplest things will confuse her until she not only forgets to eat, but forgets how to eat."

For the first time in a long time, Robbie thought about his grandfather and wondered if he were still alive. He vowed to write a letter to his father.

His father. Shellshock sounded like a type of senility. It would explain how you would forget you had children, a wife, and a father.

"What does shellshock do to you?" he asked the doctor when they were on their way to the next patient in the automobile.

"What have you heard?" said the doctor, jerking round to look at him. His usually waxen face was flushed. His voice trembled.

Robbie, after glancing at his reaction, managed to keep his eyes on the road and say evenly, "It's my uncle. He came back from the war very different." By the doctor's reaction, he knew that he had touched a nerve. "They say he suffered shellshock. He left my aunt and cousins. I think he forgot who he was."

The doctor took his hat off and ran his fingers through his hair. "Your uncle." He let out a long breath.

When he spoke, he was calmer. "I think the consensus now is that war can change people permanently. Some people lose their minds completely, forever. Some are changed. I saw things…" the doctor stopped.

"You were over there?" asked Robbie. *Maybe that's why he drinks.*

"Yes," said the doctor. "I was over there and I saw…terrible things." His voice was rising again. "I don't want to talk about it. But you're right. The war changed everyone that was there. Call it shellshock or whatever you want. And no, it is not like senility. You never forget."

They made all kinds of house calls. There were pregnant women who were ashamed of showing their bulk in public; there were cuts that needed to be stitched; limbs to be straightened; boils that needed to be lanced; fevers that needed to be reduced. These patients either had no way of getting to the doctor or were so incapacitated that he had to go to them. Some of them would have been better off in hospital, but they didn't have the money.

Another old woman they visited had an infected toenail bothering her. Her house was so cold you could see your breath inside. The stink almost bowled him over.

The doctor took Robbie aside, "She has to go to hospital. Gangrene. I knew that smell as soon as we walked in that door."

Robbie shook his head. Another poor old woman living alone and afraid, in so much space. Too bad there wasn't some kind of Homes where abandoned seniors and children could live together. And he didn't mean a place like the Poor House. A place where they could help each other.

As he dropped off the poor woman at the hospital for a probable amputation, he knew that he was learning invaluable lessons that somewhere, sometime would come in handy. *You never know.*

CHAPTER NINE

By late November, the cold had set in. He had held out as long as he could, but staying there over winter was impossible. He'd had to move to the house.

Since he'd been sleeping there, he'd been woken up frequently. He couldn't put his finger on the reason, but something had changed in the room: there was a swirl of displaced air or the ghost of a sound, like raspy breathing or a sigh.

Whatever it was, when he woke, he'd always just caught the end of it and was unable to identify what it was. At first, he'd dismissed it as part of a dream, but it was happening too often and was too real. After the first few times, he lit a candle and got out of bed, sliding into his slippers and looking into the corners. Nothing. Except one time the shirt he'd hung on the door handle was on the floor.

He asked Miss Bruce about it, but she shrugged and said, "It's probably a draught."

"A draught? No, Miss Bruce, it can't be. The candle flame doesn't even flicker."

"Well, I don't know, then," she said sharply for her. "You must be dreaming."

He slipped a hard, heavy two-by-four under the bed. And then, every night he lay awake, waiting for it, whatever it was. But invariably, he was so tired that he fell asleep.

***

The doctor and his old maid sister were driving him around the bend. At least in the carriage house he'd been able to escape. Now, he had to go for a long walk in the evenings or he had to go to his room early. It was bad enough to be with one of them on their own, but, when they were together, it was like the light of life had been extinguished from the room.

One night, he was sure it was the click of his door closing that had awoken him. He jumped up and ran to it. He saw Miss Bruce's door close. In the morning, he confronted her in the kitchen. "Miss Bruce, you were disturbed by the same noise as me last night, weren't you?"

"No, I wasn't." She was busy putting dishes away. "I told you before it was probably a draught."

Dr. Bruce had come into the kitchen at this point. He was having trouble knotting his tie with his fluttering fingers. His sister took over for him. As she tied it, he looked down at the ground, and her eyes didn't stray from her task.

So what was it?

The telephone rang. Everyone listened. Two short rings, one long. That was their signal on the party line. Miss Bruce answered and wrote some information on the roster. "Three calls this morning. The first two sound urgent. The second is a high fever." She was curt.

In the car, Dr. Bruce said, "Is something going on that I should know about?"

Robbie explained. The doctor wiped the sides of his mouth. "Well, I guess she's started again."

"Sorry?"

"She sleepwalks," he said. "That's the reason why the last young man left. It unnerved him."

"Is there nothing that can be done?"

"No. Nothing," said the doctor looking at the notes his sister had written. "We've tried all the cures. I'll have to up her dosage of laudanum."

"Is there a reason?"

Dr. Bruce glanced at him, with that irritating look over his glasses.

"Not that I know of," he said. "Just lock your door and she won't bother you anymore. Now let's get on with the day."

***

One late evening when Robbie came back from a long walk, he saw a light on in the sitting room. Dr. Bruce was usually in bed by this time unless he was well under the influence. He pulled off his overcoat and his scarf and hung them up at the back door.

"Lydia has gone to bed early. I've already given her the tonic. She had a headache." Dr. Bruce's eyes were a little out of focus. "You know that she doesn't like it when I drink. But don't worry, she'll sleep through anything tonight." He was holding a large glass of scotch. "Throw another log on the fire. Grab a glass. Sit down." He gulped and grimaced.

As Robbie held out his glass, the doctor took his wrist. He filled his glass halfway, smiled and didn't let go. When Robbie pulled away, he laughed. He was well gone.

Robbie sipped his drink. Funny, he was Scottish but he had no stomach for scotch. It unsettled him. He straightened up in his seat.

"Bottoms up," said Dr. Bruce as he drained his glass. He filled it again. "And, Robbie, call me Larry."

"Thank you, Dr. Bruce, Larry."

"Don't you like Toronto? I do. Everybody minds their own business here." It was the first time he'd seen Dr. Bruce with his glasses off. His words were slurred. "Let's drink to Howard Ferguson, his Conservatives and the end of this bloody prohibition! Let's put on the gramophone. Have a little music. Why don't you put on, hmmm, *The Old Grey Mare."*

Robbie got up and shuffled through the records. An opportunity to play the gramophone! The doctor was singing, "The Old Grey Mare ain't what she used to be, ain't what she used to be…"

"Yes, Dr. Larry. It beats living in the sticks," Robbie said while he took the record out of its sleeve and put it on the turntable. "It was lonely out on the farm."

Dr. Bruce wasn't listening.

When the record was over he laughed. "The old grey mare," he said, "My sister. And that's all she'll ever be now." He took another drink and his smile faded. "One mistake. One lousy mistake and I'm saddled with her for the rest of my life."

Robbie sipped his drink, saying nothing. The doctor was staring into his drink uncertainly like it held a message.

"She asked me to do it." He looked up but his gaze was unfocused. "But you wouldn't know about that. You don't have a sister."

"Yes, I do," said Robbie painfully. "Her name is Emma."

"Oh, my dear Sir. You're a man of mystery." The doctor raised his glass. "Emma. What a pretty name. Is she pretty? Do you love her?"

"I haven't seen her in a long time," said Robbie.

Dr. Bruce leaned forward confidentially. "She asked me to do it, she begged me to do it. We were so young."

Robbie recoiled. He got up and moved toward the gramophone.

Another record. Quick. Drown him out. I don't want to hear any more.

Before he could get it on, the doctor said, "Her hands, her lips, her thighs. There was no one else in our small town that came close to her beauty." He took a breath.

"When I came back from the war, I had terrible nights. I screamed. She slept on the divan in my room but often had to lie in bed and hold me till the fit passed. She was the only one who helped me get over the horrible things." Dr. Bruce blew his nose. He got up and paced awkwardly, wiping his eyes on his sleeve, sloshing his drink. "She was so kind and so beautiful and sad." He lit a cigarette and offered one to Robbie.

"Her fiancé died in the war. We were each other's comfort." He took another large gulp and looked at Robbie, "Do you know what I mean?"

Robbie put the record on the turntable.

"Wait! And then…I had to help her. Something went wrong and there was so much blood. Blood and…"

Robbie dropped the needle on the record.

"Hey, be careful with that!"

Robbie's head was beginning to pound. *"The Turkey Waltz"* started. The doctor was holding his glass tightly in his hands. He looked up and yelled, "Take that shit off and leave me alone!" He threw his glass across the room.

Robbie picked up the needle and made his way toward the door. As he opened it, Dr. Bruce said, "Ever mention this to anyone and I'll wring your neck." Then he sat back in his chair and closed his eyes.

Robbie tossed and turned until the grey winter light filled the room.

In the morning, Dr. Bruce was his same cold self and Miss Bruce handed Robbie the roster. For her sake, Robbie tried to act as normally as possible. Those two were both still paying for what had happened.

CHAPTER TEN

Robbie picked himself up off the ice. He dusted the snow off the knees of his trousers and noticed that there was a tear in the fabric. Sighing, he painfully skated over to the bench at the side of the rink. His feet were sore, mangled by wallowing around in the two-sizes-too-large borrowed skates; his knees and back were killing him from falling every five seconds, but worst of all, his pride was hurt. He absolutely hated being the jackass of any sport. Led by Fred, the boys laughingly told him to get a pair of girly skates.

If he didn't like Alex so much, he'd have a go at that smarmy Fred. He could knock the chip off his shoulder with one hand tied behind his back. But Fred was Alex's good pal.

Alex sailed by him on the ice, with glowing cheeks and an ease that no amount of practising could ever help Robbie match. She called for him to join her but he waved and smiled bravely. He unlaced the skates and when he got them off, massaged his feet. He really didn't know how he was going to get his shoes on. Alex, on her next lap, stopped.

She looks so alive.

In the short time he'd known her she'd grown up. The sharpness of her tomboyish body had softened as well as her demeanour.

"Giving up so soon?" she asked.

Robbie pulled down his sock to show her the bloody blister on his heel. "I like skating but it doesn't like me."

"Oh," she said. "That's looks terrible. Why didn't you say anything sooner?"

Robbie shrugged. "It doesn't really hurt."

"Of course it does," Alex said, unlacing her skates. "Let's go."

They walked away from the rink arm-in-arm, Robbie with his jaw set and trying not to limp, Alex trying to help him take the weight off his heels.

"You just need to get the right size skates," she suggested.

Robbie stopped. "Alex, skates are expensive and I have to save some money, if we ever want to…"

"Want to what?"

"Never mind," Robbie said. "We'll cross that bridge when we come to it."

Alex hugged his arm more tightly.

Robbie had met Alex at a lightly drizzling Remembrance Day service that he'd attended more to see the ceremony than out of respect. He'd been chain smoking, and moving from one foot to the other, trying to keep warm while watching the soldiers in uniform march toward him, most of them out of shape and out of breath.

The Union Jack flew at half mast in the park and as they passed it, the soldiers saluted it.

The poor suckers. They all look so proud.

Most of the veterans that Robbie had asked, didn't really know much about the war - except that the Germans were trying to beat the rest of Europe into submission. But Robbie knew it had been much more full of twists and turns than that. Complicated, yet as simple as children taunting other children in the playground. The politicians, the ones pulling the strings on both sides, had let them down, like they always did. Those bastards had conned tens of thousands into dirty, stinking holes for four years and let them kill each other in increasingly malicious and hair-raising ways.

For God's sake. Why did I come here to watch guys who were content to be their pawns and hear about how they fought for our freedom? It never gave me mine.

He inhaled and then coughed. He tossed his cigarette. He was starting to get cold. He rubbed his hands and then stuck them inside his jacket under his arms.

It would disrupt too many people if he started to push through the widows and their children. They still had to believe their loss was important – just so they could carry on.

He listened to the chaplain's empty words of honour and glory, heard the *"Naval Hymn"* and *"O God Our Help in Ages Past"*, and watched as different contingents laid wreaths. His stomach churned. He hated remembering about what the war had done to his family.

He was looking down at a fallen, brilliantly red maple leaf when he heard the stanza from the poem, *"In Flander's Fields"*.

If ye break faith with us who die, we shall not sleep.

He hadn't heard it before but it stirred something deep down inside him. In the two minutes of silence that followed, as if in slow motion, he heard the sound of a boy sniffle and then wipe his nose on his sleeve, heard the flap of wings of a bird landing on a branch overhead, listened to a dog with bared teeth bark. People shuffled their feet.

Tears came to his eyes. He brushed them away. He clamped his mouth tightly shut when the lone piper played, *"The Lament"*.

A girl, a very pretty girl, standing next to him, nudged him and handed him a hankie. After they sang, *"God Save the King"*, everyone placed their poppies on the ground around the wreaths. As the crowd dispersed, a gust of wind scattered the blood red felt flowers.

The girl, wearing a tam and matching gloves, spoke to him, "All those men going off to get killed was so terribly wrong." She turned her head away. "I shouldn't be saying that."

Robbie offered her a cigarette. She declined. He lit his last and crumpled the packet.

"I am trying to remember what my father looked like, but I can't. He died on the battlefield when I was seven. My uncle made it through the war unscathed but died of the Spanish flu in England after everything was over," the girl said. "Wasn't that ironic?"

"What about you?" the girl asked him. "That is, if you want to talk about it."

"I lost my father and my Uncle Duncan to the war."

"Oh, your father and your uncle, too? Just like me. How awful."

"Yes," Robbie said. "But you're right. I don't want to talk about it."

The girl misread his coldness for grief. "Yes, of course, I didn't mean to intrude."

"You're not."

"Where are you from?"

"Scotland."

Her green eyes sparkled.

"My background is Scottish and English."

This put Robbie off slightly. He sighed.

Why do Canadians always have to clarify their heritage, as if being Canadian is never enough?

"And a touch of Irish. But I am really Canadian. I was born right here in Toronto." She tucked a piece of errant hair away. *What have I said to annoy him?*

"What is a Canadian anyway?" There was a tinge of sarcasm in his voice. *For God's sake, stop it.* Then he said, "Sorry. The service upset me. You look cold. Would you like a cup of tea to warm up?"

She looked at him, deciding.

He reddened. *I've blown it.*

"Well, oh yes, why not?" she said. "But where?"

"Anywhere you like."

"Fine but before we go, there's one thing you need to tell me."

"Yes," said Robbie warily. "What?"

"Your name. Mine's Alex for short. Alex MacRae."

"It suits you. I'm Robbie James."

Robbie had tea and Alex had coffee and Robbie splurged on biscuits for them both. When he accidentally poured too much sugar into his tea, Alex raised her eyebrows at the amount. "I always drink tea like this," Robbie said grimacing at the sweetness.

"Oh, sure you do," she laughed.

She was the easiest person in the world to talk to. Maybe because she did most of the talking. In fact, she was a regular chatterbox. Robbie wondered what in the world she saw in him.

After finding out that Robbie was fairly new to the city, she had invited him to join their gang, as she called it. It certainly beat hanging around old Paddy and the men at the Legion. They went to the moving pictures, dances at local clubs and when it got cold enough, out came the skates.

The boys in the gang all played hockey; the girls, giggling and holding hands, tried twirls and figure eights on the ice. Robbie stayed in the corner, stiff as a board, trying to get his feet to glide. But he fell and he was cold and his feet hurt, every single time.

As they walked away from the rink, Robbie swore nothing would get him back on the ice. Never again. Not even Alex.

***

Alex's friends had recognized them as a couple almost right from the beginning. They all had British roots. The first time he met them at a dance, Fred was the first to stick his hand out to him, saying, "Scottie, a friend of Alex's is always a friend of mine." Of the boys, Fred was by far the more smartly dressed and well-manicured of the lot but that didn't make him the best-looking. He had an oblong head, covered by thick, well-cut gingery hair. There was something Robbie couldn't put his finger on, right from the beginning, that made him dislike him. He was sure the feeling was mutual.

The others introduced themselves. All the boys had nicknames except Fred. There was 'Sec', who couldn't decide quickly; 'Fish', who swam like one; 'Joe', whose real name was Harry and 'Hap', who was always in a good mood. They were all around the same age.

Robbie was proud of being with Alex, who everyone said was such a good sport. Yet, he had trouble making her out. She said she was a good church-going girl, indignant with any of the boys who took the Lord's name in vain, yet she sipped on the illegal silver flasks and wildly abandoned herself to dances. She was especially good at the shimmy and Robbie didn't like the way men looked at her when she let herself go, eyes closed.

Alex also danced with other men whenever he wouldn't dance with her.

For the slow dances, she came back to him breathless and would whisper in his ear until he smiled again. And then, with a wink she would run off with her girls to do the Bunny Hop or the Butterfly. The fringe that was sewn to her white dress whipped about her twisting body.

After a few times out, Robbie realized that Fred was always hovering nearby. *Big Brother is a good nickname for him. Or Greyfriars Bobbie, the dog who never left his master's grave.* Then he had it. *Neeps. Turnip in Scottish. He is the colour of one.*

One night when Fred offered him a cigarette out of a silver monogrammed case, Robbie took one and lit it from the proffered silver lighter. "Scottie," Fred had waited for a lull in the music, "enjoying yourself?"

"Fine, 'Neeps', just fine."

"What's that mean, Scottie?" He said that in a threatening tone. The gang was on his side. He was their link to all the clubs.

"It's a Scottish word for a natty dresser, Neeps."

"Don't know if I like it, Scottie."

"Don't know if I like Scottie, Neeps." Robbie crushed his cigarette in the ashtray. "My name's Robbie. That's a good enough nickname for me."

Fred glared for a moment, then took out his flask, "All right, Robbie." He offered him a swig. "Don't you work for a doctor?"

"Yes, I do."

"Do you think you could get him to write some prescriptions for us?"

"For what?"

"For booze, of course. The doctors call it nerve tonic. They are filled at the pharmacy. How else do you think we get the good stuff? It's safer than from a bootlegger or moon shiner." The penny dropped. That's how the doctor got his liquor. He had his finger on the source.

"I can try," Robbie said. The music swelled into a sad song. Alex came over and slung her arms around his neck. "Come on, Robbie, my handsome Highlander."

Robbie had it made, so he thought. Not only had he captured the heart of a beautiful girl but his ability to procure prescriptions from the doctor made him sought after. And although he knew the reasons for the sudden change in his status, he was still pleased.

Things are finally going my way.

***

Robbie had decided that she was the one. He had to tell her about his past, though, before things went any further. He needed the right moment. He waited for it.

Flu season settled in and it was a hard few months leading up to Christmas. The poor old people suffered the most and Robbie spent extra hours trying to make them comfortable. He went to a few parties with Alex but they were rarely alone and then they always seemed to be rushed. He decided to wait until she got back from her annual Christmas trip to visit her grandmother in Kingston.

During her absence, Robbie was hit with a bout of horrible stomach flu and was confined to bed. Miss Bruce hadn't been too sharp in the mornings since her brother had strengthened her nerve tonic, but, when she was able, she brought him tea and toast. He spent a lonely festive season in bed, sweating it out.

On Christmas Eve, when he finally felt good enough to come downstairs to sit by the fire, carollers came to the doctor's door and, as if on cue, while they were singing *"O Little Town of Bethlehem"* and *"O Holy Night"*, snowflakes drifted down, sparkling in the moonlight. Robbie suddenly longed for Mount Zion, the church at the Homes back in Scotland and the children raising their voices together. He missed the anticipation of the gift trees, *"The Ham and Egg Song"*, the treats on New Year's Day.

Strange. He had never thought he would miss the orphanage.

Miss Bruce gave the carollers oranges and one of her rare smiles. Seeing the oranges made Robbie remember Tom and his first Christmas at the Homes and he grew melancholy and withdrew to his room.

The rest of Christmas was a quiet affair with Dr. Bruce, his sister and Robbie having dinner and unpacking a few presents. The doctor and his sister indulged each other with chocolate and Turkish Delight, Miss Bruce's favourite jellied candy. Robbie was given a plaid scarf. He gave the doctor a cigar and Miss Bruce a little vase.

After he came back in from a short after dinner walk, he excused himself. He went to his room and threw himself on the bed and cried softly into his pillow. At that very moment, he really felt like he was an orphan. This had been a bad Christmas and this house was sadder than anywhere he'd lived before. Dr. Bruce and his sister had been dead longer than they had been alive.

CHAPTER ELEVEN

He used a toothpick to pick his teeth clean. Like every Sunday, the Irish stew at the diner had been nicely seasoned except the beef that they had used today must have come from an old bull. It was stringy. But he had eaten it all anyway, and used his bread and butter to clean the bowl. Water was all that was to be had for drinking but he didn't mind. He could take or leave drinking. Right now his money was better spent on food.

He splurged on dessert, getting a beautiful piece of lemon meringue pie. He was tempted to lick the plate, it was so good. And like every Sunday, he got up off the round stool and went out for a walk. It was such a beautiful sunny day that he bought a newspaper and went down to the beach to read it and relax. *The sky is blue, the birds are singing and I have a job.*

***

He left the Bruce siblings almost exactly three years ago. That winter was cold and bitter and there was plenty of snow to shovel and ice to clear. After the flu epidemic waned, there were many broken bones to set, temperatures to bring down and heart attacks to nurture back to health. He was kept busy.

Despite the sadness of some of the cases, Robbie was happy to stay on at his job. He had a girl, was saving money and was well-respected. When Alex finally got him to meet her mother, even she gave him a polite smile, although she was such a bitter old widow.

***

Robbie, like everyone else, got caught up in the euphoria of growth and prosperity of Toronto in the summer of 1927. There were buildings shooting up everywhere. Robbie began to think that there might be something bigger in his future. Maybe he could start up a business.

"But what could you do?" Alex said.

"I'll find something," he replied, surprised.

"Make sure you talk to me before you do anything."

"Yes, of course. I'll ask for your permission the next time I tie my shoes."

"Robbie, don't be childish," she said. "I know the city better than you do."

She sounded like her mother.

Robbie said, "Thanks for your vote of confidence."

But she kissed him then and everything that had been said was *almost* forgotten.

On the golden wave of affluence, even prohibition was being lifted, despite the year-old referendum that had narrowly upheld it. Robbie's flow of so-called pals, who had been dropping by frequently before, slowly dwindled off into nothing. They didn't need the prescriptions anymore.

June, July and August went by in a haze of heat. And as he walked along the boardwalk one sleepless night to get some relief, he tried to, but found it hard to imagine, what this same stretch of beach was like in the winter. He sat down and looked up at the stunning moon.

He was a coward. He still hadn't told Alex.

Not being sure of her reaction, distressed him. He had nothing to be ashamed of, but there was something in the upward tilt of her chin whenever they discussed the unemployed or poverty that was like a red flag, stopping him in his tracks.

One day, the perfect lead-in occurred when Robbie took off his top after swimming to change into something dry and Alex caught sight of his disfigurement. But he only told her that he tipped hot water on himself as a child. She put her hand on his chest lightly and the moment passed.

Instead, he chose to bask in the innocence of that summer; throwing rugs on the sand and having picnics. Dancing under the stars with his girl in his arms, swimming, boating or just strolling along the boardwalk.

The boys tried to teach Robbie baseball but he always seemed to have the sun in his eyes when he was trying to catch the ball. They laughed at him just like they'd done when he'd been trying to learn to skate.

At the end of August, although it was still hot, there was that familiar nip in the air in the evenings.

Robbie was losing control. The alluring scent of her, the fluid way Alex walked, the way she blushed when she caught him hungrily eyeing her. He could look at no other girl. He had to ask her to be his wife.

And what better way than an upcoming marriage to force the doctor into giving him a raise. But away from her, sanity prevailed. His was a no-win situation. If he told her about his sorry past, she'd think he wasn't good enough. If he didn't tell her and she found out, which she was sure to, she'd be wondering what else he was trying to hide.

***

In October, Tom appeared on his doorstep. He decided to see what the big city was like for himself. He ran away from the farm he'd been on because he was bored, he'd said. He was going to British Columbia for the winter to cut down trees. "Why don't you come with me? They need strong men like us."

"You're fifteen," Robbie said running his hands through his hair. "You have to stay on a farm until you're eighteen. That's the deal."

"Who's going to make me?"

"You've got bats in the belfry. You have no papers."

"What do I care about papers?"

"You can't go back to Scotland without papers."

Tom shrugged.

Robbie licked his lips in frustration. Tom wasn't going to listen to him. He tried another tack. "Did you ask dad what to do?"

"No." There was a look of uncertainty on Tom's face.

"How would he feel about you running away?"

Tom looked down.

At that moment, Robbie knew he had him. "And you won't get any of the money that Fairknowe House has on account for you."

Reluctantly, the next day, Tom sent off a letter to the farmer apologizing and promising to return in a few days.

Robbie made him scrub up, clean under his fingernails and bought him a new jacket.

He sat Tom down before they went out. "Don't tell my friends we're from the Homes."

"Why? Are you ashamed?" Tom asked.

"This has nothing to do with you," Robbie said. "I don't want to be a Home Boy any more. I work for a doctor. These people respect me. I am their equal."

"No, you're not, if you can't be yourself."

"I AM myself. This is what I am now."

"What lies do you want me to tell them?" The familiar sneer had come back into his voice.

***

Tom had already been in the carriage house for a few days before the doctor met him. Dr. Bruce had been under the weather and had stayed in his room. He wasn't smiling when he finally came down for breakfast. The doctor raised an eyebrow when he saw Tom, "So this is the brother you came over to Canada with?"

Tom said, "Yes."

"How old are you?"

"Fifteen," Tom said before Robbie could stop him.

"So if you are fifteen now and you came over three years ago, that would have made you twelve." The doctor raised an eyebrow at Robbie.

"Yes," an uncomfortable Tom said.

"How did your parents let you two go at such a young age?" He was sharp and irritable. "Is there something you want to tell me?"

Robbie said nothing.

"Let me help you. You two scallywags ran away from home and were stowaways on a ship."

"No," Tom said. "We were sent here. Our passage was paid."

"By whom?"

Robbie suddenly burst. He was under no obligation to explain himself. He'd worked hard for the man. He could barely control himself, "It's none of your business."

"Yes, it is if you want to work here!" Dr. Bruce said. His sister came out of the kitchen to see why there'd been raised voices. "I have my reputation to think about."

That does it.

Robbie walked over to the doctor and grabbed him by the front of his shirt.

"Your reputation?" Robbie shouted, "Let's talk about you and your sister!"

Miss Bruce blanched and ran from the room and Robbie let the doctor go. Tom looked from one to the other. "Get out of my house! You're fired!" the doctor snarled at him.

"You can't fire me. I don't want to work for the likes of you." Robbie stormed off back to the carriage house followed by Tom.

"What's going on, Robbie?" Tom said quietly.

Robbie couldn't answer him.

Miss Bruce came in as he was packing his few belongings. She looked ten years older. "I'm sorry, Robbie," she said. "You've been the best worker we've ever had. If you need a reference, I'll be happy to give you one." She got out her purse and paid his wages and included a little extra.

Robbie's feet were pulled out from under him yet again. First he had to find a place to stay. Then he had to tell Alex. They walked down to Queen Street where there were a few boarding houses.

He left it until after the pictures to tell her. Alex was so busy gushing over Mary Pickford that they'd gone to see, she didn't notice Robbie's obvious discomfort.

"I wish I looked like her."

Robbie didn't answer her.

"Tom, meet me at the boarding house."

"Why isn't your brother staying with you? Won't the doctor allow it?"

Robbie cleared his throat. "He is. I'm staying there too." He tried to sound confident. "Alex, I've given the old man my walking papers."

"What do you mean?" she stopped and looked alarmed.

"I've quit."

"Do you have another job?" she said.

"No."

"Why, then?"

"Believe me, if I could have stayed, I would have. I loved that job." He took her hands. "It's just that doctor. I can't stand him anymore. If you only knew…"

"Knew what?" she said. "Robbie, go back to him. Apologize. Maybe he'll take you back."

"I can't." Robbie had thought about the misery in Miss Bruce's face. For her sake, he couldn't tell anyone.

"But for us to have a future together…" Her voice had quavered. "Mum doesn't approve of you as it is. She keeps saying a man who doesn't go to church can't be relied upon."

"Well, you can tell her that when I was young, I went to enough church services to last me a lifetime," Robbie had said. "Don't worry about what your mother says. I just have to make sure Tom gets back and then I'll find something."

She jerked her hands away. "Something?" She looked like she was going to cry. "Where are you going to get another steady, respectable job? You said you were going to talk to me first before you did anything."

"I guess you just have to believe in me."

"You're not telling me everything."

"I can't, Alex," Robbie said, frustrated. "Some things just can't be spoken about."

"Fine, Robbie." She removed her hands from his and turned away. "Take me home."

"Come on, Alex."

"I just want to go home," she said. The walk was swift and silent.

***

Robbie was true to his word. He sent Tom back on the train. After paying for the ticket, he was almost skint but within a few days he got work finishing the exteriors of houses. It was on a daily hire basis. Soon it'd be too cold for this kind of job, so he spent every day working for fourteen hours, six days a week, saving every penny. His time with Alex was brief and rare.

He still thought about marriage when he kissed those sweet lips of hers, but wasn't sure anymore that she would say yes. Robbie put it out of his mind. He had nothing to offer, at that moment.

Alex became a full-fledged seamstress and started earning money of her own. She convinced her mother to let her hold an early Christmas party for the gang that she would pay for. Her mother thought it frivolous, but as they were going to go away for a couple of weeks again, she acquiesced. Alex spent days planning, decorating and baking.

Robbie showed up late for the party, sincerely apologetic: he hadn't been able to get away. "It's okay," she said loud enough for everyone to hear, "we were having a good time without you." And laughed, like it was a joke. The way she looked at him, he wasn't sure it was one.

Round about the same time that Alex and her mother left, the work dried up. He was lonely, tired and cold. With no work and without her, he shyly lost touch with her friends. He had enough money for the tiny, dismal room he rented, only because he saved every spare penny. There was little heat and little light. During the day, he looked for a job in the newspapers in the library at Queen and Lee. At night, he only had a few candles for warmth and shivered in his room. When he looked out of draughty window, he could see thick white flakes of snow drifting down. He started to cough. He decided he needed the money he had on account in Brockville if he wanted to make it through the winter.

Again, it took him a few days to get there. He spent a night in an abandoned rail car and two in different barns piling fresh straw on himself to keep warm. When he arrived at Fairknowe House, he was on his last legs, shivering with fever and coughing up yellow phlegm. In his despair, he prayed for the first time in ages.

Please Lord; let them have room for me.

And there was. After a bath, he collapsed into a freshly made bed and asked for a doctor. Grimsby stood in the doorway of the room, his hands on his hips. "You look like a tramp."

"Thanks," he said and closed his eyes.

The doctor left him some eye-watering drops to rub on his chest. Later, when Robbie saw the bill, he shook his head. The doctor did little for him that he couldn't have done for himself.

After a week's rest and good food, he was told that he could get some work on a farm cutting down the bush for firewood, for the few winter months left and Robbie took it, happy to be working at all. He didn't want to touch his savings unless he had to. He wrote to Alex, telling her he would be back in the spring.

He was hired at full pay, and two months slipped into three and then he helped with the planting and tending of the crops. The summer passed and it was almost his birthday, again. He was offered to finish up the season with a bonus. He thought that this would pad his pockets nicely while he looked for a job in the city.

The frequency of Alex's letters slowed and didn't she say she missed him anymore. She didn't say she loved him. She talked about swimming and canoeing at the beach and how she was busy at her job as more and more people preferred to alter their clothes than buy new ones.

When she wrote about how wonderful it was that Fred's father had given him a promotion, he had a strange feeling. He had to go back.

Stopping in Brockville to leave his money at Fairknowe House on account, he asked for news of Tom. He was relieved to hear that Tom was working full-time and they had good reports from his employer.

He thought it was about time Tom smartened up. He was, after all, old enough.

He pondered taking the train back but the rail fare was worth more in his own pocket. Back in the city, he rented a room at the same Queen Street rooming house as before. He cleaned up, put his Sunday suit on and went to see Alex at her work. A bell jingled when the door opened and there she was, pinning a woman's skirt. She blushed, "Robbie! So good to see you!" she said after taking the pins out of her mouth. "Can you come back in about twenty minutes?"

She was as beautiful as ever. But there was something wrong.

He stood across the street, watching the door, waiting for the woman to leave. When she was gone, he crossed the street with dread in his heart. The look on her face stopped him cold.

"Robbie, what are you doing here?"

What a strange question it was to ask.

"It was meant to be a surprise." He kept his distance.

"I didn't know if you were ever coming back."

She looked at a point over his shoulder. "I wish I didn't have to tell you this."

"Tell me what?"

"I'm engaged." She held up her left hand to show him the ring, "Fred and I are getting married."

"Fred?"

"Yes, I'm going to marry Fred."

"But what about us?"

"Us?"

"Yes. I thought we had an understanding."

"Yes. We did. Kind of. But you were gone so long."

"Alex... I wrote to you."

"Those two-line letters kept saying you were coming back soon. But you didn't."

"I thought you knew how I felt."

"You never asked me to marry you. You never told me how you felt."

Robbie searched her face for anything that would give him hope. She looked away.

"I waited almost a year for you," she said. "It's too late."

Robbie looked down at his clenched hands.

Fred had better not cross his path.

Suddenly, it was clear. "Your mother put you up to this." Robbie turned on his heel and slammed the door behind him. The bells jingled furiously. In front of her little shop, he kicked the mailbox that was just outside the door and then punched it. The force of his hand hitting the hard metal made him swear. A woman, who was walking by, shook her head.

Alex opened the door. "Robbie…"

Nursing his hand and fighting back tears, he strode off.

He spent his twenty-first birthday, drinking slowly but steadily. As he sat in the tavern, alone, he thought that he couldn't blame her. He was a loser and Fred was a winner. If he were her, he would have made the same choice.

***

It was on everybody's lips. The stock market crashed. Overnight, the world had changed. Nothing was certain. People stopped spending. Companies stopped hiring. Robbie's applications were turned down at place after place.

He stayed for a couple of months at a flop house that was cheaper than the rooming house. He had a few days of work here and there with builders but construction had come to a screeching halt. Even the grandiose plan to modernize downtown that had everyone talking just the year before, was scrapped.

To Robbie, it seemed like his luck turned when the doctor confided in him. If he didn't know, he would still have work, friends, a girl and most important - respect.

He thought that for God's sake, there were skeletons in everyone's closets. They just needed to be kept there.

***

He was getting nowhere in Toronto and he knew he could get work back down near Brockville clearing bush for the winter again. He had to tide himself over till the spring. A roof over his head, food in his belly and maybe he could see Tom again.

Before he left, he ran into Sec and Hap on Queen Street. "How are you, old man?" they greeted him, pumping his arm up and down. "Didn't know you were back," Hap said. "What're you doing?" All mention of Fred and Alex was avoided, just as they avoided looking at him.

"Going down to see my brother," Robbie said. "For Christmas."

"Hey, that's good news, that's great. Happy Christmas!" Sec said.

"Yeah, you too."

Off Robbie went then, his thumb out and his collar up, one last time.

***

Tom was way up north. The farmer he was working for couldn't afford him anymore and Grimsby sent him to work on a lumber camp run by a former Home Boy. He asked for Robbie's address before he left, but they didn't have one to give him.

Robbie found odd jobs like painting, fixing floors and ceilings and cleaning out eaves for the rich but it just kept his head above water. Headlines in the newspapers were alarming. In Montreal and Toronto, stocks were plummeting, people's life savings were wiped out, and unemployment was rising. Soup kitchens in the cities were doing a brisk business. Suicide rates were soaring.

The best way to get Alex out of his head was to work. Keep his head down. Work until he was so exhausted that all he could think about was crawling into bed. If he had no work, he walked until he could barely put one foot in front of the other. Gradually the pain of her subsided.

But he still felt a great sadness. The future he allowed himself to dream about was no longer to be. He didn't want to be a hired hand for the rest of his life but he didn't have much experience other than in farming, construction and being an assistant to a doctor. Alex was right. He was useless.

One day, on a farm where he had found work, one of the farmer's children came down with a terrible fever. Unfortunately, a heavy, bitter Arctic storm made the roads impassable for a few days. The farmer got his horse and sleigh out to press down the snow but it was slow-going and the farmer, after exhausting himself and the horses, came in half frozen to death.

As he had done with the elderly before, Robbie stayed with the little girl until her temperature broke, applying cold compresses to her calves and spooning liquid into her mouth. Coaxing her back to health. A few days later, when the doctor managed to get through, the little girl was sitting up. The doctor congratulated him, saying he couldn't have done more himself. Susan, the little girl, gave him a hug and a kiss on the cheek that was worth more than anything.

After this, Robbie wanted to go back to Toronto and get a job helping people.

When the crocuses started to peep up through the snow, he said his good-byes and went back to the city. He took all the money from his account at Fairknowe. He was not going back.

Despite all the jobless roaming the streets, lining up by the hundreds at building sites or down by the docks, Robbie took looking for a job seriously. After a day of pounding the streets, he took off his shirt and washed it out in the basin in his room. Then he washed his socks. Every morning, he got up at sunrise and shaved and had his tea. He didn't want to look like the dishevelled, desperate rest with their sweat-stained vests and onions on their breath.

The hospitals desperately needed help but weren't hiring. He was told he could volunteer, if he liked but that wasn't an option. He needed cash.

After six weeks, when he'd almost given up, Robbie got a job as a milkman at Roster dairies, one of the largest in the city. He was proud of himself although he conceded that he had a little luck. A Scotsman was doing the hiring. "Got to take care of our own," he said. "And you look like you mean business."

And as Robbie left the diner after his lemon meringue pie, he knew his luck had finally changed for the better.

***

Robbie took his *Toronto Star* down to the Beach on Sundays. It was one of the cooler spots in the city, with a soft breeze usually coming in off the lake. More and more, the area was teeming with unemployed immigrant picnickers, with the same idea. As he walked through Kew Beach Park right down to the boardwalk, he passed groups of people whose conversations were in languages he didn't understand. It was like the world had sent special envoys to preserve different cultures in a world gone crazy.

Like Noah's Ark.

And it was crawling with kids who ran wild, their fathers paying little attention to them as they stood around speaking loudly in angry groups, unwashed and unshaven. The men's wives always seemed timid to Robbie or perhaps it was defeat he was reading into their demeanour.

The world-wide economy was getting worse. In Ontario, with twenty percent out of work, the new immigrants were not hired or were the first to go. Single men were also badly off. Any jobs were given to men who were White-Anglo-Saxon-Protestants with families. Drifters were run out of town.

Not only that, but wages were being reduced to keep more men working. At the dairy, Robbie's were cut by half.

It seemed at work, in the tavern, at the dances or among friends, all everyone was talking about was the price of things and how they were trying to make ends meet.

By 1933, over thirty percent of eligible workers in Toronto were unemployed. On average, wages for people with jobs had dropped to sixty percent of what people were making four years before. Robbie was being faced with more and more mothers who tried to get credit. Sometimes he let their debt slide. He could all too well remember the crushing humiliation he himself had faced as a child when they had to hide from the milkman or beg stale bread from the baker. He would never be able to forget the worry of wondering when he was going to eat again.

Jimmy Cameron, who'd hired him, warned Robbie to collect.

CHAPTER TWELVE

"These people need to get their priorities in order. We'll both get the sack if you keep it up," said Jimmy.

"They have nothing to pay with."

"Come on Robbie. They have vouchers."

"It's not enough. These are families with small children."

Jimmy sighed. "Well, Robbie, you can either pay their bills yourself or you will be replaced. And you'll end up riding the rails. No one wants to hire an unmarried man." Jimmy crossed his arms.

***

Robbie scrutinized the newspaper every day. He hoped to see light in the darkness. But there it was, hidden sometimes, but ever present – the despair. And the government did nothing. They had stopped spending, too. And to top it all off, a motion to put a special tax on incomes of over ten thousand was successfully crushed. The idea behind that was the rich needed to be able to spend money to keep the economy going. But the rich didn't spend more money. The poor were getting poorer. Robbie didn't understand how things were going to change.

Robbie's social life had almost come to a halt. Not only did he have fewer wages, he was forced to work longer hours for them. When he finished work, he was usually too tired to go out anywhere.

But there were a few girls.

They were nice girls from the old country: English, Irish and Scots. All were working but they were paid such poor wages for back-breaking work that they wished they weren't.

They couldn't help but see Robbie as a big, fat fish waiting to be hooked. It got to the point where he felt he could only date someone twice before they became possessive – calling him their boyfriend, marking their territory, his cheek, with their lipstick.

If it hadn't been so embarrassing, it would have been funny. Robbie, the undesirable Home Boy; the boy whose mother had abandoned him at the Poor House; the boy, whose father, after picking him up there, had only abandoned him again at the orphanage; the boy, called a "Street Arab" right here in Canada, was now a good catch.

His problem was that he looked for Alex in each and every one of them. But none of them laughed like Alex, none of them had her green eyes and none of them drove him to distraction, like she had.

His heart still ached and deep down in his soul, he believed that he was meant to live a lonely life.

***

He ran into Sec and Alex's girlfriend Winnie, on the first warm day of May. He was truly glad to see them; they had always been genuine people. And good friends to Alex, too.

"Robbie," Winnie called. "It's so good to see you. You look well. Are you working?"

They chatted for a few moments until Winnie blurted out, "You know, Alex didn't marry Fred."

"That's too bad." Robbie cleared his throat.

"Yes. His father's business took quite a beating and they lost almost everything," Winnie continued. "I had a talk to Alex and asked her if she really wanted to be tied to that miserable so-and-so for the rest of her life. The next thing I heard was that they had split up." Winnie smiled. "She is available."

Robbie struggled with his pride for a few days. But he had to see her, even if it were for one last time. To see if the real Alex could compete with the ghost of her. Once decided, he went quickly to her house and knocked on the front door. The house looked badly in need of a paint job. A strange man, older than Robbie, answered the door in his vest. "What do you want?" The man was bleary-eyed.

"I'm looking for Mrs. MacRae and her daughter."

"Listen, buddy. All the rooms are taken." The man was shutting the door in his face.

Robbie was startled. "This is a rooming house? Do they still live here?"

The man took a stained and crumpled handkerchief out of his pocket and wiped his nose. "She don't live here. I'm in charge of the house for her." He gestured down the street. "Most of these houses are rooming houses now. Where've you been, pal?"

"Do you know where they've gone?"

"Out of town."

"Do you have an address or can I leave a message?"

"Leave a message but hurry up. I just got off my shift and I'm dog tired."

"Do you have a pencil and paper?"

"Do you want me to write it for you, too?" He looked at Robbie's long face. "Okay, just wait a minute."

Heart pounding, Robbie hurriedly scribbled his name and address and he folded it in half with Alex's name on the outside. He passed it to the man. "Can you make sure that Miss MacRae gets this?"

"Sure, buddy," the man yawned and closed the door in his face. He tossed the piece of paper on a messy pile of letters and bills on the table in the hall.

***

Robbie met Annie at a dance in August. Finally, he had found a girl who sparked his interest. Annie was a little on the shy side, just off the boat from England. Jimmy Cameron had gotten some tickets to the Beach Club dance and one of the girls had brought her friend, a young nurse, with her. It seemed like ages since Robbie had set foot in that place.

On his way there, he noticed an even more heated atmosphere on the beach than he'd witnessed before. The groups of immigrant men were animated, pounding their fists against the palms of their hands. There were no women or children to be seen. The men seemed to be gathering into one large group.

He waved it off. The gentler sex had probably been sent packing as dusk was setting in.

Then he saw the reason. At the club, Robbie saw a swastika emblem on a sign out in front. He had heard rumours that there were young men from the club patrolling the beach wearing swastika badges and this had made the hackles of the foreigners rise.

The use of the swastika surprised him but the vying for territory didn't. The Beachers were trying to keep their part of the world safe from those who were changing it. Put a new dog in a room already inhabited by old dogs and they will rarely accept it. He hurried inside.

The band was local but good, and Jimmy told him it was the latest - jazz. To Robbie, it sounded like smoothed-out ragtime with less piano and saucier trumpet. He liked it a lot.

Annie had immediately caught his attention; she had naturally wavy dark hair falling to her shoulders and deep brown eyes. She looked to be in top form and when the first slow dance was played, he tapped her on the shoulder. She was a perfect fit in his arms and she smelled like fresh air coming in off the lake.

When the faster dances were played, she passed on them, like Robbie. But she enjoyed watching, staying by his side, keeping time to the music by patting her hip. She took a sip out of his flask and after grimacing, refused more. "No thanks. Do you drink much?" There was a hint of worry in her voice.

Suddenly, there was a rush to the windows and the veranda. The band stopped playing. Someone yelled, "Girls stay inside. Boys, come on."

Robbie went outside with Jimmy and his friends.

On the perimeter of the club, there were a growing number of burly men armed with baseball bats and broom handles. On the grounds of the club, there were also a large group of youths holding bats and lacrosse sticks.

The groups stood eyeing each other. The police arrived, pushing the crowds farther apart. A voice cried out, "Go back where you came from!"

"Nazi pigs!"

"Hail Hitler!"

At this, the group of men surged forward, and blood began to flow. Girls, hanging out of the windows and on the balcony screamed, men groaned. More police arrived and using their batons freely, forced the intruders back. More insults were hurled back and forth but the police managed to nip any more scuffles in the bud.

Annie wanted to go home. She was in tears. "What's wrong with the people here? Doesn't anybody remember the war?" Robbie asked her to stay but she linked arms with her friend Beth and they left.

The boys got together in a nearby tavern over a beer. It was a dark place, with cold smoke lingering in the air and sawdust on the ground to soak up any spills. Jimmy was excited, his blue eyes glistening. "I'm going to join the Swastikas."

"You can't be serious," said Robbie.

"Oh yes, I am," said Jimmy. "You've seen the state of our beaches on the weekend. All the crowds of unwashed, filthy immigrants changing into their bathing suits on the beach. Men walking around half-naked. They don't follow the regulations. They can't even read the regulations." He looked a little dazed. "Our women are afraid to go out on the weekend."

He continued, "They even swim naked after dark and when the washrooms are closed, they piss and shit wherever they want. They're like animals."

"Jimmy, stop repeating all the bullshit rumours you've heard. Don't forget we're immigrants, too."

"We're British. It's not the same." Some of the other boys nodded.

Robbie shook his head.

Jimmy continued, "Look. Who do you think is responsible for the Depression? The rich! They ride on our backs."

"The immigrants, who come down here for picnics, are not rich."

"They're the same kind."

"I don't believe what I'm hearing. Do you follow Hitler?"

"No, but look at what Hitler's done for his people. They were worse off than we are. And now, they are on the road to recovery. People are working."

"Jimmy, they are rearming. They've broken the *Treaty of Versailles*. Do we really want a strong Germany again?" said John, who was from Belfast.

"That's not the point. Don't you read the papers? Hitler has said that Germany only wants to have the same military presence that the other European countries have, like France. Just for protection. Right now, they have less than the Treaty stated."

"Not counting Hitler's private army: the SA and the SS," said John.

"Jimmy, don't be naïve. Hitler is just spreading his propaganda worldwide and it's working," said Robbie.

"And you believe the Jewish propaganda. Anyway, the Swastikas are just patrolling the beach area to make sure undesirables don't pollute the area. They're not causing any trouble. Boys, take it or leave it. I'm getting tired. Time for me to hit the hay."

Robbie had an uneasy feeling as he walked home. He was surprised at the vehemence in Jimmy. He had nothing to complain about. He didn't even live in the immediate area. Young people who were out of work and who had no future prospects were easy targets for this kind of behaviour. Jimmy shouldn't be.

On Queen Street, Robbie passed by some young men, sporting the swastika. They'd obviously had a few and were singing loudly, "Liked by few, loved by naught, there goes the Jew, running 'fore he's caught."

What's happening? Are we all losing our minds?

***

Robbie called on Annie at her nurse's residence. She didn't want to come out. There were daily reports of skirmishes. There were rumours of stabbings and outright confrontations. And then, there was the eruption after a junior city softball championship semi-final game in Willowvale Park.

Crowds gathered, some to join in, some to watch the excitement they saw building. At the end of the game, a youth waved a Swastika. He was knocked out and then an all-out wide riot ensued. Broken bottles, baseball bats, pieces of pipe, heavy boots and fists were used as the battle took to the streets and flowed along Bloor Street West from Christie Street to Clinton. The hospitals in the area were overwhelmed.

After this incident, Mayor Stewart, issued a warning to anyone wearing the swastika badge.

In an about face, the Swastikas reported that their club was open to anyone including Jews and they would cease using the emblem. They said they just wanted peace.

Robbie didn't believe them.

When he dropped in on Annie again, she told Robbie she was going to move back to England. She didn't feel safe in Toronto. She'd started saving for her passage.

Robbie tried to persuade her to stay but the growing influence of Hitler's heavy hand, was being felt in every corner of the world and Annie wanted to go home.

CHAPTER THIRTEEN

He didn't get close to Annie for almost another year.

Toronto was in a state of semi-consciousness even though the city had just had its hundredth birthday the year before and had celebrated with concerts and rockets and poems and plays. Robbie got a glimpse of Mary Pickford in her car as she drove up to The Royal York Hotel. Seeing Alex's favourite actress made him relive the day he had told Alex he had quit his job. The beginning of the end of their relationship.

He was no longer devastated. In fact, he felt next to nothing.

The city was collectively holding its breath. Like Robbie, it was waiting for something to happen. There was no building going on, there were no improvements being made. The same gaunt faces showed up at the soup kitchens. The homeless were chased from place to place.

The only good thing, as far as Robbie could tell, was that the swastika business had died down.

Annie worked at the Riverdale Isolation Hospital next to the Don Jail at the busy intersections of Broadview and Gerrard overlooking Riverdale Zoo and Park. Robbie frequented the area, trying to catch a glimpse of her, and afterward, went down to the Don River among the homeless masses who had been forced to take shelter there. With no proper facilities, it had become a nasty quagmire of unpleasant sights and smells. He always took a bag of fresh dinner rolls and passed them out to the children that he saw.

Annie had pushed Alex out of his mind, even though he had only seen her a few times. After relentlessly pestering her friend and fellow nurse Beth, whom he still often saw at the club, she finally arranged for Annie and Robbie to meet in Riverdale Park.

When he saw her sitting peacefully under a tree on a blanket, her feet tucked up under her, her concentration on a book, he knew she really was the one. This was the woman he wanted to be the mother of his children.

"I'm still determined to leave," she said when she saw him. But she hadn't remembered how handsome Robbie was. Like Gary Cooper. It was the way he looked at her when he wasn't sure.

"You'll get used to it," Robbie told her. "The weather, I mean."

"That's easy for a Scot to say," said Annie with a laugh.

"Annie, the winters may be harsh, but most of the time, it's sunny instead of the dreary grey we have from October to March. Over there, I bet you don't go out without an umbrella."

"You're right. In any case, I won't be able to go back this year."

"You can't imagine how happy I am to hear you say that."

Annie smiled.

"Let's go to the pictures and take it slow," Robbie said, opening the pages of his newspaper. "We could see Joan Crawford and Robert Montgomery in "No More Ladies." He wanted to see "The Raven" with Boris Karloff but women preferred romances. She surprised him by pointing to the ad above.

"Look. There's a double bill at The Imperial Theatre. "Hooray for Love" with Ann Southern and the wicked Boris Karloff in "The Raven". I love Edgar Allen Poe. Unless of course you want to see Joan Crawford?"

Robbie jumped up. "A girl after my own heart. Let's get a bite to eat before we go."

"You're on."

Those eyes. A girl could get lost in those eyes.

***

Annie was a church-goer, although it wasn't because her mother made her, like Alex. She was Anglican and made sure that she always went to church on Sunday. Robbie went with her once but excused himself, telling her he was a Presbyterian and so, wouldn't kneel when he prayed.

That was malarkey, Irish John said.

Robbie really liked this girl but church wasn't an option. He had to tell her why. And so, again, he was faced with the task of opening up about his past. This time, better sooner than later.

He put on his freshly pressed white shirt and trousers and tied his tie. Then, despite the heat, he put on his vest and jacket. He had shaved himself closely and brushed his hair till it sat properly. He looked at himself in the mirror and licked his lips nervously. His hairline was receding slightly, but he had a lean, taut body. He thought he looked dapper as he put on his hat at an angle. And then, he fortified himself with a quick slug from his flask.

By the time he walked over from his tiny room at Pape and Dundas, he had loosened his tie and taken his jacket off. He saw her under their tree in the park, lying on the plaid that she had already spread out. He wiped his face with his hankie and then put his jacket back on and tightened his tie. Robbie had brought a couple of ice-cold lemonades that he'd picked up at the corner.

Annie was leaning back on an elbow, reading yet another book. She looked as lovely as a picture postcard. He got quite close to her before she heard the clink of the bottles. She looked up at him and smiled and said, "Hello. You're looking very formal." She had a soft blue and yellow print dress on. "Aren't you too warm? Take off that jacket and tie and stay awhile."

He was happy to comply. He rolled up his sleeves and opened the two bottles of lemonade.

"Annie, I've something to tell you."

She held her breath. He sounded so serious.

He is married.

"I'm a Home Boy," he paused.

There was the Gary Cooper flicker of hurt in his eyes, like after a friend's betrayal.

"What does that mean?" She started to unpack sandwiches and took out a jar of pickled onions and beets.

"My brother and I were abandoned at an orphanage by our parents and were sent to Canada as child labourers." It all came out in a rush. He wasn't looking at her. "I don't know what happened to my sister."

Annie stopped what she was doing and paid full attention.

"How awful," Annie said. "It must have been terrible for you. Are you in touch with any of them?" She was relieved. She leaned over and squeezed his hand.

"For a while, Tom and I were. I never found out where Emma went," he managed to get out. He wasn't prepared for her genuine kindness. He stood up and walked a short distance away. It took him some time to compose himself. When he got back, Annie had calmly gone back to her book.

"Are you all right?" she said. Robbie nodded and sat down.

"Have something to eat." The egg and cucumber sandwiches were good but warm. He ate them anyway. Food was too precious to let spoil. "Let me tell you something." She took a deep breath. "My father was a gambler and lost everything. My mother turned to alcohol. I had to bring up my three younger brothers."

There was a momentary silence.

"We're not to blame for our backgrounds," she said. "And can't change them."

This time Robbie grabbed her hands. "Aye. We can only make sure that our future is different."

Before he could get another word out, Annie was offering him another sandwich. She said, "Robbie, you don't have to tell me anymore right now." She looked at him and smiled, "Unless you've murdered someone."

"And by the way," she continued, "everyone has skeletons in their closets."

"Come on," he said, "let's go for a walk down to the Zoo."

***

By the summer of thirty-six, Robbie had told Jimmy to stuff his ideas and his job and Annie got him in as an orderly for the Isolation Hospital. His experience of working for the doctor came in handy.

Polio season was approaching and the year was promising to be bad. Scientists had studied how polio came in waves across the country. Last year, there'd been quite a few cases in the Prairie Provinces. The hospital was gearing up to be ready.

But instead of infantile paralysis, a heat-wave engulfed the city. Record temperatures soared, a clean water shortage was announced, and there was a ban on watering gardens and grass. Hundreds died in the heat, as always, the most vulnerable: the very young and the very old. Robbie and Annie worked hard to help ease the patients' suffering.

Annie was patient with Robbie and never enticed him into proposing. There had been a few times that he had come close but he always stopped short of asking her.

She understood. Times were bad and poverty for people like them lurked just around the corner. It was not the time to start a family.

When the weather cooled, all the talk was about the Berlin Olympic Games and the mad fervour of the participants and the observers. For all the world to see, Germany had not only rearmed but was stronger than ever before. In fact, they were flaunting it. The newsreels at the theatres showed the mass hysteria that had enveloped the country and how it was spreading like a malignant disease. The blood-red Nazi flag overpowered flags from other nations.

Everyone knew how powerful Hitler was, but Robbie had not expected the Canadians to salute him Nazi-style – right arm out straight. The crowd cheered them wildly. The Canadian Ensign was also dipped to him as were many other national flags.

By the closing ceremonies, Germany had done what it had set out to do: showcase their power. They had never won a gold medal before. This time they won a total of eighty-nine medals, thirty-three of which were gold. Hitler had proved his Aryan point.

Everyone was watching as preparations were made to take on the world.

***

Christmas was the best Robbie ever had. When he found out that Annie had to work, he volunteered so that they could be together. After they got the patients settled down for the night, the nurses and orderlies had a party in the staff room. Those who were on duty and those who were in residence, made a punch and put out thinly sliced pieces of roast beef, cheese, loaves of fresh bread, butter, pies, cookies, plum pudding and Robbie's favourite:

mince pies.

They spiked their punch with a little medicinal rum, just to be merry and nothing more. Annie started singing carols in her soprano and the others joined in. They had Christmas crackers which, when cracked, spilled out a little treat and paper hats that they all wore. Someone brought a fiddle and they danced. Then, out of breath, they played word games, guess it if you can and musical chairs. They took turns making the rounds.

CHAPTER FOURTEEN

Robbie turned around and went back to have a last look at the building, which had given him the most happiness in his life, before he left. Everyone had gone back in.

He should have married her. They had been engaged for a year, but Robbie was finding it difficult to take the final step. Yesterday, he had told her, if she wanted, they could break if off while he was away. So she wouldn't be waiting for him and if someone better came along, she would be free.

She had been so upset she had started to cry. He thought she was going to slap him, but her raised hand had dropped helplessly to her side. "What do you think of me?" she had sobbed. "I love you and there'll never be anyone else. I keep my promises." She wiped her eyes. "Don't you?"

Robbie swept her into his arms. He kissed her forehead. "Yes. You are my one and only. But if something happens…."

"I'll be waiting for you."

It was like a scene out of the pictures. He hugged her and she didn't mind the roughness of the uniform up against her cheek.

When they parted, she was surrounded by their friends. Beth put an arm around her shoulders. He gave her a kiss, turned on his heel and walked quickly down the front steps. He was the first of their lot to go.

The war had been no surprise. Not only had Germany been

rearming, there had been bloody conflicts in different parts of the world with Italy meddling in North Africa, the Japanese and the Chinese battles over Shanghai. Never mind the conflict in Spain.

But in the end, it had happened fast. Germany had invaded Poland and countries had scrambled to take sides.

The world had listened in horror to the bulletins.

"You know, Annie, I used to think that soldiers were the biggest suckers in the world. But somebody has to stop this madman."

She agreed.

And on the same day as war had been declared, a tragedy had struck that upset Robbie on the most personal level. Robbie, Annie and some of the other staff had been listening to the reports from Poland. A sombre voice interrupted and said that The *S.S. Athenia*, a ship carrying British, Canadians and Americans, had been torpedoed. There were one hundred and twenty Torontonians aboard. It was a ship full of civilians. It was the beautiful ship that had brought him to Canada fifteen years ago.

He had made the decision to enlist right away. He was going to do his bit to stop this rabid Hitler.

Annie didn't protest when he told her, although he could also see the worry in the creases around her eyes.

His Annie was an angel. In fact, Robbie believed most nurses were. They did far more than the doctors did for the comfort of their patients. Her ability to make crack decisions had saved many lives. Her kindness had provided patients relief in their dying moments and she knew the right words to console grieving mothers.

He wouldn't forget how two years ago, when Toronto had been in the middle of the worst polio epidemic since 1930, Annie still found time to spend with the frightened ten year old girl stuck in the Drinker Respirator, the 'Iron Lung'. She would take her lunch and sit with her, telling her stories about her own childhood in England.

He would also never forget, as more and more children were sent to them, that life at the hospital had become a whirlwind blur. No one grumbled about long hours when they experienced the tough little ones bravely fighting for their lives every day.

Robbie was going to remember those little children when the going got rough over there. He wiped his eyes. He was leaving to protect the way of life in Canada he had grown to love. He was going to fight for the safety of his Annie.

Damn it, I should have married her.

***

The voyage over was rough but the worst thing about it was the night. The submarines always surfaced when it was dark and you never knew where they would strike. Robbie, like the rest, spent late nights on the blacked-out deck in small groups, smoking cigarettes.

When they landed they were sent to their secret destinations in England for training. Robbie, because of his background, had been delegated to the medical corps.

He was stationed in England. The locals in the pub cheered whenever Robbie or any of the other Canadians showed up for a drink. They were slapped on the back, bought drinks and invited for dinner into local homes. The girls treated them like heroes even though they hadn't done anything yet. It made Robbie, in his shyness, feel awkward.

There was a heady excitement in the air. The soldiers urged each other to have a last fling before they were shipped to France. Robbie knew that if he gave in, things would never be right for Annie and him. And so, when he was given a weekend furlough, he decided to search out his father in Edinburgh.

When he reached the last address he had for his father on Brighton Street, he rang the bell. There was no answer. It was Saturday and he supposed his father was at work. He stood uncertainly outside the door and smoked, trying to figure out what to do with the rest of the day.

When the door opened, it startled him. A man nodded to him. "Good morning, soldier. Looking for someone?"

"Yes," Robbie said. "My father. Mr. James. I mean Mr. Lapointe. I'm one of his sons who live in Canada."

"Oh," said the man, "I didn't know he had any sons."

"Can you give me the address where he works?" Robbie's mouth was dry. His heart pounded.

"I can do one better. I can take you there. It's on my way."

"Robbie James, sir." Robbie offered his hand.

"James MacIntyre." They shook.

***

Mr. MacIntyre pointed out the kilt shop on Princes Street and lifted his hat in a farewell salute.

Robbie walked in and looked around. It was filled with yards of tartans, in every possible clan's combination. A grey-haired man glanced up from his measurements. A man with a scar on his lower lip.

"Can I help you?"

"Mr. Lapointe?"

"Yes?"

"Dad?" Robbie's voice quavered. "It's Robbie." He took off his cap.

"Robbie," said his father, "Robbie?"

"Yes, dad," said Robbie. "It's me."

His father put his pencil down. He didn't move.

"You're in the Canadian army."

"Yes," said Robbie. "We expect to be shipped out soon."

"You look well."

"I am. And you?"

"Can't complain."

William came around from behind the counter. "Have you heard from Tom? He hasn't written in a long time."

"I don't know, we lost touch years ago. The last I heard he was in British Columbia."

"That's too bad."

Robbie said, "What about Emma?"

"She's somewhere over near Glasgow, married with two sons."

Emma married with children!

"Do you have her address?"

"No, no. She didn't really keep in touch."

No bloody wonder.

The stooped old man's hand began to tremble as he reached out to

286

Robbie. There was a pause before he said, "Good Luck." Robbie hesitated and then took his father's hand. They shook. Before his father let his hand drop, he said, "Robbie, always remember to keep your head down."

"Yes. I will."

"Good-bye."

Robbie saluted, put on his cap and then turned and left. Outside, he lit a cigarette and watched his father through the window. His father had gone back to his table and looking down, reached into his pocket and pulled out a hankie, wiped his eyes with it, blew his nose and then put it away.

He picked up his pencil and went back to work.

Robbie watched him for a few moments, and then, he dropped his cigarette and crushed it under his heel. He made his way back to the train station slowly, not able to see the beautiful city he was walking through anymore.

ACKNOWLEDGMENTS

Throughout the four years it took me to research and write this tribute to British Home Children, there were a few people who kept me motivated even when the going was rough. Because of their support, I continued to write and even took a trip to Scotland, while undergoing surgery, radiation and chemotherapy.

Revital Mula, I can't begin to thank you for your belief in me and your countless hours of reading, editing and ideas.
Ron Dorman, my partner, for your generosity and faith in my work. You've kept your promise to my dad.
Sandi Cox, for being my initial driving force and my friend for so many years.
Lynda Joyce, my sister and friend, for being my co-researcher, editor, proof-reader and general Girl Friday.
Leigh Voigt, for your remarkable cover design and images. You hit the nail on the head.

Thanks also to Will and Lise Robertson, for putting up with me and putting me up as well as their daughter, Keltie Robertson for proof-reading and helpful hints; Fred Wardle, for the loan of Home Child videos, Beth Bruder for her sage advice, Lyma and Walter McIntosh and Don and Janice Blaney, for help in understanding farming in Ontario; Sandy Drysdale and his uncle, "Joe", Maurice Taylor, who gave me great insight into growing up on a farm in the thirties in Smith's Falls; MPP Jim Brownell, who wrote the foreword to The Street Arab; the people of Glengarry, who welcomed me into their midst and all the members of the Quarrier's Canadian family, especially those who made the trip to the Orphan Homes of Scotland now known as Quarrier's, in remembrance of our remarkable ancestors.

Thanks also to the rest of my family: Claire, Penelope, Cynthia and Ryan and Sascha, for their patience and love as well as Kirsten, Keegan and Steve.

In researching this book, I would also like to thank the staff of the libraries of Kirkcaldy, Scotland, The Royal College of Surgeons, Edinburgh, Scotland, the Brockville Public Library, the Cornwall Public Library, Martintown Public Library, the Toronto Reference library and the Toronto Archives as well as Quarrier's Narrative of Facts from 1919 to 1925, available on the website: www.iriss.org.uk/goldenbridge.

I would like to recognize the use of the poem that every Canadian knows by heart: "In Flander's Fields" by Lieutenant Colonel Dr. John McCrae.

I would like to recognize the use of a part of: "The Old Grey Mare" (traditional)

And, "It's a Long Way to Tipperary" (1911) by Jack Judge, co-credited to Harry Williams (public domain).

SANDRA JOYCE, a Toronto-born writer, graduated with a B. A. A. in Journalism at Ryerson University, in Toronto. After graduating, she became the National Publicity Coordinator and Staff Photographer for CBS Records. During her tenure at CBS, she won Top Publicist at the Canadian Black Music Awards.

She has managed three rock bands, worked for the German Department of Defence as a contract specialist and negotiator, as a freelance sports writer, and as a consultant at an Independent Music Company.

Aside from writing, she is VP of Media for a Terry Fox Run site, a storyteller at the Harbourfront Centre and an English teacher.

Sandra is the daughter of a British Home Child.

Portrait of the author by Leigh Voigt